OUR FINEST HOUR

THE TIME SERIES BOOK ONE

JENNIFER MILLIKIN

JNM, LLC
Scottsdale, AZ
jennifermillikinwrites@gmail.com

ISBN-13: 9780996784559

Time passes at the same rate of speed no matter how it's used. It's up to us how we spend it.

Do we harbor fear or hate? Do we wage battles on others or within ourselves?

What if we used the time to forgive and love? How much more enjoyable could our hours be?

APRIL FOOLS.

I'm still waiting for Owen to yell the words.

How many seconds have passed now?

Nine?

Ten?

Each one is excruciating.

The longer we're quiet, the clearer it all becomes.

This isn't a joke. He means what he said.

Still, with a shred of hope left in my rapidly deflating heart, I ask, "Is this just a really bad April fool's joke?" I despise how my voice shakes.

His sigh is my answer, but he speaks anyway. "No, Aubrey. It's bad timing. I'm sor—"

I pull my phone away from my ear and stare at it, the rest of his *sorry* floating out into the air. With my thumb I end the call and toss my phone on the bed beside me. I don't need to hear his apology.

Eyes squeezed tight, I try to numb myself. Despite my efforts, the feelings come. Horrible, terrible feelings.

How could I have allowed this? The real question is, how could I have allowed this *again*?

It's my own fault.

Ignoring Owen McNamera would've been the very best thing for me. And I tried. My guard was perfectly intact despite all his persistent visits to the overpriced juice shop where I work on campus. It was obvious he had no desire to drink his vegetables, but every day he came. It was his slow smile that broke down my walls. The way only one corner turned up the tiniest bit, and then, after a few moments, that one side would finally give rise to the other corner. That smile was special. Just for me. Like I was the chosen one. And it was what ultimately took down my walls. No cannons or torpedoes needed. Just something nice and kind, something masquerading as love.

My vision swirls until the water clouding my eyes spills over. How long have I been lying here? Long enough for the shadows on my bed to lengthen. With the back of my hand, I wipe away any remaining moisture from my cheeks. I will not cry anymore.

All my emotions have been rounded up and locked down. My walls are rebuilt, even higher than before.

It's a crappy way to live, but it's what I know. There's comfort there, even if it's not the kind of comfort that comes with happiness or ease. Sometimes comfort is really just doing what you've always done, simply because it's what you know.

In this case, I'm a pro.

I've been here before. I know how to watch someone I love walk away.

"It's not that I don't believe in ghosts," I explain to Britt as she rubs her eyes. She mumbles something about accidentally looking too closely at the sun, and when she pulls her hands away from her face, I see the water pooling on the lower rims of her eyes.

"Here," I grab my backup pair of sunglasses from my backpack and hand them to her.

She slides them on. "Thanks. I couldn't find mine this morning."

I'm not shocked, considering the state she keeps her room in. But I don't complain, because she keeps the rest of our place spotless.

"So what were you saying before I tried to stare down the sun?" She throws her backpack's second strap over her other shoulder and starts toward our apartment.

"Just that I don't believe in ghosts, exactly." Not the ghosts of people who've died, anyway. But the ghosts of those who are still living? I believe in those.

Britt gives me a look as we come to a stop at a light. She presses the walk button and folds her arms across her chest. For a moment she studies me. I'm waiting for her to ask just what it is I believe in, *exactly*.

Three minutes ago, the very moment we stepped away from her last class, Britt asked me about ghosts. Her knitted brows and worried expression tell me her opinion on their existence.

I'd like to poke a fork into the arm of the lab partner who told her the apartment building we live in is haunted.

"Well," Britt tucks one side of her blond bob behind an ear, "We don't all have an Owen to protect us from the spirits of the undead."

I peer around, hoping to find something interesting to warrant a subject change. We're standing in a cluster of pedestrians on a busy street corner, and most people are wearing headphones. If they aren't, their necks are bent at an awkward angle, staring at their phones and using a finger to scroll. Nothing interesting to comment on.

"Yes, I'm so lucky to have Owen," I murmur. The light changes, and we step off the curb.

She walks with purpose, even though we're headed to our apartment for an afternoon of absolutely nothing. Maybe some studying. Probably some bad TV.

It's not hard for me to keep up with Britt. I walk with purpose too. I always have. We pound the stairs to our second-floor apartment. Neither of us is out of breath, a welcome change from nine months ago when we first moved in. If Britt hadn't been gasping for air each time she scrambled the stairs, she would've punched me for choosing the second story.

When I promised my dad I'd get the safer second-level apartment, I didn't know Britt Pomeroy was going to answer my ad for a roommate. Nor did I know the wheezing, blond ball of sarcasm who knocked on my door was going to become the best friend I've ever had. What mattered was my dad and the promise I made to him. And promises? They mean something to me.

When we get home, Britt takes out her laptop and navigates to Facebook. "Yesterday was April fools," she says without looking up. She scrolls through posts, laughing at some, and tossing chip after chip into her mouth. "I totally forgot."

Not me.

I haven't told Britt that Owen broke up with me. I can't stand to say the words. I'm humiliated. Mortified I even dared to be happy. Worse, I'm sad. The kind of sadness I promised myself I'd never allow anyone make me feel again.

Through fake smiles and an early bedtime, I hide it all from her.

By the next afternoon, the misery has seeped through the cracks in my walled-off heart, and Britt notices.

"I've never seen you like this." She leans over, plucks a mandarin orange from an old, chipped fruit bowl on the counter, and tosses it in the air twice before her eyes come to rest on me. "What's your deal?"

"I don't know what you mean," I murmur. Obviously I know exactly what she means. Call it a reflexive action, like putting your arms up when a ball comes flying at your head. No need to analyze the hows and whys of my automatic denial. Thanks to the therapist I stopped seeing long ago, I already know. *Fear of abandonment*, she said. When I left my session that day I told my dad he should get a refund. The only gem in our entire session was when she said it's a natural reaction to what I've been through, that she would expect me to push everyone away. *If you didn't push people away, I'd wonder if you were facing an inability to feel. And if that were the case, our visits would be very different.*

I should have told my therapist not to worry, that I'm not facing an inability to feel. If anything, the opposite is my problem. *I feel too much.* I feel every part of my mother's departure like little stabs of pain all over my body. Most of the pain is concentrated in my heart. That's where the pinches and pulls hurt the most. Right in the center of my chest, where my breath stops in my throat and my chest tightens. Even after thirteen years, I can't get rid of what my mother left behind when she walked away.

So, no. I don't believe in the ghosts of the dead. But the ghosts of the living? Yeah, those are real.

· · ·

THAT NIGHT I tell Britt what happened.

She flies off the handle, cussing and pacing, talking fast and making references to mob movies. Which is almost funny, considering she's five-foot-two, and only when she straightens her shoulders. Hardly a formidable foe.

"Nobody is going to sleep with the fishes." I speak with my most placating voice.

My chest warms as I watch her from my spot on the arm of the couch. For once I feel cared for, like someone worthy of defense.

It's not fair for me to think that way. My dad would defend me to his dying breath, if I ever gave him the opportunity—which I don't. I like handling things on my own.

"Aubrey, we can't just let him get away with this." She throws a hand up in my direction. "You need to call him back. We need to call him names. Lot's of bad names." She wrinkles her nose and makes a sound of disgust.

I shake my head. "Let it go." Calling Owen ranks very low on my list of things I want to do, falling somewhere near using pliers to pull out my toenails.

Britt blinks twice. "Why aren't you having the right reaction to this?"

I give her an answer, something about having a forty-eight-hour head start on feeling angry. Truthfully, as devastated as I am, a part of me knew Owen would leave me eventually. On some level I've been mourning the demise of our relationship since the second I let his smile carry me away.

"Owen is going to regret his choice." She wraps an arm around my shoulders. "I promise."

I smile because it's what I'm supposed to do.

Just before I fall asleep that night, I see her. From behind, like always. I think maybe this time she'll look back, because my heart was broken by a boy, something that's never happened before. Shouldn't mothers be there for their daughters?

Even my imagination can't make her turn around.

MY MOM WAS PRETTY. No, my mom was beautiful. A kind of beauty that belonged in the pages of the fashion magazines she kept stacked on the side table in the living room. My friends wanted to come to my house because they loved my mom, and I loved that they loved her.

Not only was my mom beautiful, she could bake like Mrs. Fields and Betty Crocker all wrapped up in one. She made the very best blueberry muffins that anyone ever put in their mouths. They would sigh as they took a bite, saying things like, "It's a crime how good these are."

The mothers of my friends liked to visit my mom too. Maybe they were envious of her. Beautiful woman, happy home, husband with a good job. My dad wasn't the president of the bank or anything, but he was a journeyman. Working with electricity is a dangerous job, but the trade-off is that it pays well.

Despite his good-paying job, he insisted on keeping an old Chevy truck that never ran well. "Broken more than it runs," my mother would grumble. She had a car that worked just fine, so she didn't complain too loudly about the old Chevy.

The Saturday she left was like all the other Saturdays before it. I sat playing with my dolls in the living room. My Barbie could bake blueberry muffins that were better than all the rest, just like my mom could. Dad was in the garage, probably lying under his truck, rolling out every so often for a tool.

Mom came through the living room, her chin tucked against her chest. That's what I remember most about the day she left. Normally she walked with her head up, her eyes calm and clear. But on that day, she rushed past me, only five feet away from where I sat. I looked up as she passed. I couldn't see her eyes.

"Mommy, will you please get me yogurt-covered-raisins?" I knew she was going to the store. She'd told me ten minutes ago when she'd gone to change her clothes.

She never responded. She just kept walking.

Her elbow jutted out, bent at an angle on the side of her body, and for years I would see that in my dreams. At eight I didn't understand why it was bent that way, but eventually I figured it out. She was covering her mouth.

My heart told me it was to keep her sob inside, because even she knew what she was doing was going to damage me forever. My brain told me it was to keep her from telling me what she was doing, knowing I would find out soon enough.

I found the piece of paper first. Only five words written.

I can't do this anymore.

Can't do what? I wondered.

The longer she stayed gone, the more I understood.

I can't be a wife.

I can't be a mother.

I can't make myself want this life.

I can't make myself love our daughter.

I can't do this anymore.

My dad threw away her note, but I grabbed it from the trash when he wasn't looking. For three years I studied the familiar handwriting, the scrawl matching the loving sentiments she'd written in my birthday cards. Words penned by the same hand, but the message vastly different.

OWEN and I used to see each other all the time.

Meet me for a kiss before my afternoon class?

I have a twenty-five-minute break at ten. Let's grab coffee.

Can I come over after your last class?

But now it's like he has vanished. I've been waiting to run into him, a moment I assumed inevitable, but it still hasn't come.

One week went by. Then two. I didn't know Owen was a magician, skilled in disappearing acts.

But I did know a person could live with a broken heart, and that's what I was doing. Waiting for the pieces to go back together, to drift towards one another and form a makeshift semblance of what they had been before.

I thought about calling my dad, but our relationship wasn't really prepared for phone calls about boys. He's always provided the basics for me, the base of Maslow's hierarchy of needs, but warm fuzzies? Not so much. He tried, I think, to give me a mom. He went on dates, and sometimes he'd go on more than a few with the same woman and bring her home to meet me. After a while, I felt like the lost baby bird in the Dr. Seuss book, *Are You My Mother?*

Eventually he quit trying. Then it was just us, two planets orbiting each other, not certain how to break the orbit and collide. Once I could drive, I did all the grocery shopping. Prepared meals, cleaned the house. When there's a hole, it's natural for whatever is left around it to slide toward the crater, to fill the space. That's what we did, slowly. Day by day, year by year, we slid into the void, until we became a fully-functioning, two person unit.

Right now Dad and I are both living on our own. I see him on Sundays, unless he's gone hunting. And we're not robots anymore. We're friends. Partners. Two people felled by the same foe.

Living with Britt is the opposite of living with my dad. She's talkative, secure, and well-adjusted. She hails from a happy home with a mom and a dad, a sister and a dog and a two-car garage. When I picture her house, I add a white picket fence around the green lawn, even though I know it doesn't have one. I'm not jealous of Britt. I'm happy my best friend had a glorious childhood with a mother who showered her in snuggles and love. I just wish I'd had the same.

And Britt, my beyond-lucky best friend, has decreed that today is the day I stop thinking about Owen. She has just burst into my room with her freshly highlighted blond bob cocooning her face, eyes bright.

"I'm taking you somewhere tonight, and you're not saying no. I'll drag you bound and gagged if I have to."

I point toward my window, where the driving rain pelts the glass and runs down in rivulets.

She crosses her arms. "It's supposed to let up soon.

Besides, you won't melt if you get wet. Actually, you'll dry first. Can't keep Arizona heat behind the clouds for long."

I want to keep arguing with her, but I don't have the heart. Britt is used to getting her way. And she's never had a guy dump her. Britt dates but doesn't get involved. It's her thing.

Because I love her, and because her intentions are good, I get ready like she asked me to.

Under a shared umbrella, we walk to the street of bars near our apartment. It isn't until she pulls me to the last in the row that I balk.

I point to the neon sign with the cowboy on a bull. "Rodeo Mike's?"

Britt rolls her eyes. "There's no way Owen will show up here. That's why I chose it. It's not his scene."

She's right. I guess tonight this is *our* scene. Britt invited the three girls who live in the apartment below us, and they've texted that they're already here. Jasmine, Maize, and Erin never say no to a bar. Or a good time. Or a party. Or much of anything, really.

The bar is loud and bright. I take three steps inside and turn around. This was a mistake. I can't take the band with its upbeat music, the couples on the wooden dance floor twisting and turning. Britt was wrong. What I needed tonight was something dark and brooding, like a martini bar where you could barely see a hand in front of your face.

Someone's grabbing me, pulling me back. "Just give it a chance." Britt whispers. She tugs me along with her.

Jasmine orders a round while Britt leads us to an empty table.

"Sit," she orders. "Close your eyes and take a deep breath." I do as she says, taking in the scent of wood, perfume, cologne, and beer. When I open my eyes, she's watching me.

"You made it." Her chin tilts up, pride shines in her eyes.

"To where? Here?" I tap one finger on the table. I know what she's getting at, but I don't want the accolade.

Jasmine returns, her arms full of drinks, and sets them on the table. Britt grabs a bottle for me and a bottle for her.

"You made it through the first two weeks. It'll only get easier from here." She gently knocks the top of her bottle to mine.

I drink with her. "You're not exactly an expert."

She shrugs. "I have eyes. I've seen it enough times to know."

A twirl of yellow behind Britt's head catches my attention. I lean left so I can follow the movement of the yellow dress, and the woman it's attached to, on the dance floor. She's as affixed to the man with her as the clingy dress is to her. The music is up-tempo, but they dance slowly, swaying to their own song. In my head I hear something old and sultry, maybe Etta James. My cheeks heat just watching them, the way their bodies mold against one another. I look away, feeling like an intruder despite the fact that they're in a public place.

Britt's upper half swivels, and she watches them too. When she turns back to me, her eyes light up, mischievous.

"You know what you need?" She smiles around the mouth of her beer bottle.

"Nope." My lips make a popping sound as I enunciate the p. I know what she's thinking, and it's not going to happen.

"Ohhhh, yes, you do." She lifts a solitary finger. "One night. No strings attached."

I wrinkle my nose.

"Stop." She holds up a hand. "Just stop. You're heartbroken." Her hand moves to her chest. "Owen let go of the best person I know. Forget about him tonight. Forget about *everything*. Please?"

Her blue eyes plead, and I know what she's really asking of me. She wants me to stop lingering in that place, the one where my thoughts grow maudlin. She wants me to stop before I begin to compare Owen's departure to that of my mother. She's asking me not to do what I've already done.

I'm so flawed they couldn't stay.

I'm the atrocity.

It's my fault they've left.

I LOVE BRITT. I really do. I love her so much I don't blame her when a cowboy with a big, shiny buckle and an even bigger hat comes to our table and sweeps her off her feet.

His name is Dane.

Or Dax.

Or...something that starts with D.

The point is, Britt's gone.

It doesn't take long before the other girls I'm with have caught the eyes of other wannabe cowboys and left the table. They all offered the requisite *Are you sure?* before walking away, and I reassured them it was fine. I like being alone, and I happen to be really good at it.

My fingers are slick with condensation as I peel the wrapper off my beer and rub the wet paper into a tiny, hard ball. I flick the small wad and watch it roll across the table and onto the floor.

The slow-dancing couple from earlier is back on the

dance floor, but now they're moving to the tempo. Even though they're moving appropriately this time, there's something different about them. Some kind of sensuality. Maybe it's magic. Or chemistry. Whatever it is, they have it.

I push the bottle to the middle of the table. Time for me to leave. I may like to be alone, but I don't care for torture. I stand, grab my purse from the table, and spin.

I take a step away from the table and bump into something. Or, rather, *someone*.

"I'm so sorry, I didn't mean to..." My sentence hangs unfinished as I look at the person I've run into.

I must have a thing for smiles, because that's what grabs me first. The left side of his mouth pulls up more than the right. It's a happy grin. Immediately I picture a light shining from somewhere inside him. An inherent, ambient light.

He extends one long, deeply tanned arm. "No worries. I'm Isaac." The smile doesn't waver.

I place my hand in his. "I'm Aubrey." *Am I smiling? My face feels numb.* My whole body feels numb. *God, I hope I'm smiling. That's what a normal person would do.*

"Nice to meet you, Aubrey." He nods when he says my name. "I hope you aren't leaving. I was just coming over here to offer you one of these." He lifts his left hand to show fingers intertwined around the necks of two beer bottles.

My lips twist. A few miles away my bed is calling my name. "Actually, I was heading out."

Isaac's frown is partly a pout, which accentuates the fullness of his lower lip. "Can I convince you to change your mind? It would be a terrible waste of good beer to let it get warm." He holds one bottle out to me, eyebrows raised. "This beer needs to fulfill its destiny." He moves the bottle a fraction, so it swings gently side to side.

I eye his hopeful face. *I was headed home. To my TV. And*

ice cream. In my head I see Britt's stern look, and it makes me wonder if she's staring me down from the dance floor behind me.

"OK." I nod. "But I'm not taking an open drink from someone I just met."

His lips shift like he's trying not to laugh. "You think I've poisoned your drink?"

I shrug. "I have a rule, that's all." Actually, it's my dad's rule, but it makes sense, and I've always followed it.

He nods and curls the beer back into his chest beside the second bottle. His grin turns crooked as he watches me for a few seconds. I don't know what he's looking for, but I'm sure I won't measure up.

Tears burn in my eyes, but by sheer will I hold them back. The last thing I want to do is show emotion to another man. I've learned by now that men use emotions as weapons. There is no way I'll give someone the power to hurt me again.

I should go.

My breath whooshes up in surprise when Isaac grabs my hand. Without looking back to see my reaction, he pulls me through the crowd and to the bar. Two people leave, and he quickly claims their seats. He sets the bottles down on the bar and pulls out the stool on the right.

"Let's try this again." He winks at me. "Aubrey, it's nice to meet you. Please sit and have a drink with me from a bottle you see the bartender open and hand to you."

Laughter bubbles up my throat as I sit.

Isaac bypasses his seat, leaning over it and setting his forearms on the edge of the bar. I try not to notice the ripple in his arms. Or the way his shoulders pull back. Or his stunning profile. *How does a man get lips like that?* Fillers. That must be it. I pinch my average-size lips together to keep from laughing.

He focuses on the bartender, and, when he gets his attention, lifts his head back slightly. Isaac points down at the bottles in front of us and lifts two fingers in the air. He smiles politely and thanks the bartender when he delivers the beer.

The stool doesn't seem tall enough to fit Isaac, but he manages, folding his long legs awkwardly beneath the bar top.

"How tall are you?" I blurt out.

"Six-three. How tall are you?"

"Five-seven."

He nods and grabs the neck of his beer with the same two fingers he used when he first approached my table. "Can we have that drink now?"

I tap the bottom of my bottle against his, take a small sip, and watch Isaac take a long pull. I like the way he holds his bottle. Just those two fingers wrapped around the neck and a thumb underneath.

Leaning a forearm on the bar top, Isaac pins me with his gaze. "So, Aubrey who's five-seven and doesn't accept open beverages from men she doesn't know, what were you doing trying to sneak out of here so early?"

"I have a hot date." I toss my hair over my shoulder and look at my wrist, despite the fact I'm not wearing a watch. "And now I'm late."

Isaac's gaze moves around my face and, slowly, reaches my eyes. He grows intense, and when that happens, his lips move, the tiny muscles around them twitching.

"Finder's keepers." The words are languid, sliding from his lips like caramel.

I take a deep breath and force myself to look away, even

though so much of me wants to let him sweet talk me. My heart and my ego could use the attention, but I know better.

"What did he do?"

His words make me turn back to him. I give him a side-eye and gulp my beer. "What makes you think somebody did something to me?"

"You're defensive and hesitant. In my experience, that usually means a woman's been hurt."

I glance at the door, just ten feet away. How easy it would be to escape. Part of me wants to run for the hills. But the other part wants to know what it would feel like to tell a total stranger the whole ugly truth.

"Excuse me?" I stop the bartender as he's passing by. "Two shots of Jack, please."

Isaac whistles, low and disbelieving. "That bad?"

"Ugly truth?" I ask.

"The whole thing." He says. "Don't leave anything out."

He asked for it. By the time I finish my story, Isaac will be sprinting away from me, just like Owen did. But maybe he'll turn around as he's running and yell the reason back to me. Maybe I'll finally understand.

The bartender sets the tiny glasses in front of us. I grimace as the shot burns my insides on the way down.

Isaac pushes his glass to the back of the bar top and signals for another. "Hit me with it." He says to me. "Let me in. Tell me your big, bad, ugly truth."

So I do. I tell a perfect stranger every detail. And it feels so good.

He doesn't run. He doesn't say something trite. He doesn't even say anything to make me feel better. All he says when I'm finished is, "That really fucking sucks."

And that's when I decide I like Isaac.

"You're the third person I've told that story to." Britt and

Owen are the other two, but does Owen even count? "Can you believe that?" My brain feels fuzzy. We stopped twice during my long story for shots. "Let's take a picture to commemorate the night I told a stranger my darkest, dirtiest secret." Digging in my purse for my phone, I find it and present it with a silly flourish.

Isaac waves his hands in front of him while I swipe open the camera. "Pictures steal a piece of your soul." He protests. "I don't believe in pictures."

I swivel so my back is to Isaac and snap one anyhow.

"I just stole a piece of your soul." I do a goofy celebratory dance with just my upper half.

He laughs and shakes his head, then returns his eyes to my face. *Those eyes... So intense, so dark.* Their depth seems to go forever.

"What now?" I ask. "I can't keep drinking or I'll stop functioning. And no more stories for a stranger. Unless said stranger is going to start sharing a few of his own."

Isaac watches me, and for a moment I think maybe he's going to tell me why he's there, but instead he says "I have an idea, but you're going to have to stop calling me a stranger. Considering I know more about you than most of the world, I'm pretty sure that makes me your second-best friend."

I frown as I consider what he has said. "You're right."

"I like those words."

I laugh and nearly fall off my barstool. Isaac catches my arm and steadies me.

"See what I mean?" I point at myself. "No more shots for this girl."

Isaac laughs. "I'm convinced."

His grip on my arm loosens, but he doesn't let me go.

"Do you want to go somewhere with me?" he asks.

"Are you planning on killing me and tossing my body in a dumpster?" I squint at him as if I'll be able to tell by his facial expression if he's a madman.

He makes a disgusted face and releases me. For a second I think I've upset him, but he grins as he reaches into his pocket and pulls out his wallet. Tossing a few bills on the tab, he turns to me. "My job is to do the very opposite of hurting people. And I have no plans to hurt you." His thumb runs over the sensitive length of skin on the inside of my forearm. "Unless you want me to, of course." His voice is deep and low, his eyes burning into mine.

All I want to do is play it cool, but I can't stop the widening of my eyes. He laughs softly when he sees my response, and his Adam's apple bobs.

I want to know why he's still here. Why he isn't running in fear of the woman who caused not only her first boyfriend, but also her mother, to leave and never look back. I'm too afraid to ask, because I don't want him to change his mind.

I catch his hand and run my fingertips across the top of it. Something twists in my stomach, and thanks to Owen, I recognize the feeling. *That may be the only thing I ever thank him for.*

"I've never been hurt before... not like *that*, anyway. But I wouldn't mind if you did other things..." My upper teeth catch my lower lip, and heat burns across my face.

His ever-ready smile is back before I've finished my thought. I wonder what makes a person smile so readily? He probably has the perfect life. Raised in the perfect home with a mom who made him cookies after school and helped him with homework and a dad who played catch with him in the front yard. A perfect little sister who's the perfect amount of sweet and sassy. No doubt his parents have the perfect marriage.

Perfect, perfect, perfect. That must be why his smiles are always ready, lined up and waiting in his body like candy in a Pez dispenser.

Tonight, I want a taste of perfect.

4

BEFORE I CAN RETHINK my decision, Isaac holds out his hand. "Do you want to find your friends and let them know you're leaving? I mean, assuming you've decided to leave with me. A non-killer." He laughs at his own joke.

I take his hand and pull him away from the bar. I've already made up my mind about him.

I find Britt line dancing with a different cowboy than the one who first asked her to dance. I think, anyway. It's hard to tell what they really look like with their cowboy hats on. I wave at her, and she ducks out of the dance and comes to my side. She has a sheen of sweat on her chest, and her cheeks are pink.

"What's going on?" she asks breathlessly, glancing from me to Isaac with excited curiosity.

"I just wanted to let you know I'm leaving." I clear my throat, my nervousness getting bigger by the second.

Britt evaluates Isaac. "*Leaving* leaving?" she asks without looking my way.

"Yes."

She sticks her hand out to Isaac. "I'm Britt, Aubrey's roommate."

Isaac shakes her hand. "I'm Isaac. Non-killer."

Britt makes a face, and looks at me with worried eyes. "Inside joke," I explain. "We've established he's not a murderer."

She nods and walks to Isaac's other side. She lifts her face to his ear, and he bends down to listen. I watch him nod as she talks, then he says something to her. I can't hear him, and I can't read his lips, because he's turned his head to look at her.

Britt points a playful warning finger at him while she walks around him and pulls me in for a hug. Isaac still has a hold of my hand. "Have fun tonight." Her voice is a whisper in my ear.

She steps back onto the dance floor and is reabsorbed into the dance.

"Do you want to dance?" Isaac leans closer, his words caressing the top of my ear.

Watching the timed twirling and foot stomping, I say "I don't know how to do...whatever that is."

"Me neither. But we can make our own dance." Isaac pulls my hand, spinning me in to him. I grunt as I catch myself on his chest.

My hands move to his shoulders. The scent coming off his neck is dizzying. He smells sweet but also spicy, clean but a bit like a forest. He paints a design on the small of my back with his fingertips, making me shiver despite the heat of the bodies around us.

The longer we dance, the harder it is to remember where we are, and suddenly I wonder if we look like that couple I watched when I arrived tonight.

I lean in even closer, cupping Isaac's cheek, and whisper, "I'm ready to leave."

Isaac's fingers trail over the back of my neck, across my shoulder, and down to my hand. His face is next to my ear. I listen for his words, but none come. He presses a cheek to my hair, and I barely make out a soft groan.

Isaac pulls back, my hand still in his, and leads me through the crowded bar. Outside, a line of cabs wait. He walks up to the first one, holds open the door, and climbs in after me. He gives the driver directions, then asks me for my phone.

"Why?" I ask, taking it from my purse.

"I told Britt I would tell her where I'm taking you. And give her my address." He takes my phone.

"Why not from your phone?" I ask as he opens my texts. Britt's name is my most recent conversation.

"I didn't bring my phone with me tonight. I didn't want to be reached." His voice is strained, and I'd bet a million dollars it has to do with why he was there.

He types out a message and hands it back to me. The phone slips from my sweaty palms twice before I get it back in my purse. I'm not sure how to say what I'm thinking, so I blurt out, "Do we need ground rules?" I feel like an idiot for not knowing how these things go.

Isaac looks confused. It relieves me. If he'd known just what I was asking, it would've unnerved me.

I groan and push my hair out of my eyes. "Are we exchanging last names? Because it just occurred to me we never made it to that minor detail."

He shifts so his body faces me. "Do you want to?"

"No..." I say slowly, but I'm still thinking. Knowing his last name might make him more real. Maybe the less I know, the better. "No," I repeat, my voice confident.

"OK, then." He smiles and takes my hand. "Aubrey with no last name, do you like ice cream?"

I lift a finger and shake my head. "Oh no no no. I'm not getting all Fifty Shades of Grey with you. Even if you are my second-best friend."

Isaac's laughter fills the back seat. "I'm not talking about that. I meant the question literally."

"Oh." I giggle. "Sorry."

He pushes a strand of hair out of my face, his fingers running the length of my ear as he tucks it away.

My breath slams up my throat, thick and hot. *All he did was touch your ear. Calm down.* A change of subject is needed. Now.

"You didn't say what brought you into the bar tonight," I say. "Is there a certain female that caused you to seek refuge in a bottle?"

Isaac looks down, lightly punching the empty space on the seat between us. "In a sense, yes." He winces, like he's remembering the hurt.

"Do you want to tell me the ugly truth?" My voice is soft.

He shakes his head. "It's not my ugly truth to tell."

He falls quiet, and so do I. Questions pop into my mind.

You're job is to help people? How so?

Do you have a roommate?

How old are you?

I ask none of these questions, because I'm not supposed to know the answers. That's the point of tonight.

His hand creeps across the seat and grabs mine, fingers intertwining. He has strong, long fingers. Big, thick, tan hands that look capable. *Since when are hands this interesting?* Somehow Isaac's are.

"I'm leaving the country in a few days." He says it so suddenly that I jump a tiny bit. "It's a long trip. I can extend it and stay longer if I..." He trails off, surveying me. "Sorry. More than you need to be told. I just wanted you to know I'm leaving, before this goes any further."

"I'm OK with that," I say. It's a good thing, actually. Cut-and-dry is what I need.

He nods, scraping his free hand across his chin. "I hope you don't mind that my place is mostly packed up. All my stuff is going into storage."

"I'm OK with that, too."

The cab comes to a stop in front of a row of brightly lit storefronts. Isaac drops my hand and removes his wallet, swiping his credit card through the machine on the back of the drivers seat. He steps out and I open my door. I'm halfway out when Isaac rounds the back end of the cab. Making a face, he hustles to grab the open door.

"You should have let me get your door," he chides.

"That's what people do when they're on dates." I step onto the sidewalk. "We're not on a date."

"True. If we were on a date, I would've picked you up at your house, not at a bar." He steps closer to me.

"Oh yeah?" My eyebrows raise. "What else would you have done differently?"

"Probably brought you flowers."

His hand extends across the short distance between our chests. I take his pretend flowers. "I don't understand why guys give girls flowers. They are literally dying plants wrapped in tissue paper."

Isaac laughs and takes another step, closing most of the space between us, and his arm cradles my lower back. "So you're saying you're a romantic?"

A disbelieving sound bubbles up from the back of my throat. "Hardly."

He pulls me in closer until we're pressed up against each

other. My hands fall on his upper arms, and my furious heartbeats pound a loud rhythm in my chest.

"If I kissed you now, in front of all these people, would you think it was romantic?" He's so close I can almost feel his words hit my lips.

Confused, I lean my head back and look to the rain slickened street, where I see nothing but the red and yellow lights of cars driving past. I look the other direction and see what he's talking about.

Behind us, there's a packed ice cream shop, tables full, and here we are standing in front of the long window. My eyes sweep over all the interested gazes, and my cheeks catch fire.

"Romantic?" Isaac asks when I look back at him.

"Yes," I breathe the word.

His mouth is on mine before I finish my breath. He pushes me back, past the window, and up against the brick wall that separates the ice cream place from its neighbor.

His hands are in my hair, running down my neck, tracing my collarbone. My fingers skim the muscles in his upper back, cling to his shoulders. I'm feeling things, good things, but my nerves are back, pushing into the rational part of my brain, trying to make a stronghold before I'm swept away by hormones. *Is this a bad idea? Am I going to get hurt?* I'm still kissing him, but I'm hesitant, and I wonder if he can sense it.

Isaac puts one hand on the back of my head, protecting it from the wall. Sensation takes over, and I feel his desire. It's hot like a flame, thirsty like a parched throat.

I ache for him in a way I never expected and never wanted.

"I'm not in the mood for ice cream anymore," I whisper, then pull his lower lip into my mouth and suck on it. He moans into my mouth and pulls back to look at me before diving back in. His kisses are hot and wet and his hand keeps sliding up my stomach and then back down to my waist, like he's reminding himself where we are. I'm glad he still has some sense because I have almost none right now.

Isaac pulls away, a new smile on his face. This one is lustful, a half curl of one side of his mouth.

My breath is long and loud, dragging, and it clears my mind a tiny bit. "Is this a bad idea?"

Isaac stares at me. With his back to the streetlamp, I can't see into his eyes. I wish I could, but his eyes are so dark it probably doesn't matter. I just want to look into them, to see if he's doubting this like I am.

He takes my hands and squeezes them. "I could use some comfort tonight, and I think you could too. Let's make a deal. One hour. We'll give one hour to each other. When one hour is up, you can tell me if you want me to come to your door sometime with something other than flowers. How does that sound?"

"Have you forgotten you're leaving the country on a long trip?"

He shakes his head slowly. "I don't have to extend my travel, and by the time I get back you'll be over the guy who broke your heart."

I purse my lips and look at him. Knowing he's leaving makes this decision as safe for my heart as possible. Our ending has already been decided. It's one hour, for one night, and then it's over.

My hand wraps around his neck, pulling him in. When my lips are at his ear, I whisper, "I hope your place is close."

The vibration of his groan grinds against my cheek. He surges forward, pulling me along behind him. Our pace is quick until he stops abruptly and looks back at me. This time the streetlight illuminates his face, and I can clearly see into his eyes. They look hungry.

"I don't know if one hour with you will be enough for me, Aubrey." He turns back around and keeps going.

I follow his quick footsteps, fully in the knowledge that one hour is all I have to offer him.

This isn't about love.

I have none to give.

This isn't about my heart.

It's not whole enough to break.

This is about one hour of forgetting, one hour of letting my body rule while my mind shuts off. I'm going to spend one hour with this man.

And then I'm never going to see him again.

5

I WAS certain of the outcome before I arrived, but I came here anyway. Hand poised to knock, I blow out my last deep breath. Three quick taps on the door and my hand falls back down to my side.

Hope isn't what I should be feeling right now, especially when it defies logic, but it's there anyway. Winding it's way into my veins, creeping into my heart.

When I've stared at the closed door for long enough, I turn to leave.

Isaac can't answer a door to an apartment he isn't in.

I had to check. I need to be able to say I tried.

I'm three steps away from the question I already knew the answer to when a door behind me opens.

My stride halts and I freeze. My heart leaps into my throat. *He didn't leave.*

"Excuse me? Did you knock on my door?"

It's a man's voice, but it's not the voice of the man I'm foolishly looking for.

Turning around, I nod and take a step closer.

The guy in the doorway is average size and his red hair is

pulled into a man-bun. He's so opposite of the home's previous tenant that it's comical.

"I was looking for the person who used to live here." My voice is steady but inside I'm quaking. For the shortest second I thought maybe Isaac stayed.

He holds up his palms and shrugs helplessly. "I moved in a few days ago. I'm not sure who lived here before. Or where they went."

I nod. "That's OK." Turning to leave, I say "Have a nice day."

"Good luck," he calls out. "I hope you find the person."

I throw back a smile and a thank you as I walk away.

Why am I this disappointed when I knew the ending?

My hope is gone, and that's a good thing, I guess. Better than having it hang around and haunt me.

Isaac really left.

For us there will be no first date. No showing up at my front door with something other than flowers.

The confirmation is a deliverance. I don't need to keep torturing myself with thoughts about what might have been.

I can stop dwelling on that night and focus on the future.

And my first step in that direction starts with a conversation I don't want to have.

SOME PEOPLE THINK self-reflection is a good thing, and I suppose it can be. But after a while, for someone as good and practiced at self-reflection as I am, it's more like a prison.

Right now, I'm in prison.

What if I hadn't gone out that night?

What if I'd told Britt no?

What if I told Isaac to take a hike instead of letting him hike up my skirt?

I wouldn't be where I am now, that's for sure.

I've thought of that night enough times that at this point, I'm sick of it. No matter how hard I try, I can't make the one picture I took at the bar capture more than it did. My forehead and Isaac's dark hair dominate the lower left corner, and the scene behind us is a blur of bodies and bottles. Nothing I can do will make any of this different.

My dad's truck engine can be heard down the block, long before it reaches our driveway. I sit on the living room couch and listen as it comes closer to our house. It sounds more like a slow march toward the guillotine.

He pulls into his spot and kills the engine. By now he's seen my car and is wondering what I'm doing here. It's Thursday, not Sunday. If I come over during the week, I tell him first, but this time, I couldn't spare any extra words. As it is, I'm not sure I'll have enough words to get through what's in front of me.

My shoulders jump when his truck door slams. I count backward in my head, picturing his walk up the path to the front door. *10...9...8...7...6...5...4...*

"Aubrey, what are you doing? Everything all right?" My dad stands in the doorway. It's an average size entry, and his large body fills a majority of the space.

The concern in his gaze causes tears to well up in my eyes.

He rushes across the foyer, forehead creased. His keys smack the coffee table. The couch dips beneath me as he sits.

"Aubs, what is it?" His voice is panicky. "Is it Grandma?"

I shake my head. "No, no. She's OK. I'm sorry, I didn't mean..." My voice trails off as I search for the words. "It's just..." I cover my face with my hands, unable to look at him as I speak. I didn't think we'd reach this point this quickly, but here we are. There's nothing to do but say it. "I'm pregnant."

My head stays in my hands, and I keep my eyes squeezed shut as the seconds tick by. The silence continues, growing and growing until I dare to peek at him.

He's ramrod straight on the couch, eyes wide, hands in a prayer position against his lips. His thumbs hook under his chin, and he's taking deep breaths, air filling his chest until it puffs out, then streams from his nose.

"Say something." My voice is tiny.

His gaze falls to the floor between his feet. "I didn't even know you were active...in that way, I mean. I just assumed that you, I don't know, were just..." He gulps, his cheeks red.

My face is so hot, I can feel the warmth in my ears. It doesn't matter that I'm twenty-one and an adult. His baby girl is pregnant, and he hasn't even heard the worst of it yet. I open my mouth to tell him the part that's going to make this bad dream a nightmare, but he starts talking first.

"You didn't tell me you and Owen were back together." There's an accusatory edge to his tone. It would be an understatement to say my dad simply *dislikes* Owen.

I clear my throat and pick at one of my fingernails. "We're not."

His eyes lock onto mine, his expression a mixture of surprise and horror. "The baby isn't Owen's? Are you seeing someone new?"

He's trying, I think, to control his emotions, but the devastation is there, visible in the planes of his face. Knowing I put it there hurts me to the core.

"I'm not seeing anybody, Dad." I take a deep breath and

look at my poor, mangled thumb nail. "This baby is the product of one night." *One hour.*

My dad stands and strides to the kitchen. I stay where I am, waiting. Listening as the refrigerator door opens, closes. He comes back a minute later with a beer in his hand. Half of it is missing already.

He doesn't sit. He leans against the wall and tips his head back until it's propped up by the wall too.

"One night, huh?"

"It's the only time I've done that and—"

He holds up a hand. "I don't want any details."

I make a face. "I wasn't planning on giving you any."

He pushes off the wall and sits by me again. "Who's the father? What did he have to say when you told him?"

"Um, well, the thing is, we didn't really exchange a lot of information, so I don't know how to get a hold of him to tell him." *This* is what I've been dreading telling him the most.

His open palm catches his drooping head, and he holds it there, his elbow propped on his knee. "Aubrey, I failed you."

I blink. I've spent a lot of time imagining what he would say, and *I failed you* did not make the list. "What are you talking about?"

"I should have talked to you more about sex. How to be safe."

We were safe. At least, we thought we were. And as far as Isaac goes, he still thinks the condom did its job. *You had one job, Condom. One job.*

"Dad, I'm old enough to know. And we were safe. The safety failed." I blush again. This conversation is not getting any easier.

He sits back against the couch, but I stay upright. I

haven't relaxed in two weeks, not since I realized my period was late.

"How are you going to tell him? What's his last name?"

"I don't know."

My dad sighs. "What's his number?"

"I don't know."

He sighs louder. "Can you go back to the scene of the crime and find him there?" He winces as he says it.

I do too when I realize what he's asking. "It happened at his apartment, Dad, not between pallets behind a grocery store."

He lifts his face to the ceiling and mouths *Thank God.*

"Geez, Dad." I rub my forehead. "I have his address, but it won't do any good. He was moving three days after we, um, spent time together." How am I supposed to describe it? I can't use the words Britt did. *Single serving, hit and run, one hit wonder.* And then I made the mistake of telling her about our one-hour arrangement, and it became our *hour of power.*

"And he wasn't lying, either." I add when I see the skeptical look on my dad's face. "There were moving boxes everywhere. Packed."

My dad drains the remainder of his beer.

"What now?" he asks.

"I need to find a doctor."

"And school?"

"I'll figure that out. Just not yet."

"What about the father? Does he have a name?"

I bite my lip, preparing to lie. I've already decided that Isaac's name doesn't matter. Knowing his first name isn't going to make him magically materialize. It was one hour. At this point he was a sperm donor. Just like my mother was a deliverer.

"Mike," I say, picturing the neon sign of the bar. *Can't get more basic than Mike.* "But I've already decided it doesn't matter. I can't locate him, and you won't be able to either."

"The hell I won't," he growls, his chest puffing out. "I'll hire a private investigator and—"

"He left the country three days after that night. A long trip, he said. And before you ask, I don't know why he was leaving. I didn't ask. Because I didn't want to know." *The less we knew the better, or so I thought at the time.*

One hour spent trying to forget, and for that I'll spend the rest of my life remembering that one hour.

"I made my bed, and now I'll lie in it. This baby wasn't planned, but it's mine." My hand goes to my stomach, rubbing the flatness. "I'll raise it myself. I know how to be a single parent. I've been watching you for years."

Dad shakes his head. "If only your mother—"

"Don't give her that much power. Don't start thinking about the way things could've been if she'd stayed." It's a fruitless endeavor. And it does more harm than good. I would know.

His eyes grow shiny. "Can I come to your first doctor's appointment?"

"I'd be mad if you didn't."

He hugs me the same way he did whenever I got hurt when I was little. The way only a dad can.

"Do you want dinner?" he asks when he releases me.

I nod, wiping my eyes. "Of course. A lot of dinner. I'm hungry these days."

He chuckles, but the sound is more incredulous than joyful. He goes to the kitchen. I follow.

"I have just one request for you." He looks over his shoulder as he stands in the open pantry and moves stuff around. "No more life-altering surprises for a long time, OK?"

"Agreed."

The rest of our evening is pleasant, mostly, but there are some awkward moments. My thoughts move frequently to Isaac, to our hour together, the way I quietly dressed and tip-toed out. Leaving wasn't as easy as I thought it would be. I liked his deep voice, his quiet competence, the way his hands felt on my skin, like they were supposed to be there. We had a tangled rhythm, an interwoven flow. The entire hour was an apex of cast-away pain and welcome pleasure. When our time was up I thought about telling him that *something other than flowers* when he came back was possible. In the end, my rational brain won. We had placed a time limit on ourselves, and so had circumstance. He was leaving soon. So I left first.

I had no way of knowing this would happen to me.

This isn't how I pictured my life going. But this is what it is now.

And if I know anything, it's how to handle the unexpected.

It SURPRISED me how much I liked being pregnant. But what surprised me even more was the way I felt when the doctor laid my baby on my chest.

"Did you decide on her name yet?" she asked. I'd been waiting until I saw my baby's face to name her.

"Claire," I whispered through the curtain of tears streaming over my lips.

A nurse approached with her arms open. "I need to clean her and take her measurements." She lifted Claire off my chest and, even though she was mere pounds, I felt the absence of her weight.

"Be careful. Don't trip." I told the nurse, frightened for

my daughter's safety for the first of what I knew would be countless times.

She smiled warmly. "Of course."

I've hardly set Claire down since the nurse finished up and brought her back. Everything about her feels right. It doesn't matter how she was conceived. What matters now is that she's here, and she feels like everything I was always supposed to have.

For the first time, I'm seeing what my mother lost when she left. I've spent my whole life thinking I was the one who missed out, but that's not completely true.

All I needed was Claire to show me. But the funny thing about truth is that it can't be controlled. The truth can hurt. And with the knowledge Claire brought to me comes greater pain.

Now I know exactly what my mother chose to leave. And even though I've only known Claire for twenty-four hours, there's no chance I would ever leave her. Being her mother is a privilege.

Every few minutes, Isaac's image pops into my head. I see his happy grin, feel his hands on my back. He would've been an excellent dad. Somehow I'm sure of it.

Claire startles in my arms, wails for a moment, then falls back to sleep. I wonder what this will all be like once we're at home? It won't be just me and Claire, and right now I'm really happy about that. Moving back in with my dad was a good idea. As independent as I am, I can't do this alone. He was in the delivery room with me yesterday, last night he slept on the excuse for a chair, and this morning he brought me breakfast.

I just wish he would stop making comments that cause me to think even more about Claire's father. "Dark eyes," he said before he went home to shower. He gave me a meaningful look, then he kissed the top of my head and left.

His comment wasn't lost on me. Neither is Claire's skin tone.

She has Isaac written all over her.

Something tells me she'll have his smile, too.

6

FOUR YEARS LATER

"SHE'S GOOD, ISN'T SHE?" My dad asks, but it's not really a question. His eyes don't stray from the field. Quickly he rubs his palms together, over and over.

It makes me smile. He always rubs his hands together like that when he's excited. I call it his grasshopper music.

"She's good." Claire's legs seem tiny, but they move quickly as she tries to maneuver in front of another little girl who has the soccer ball. "But she's also four." I feel the need to remind him of this fact, even though there's no way he needs reminding. Her birthday was last month. "They all are. It's supposed to be about having fun, remember?"

He sips coffee from his stainless-steel thermos and leans in to me. "I can't help it if my granddaughter is more talented and cuter than every other kid on the field, can I?"

My shoulders shake as I suppress my laughter. "You need to learn how to whisper."

We laugh together, our eyes on Claire as she charges down the field the same way she does in our backyard. She's an intense child with a take-no-prisoners attitude. She loves hard, she plays hard, and she's almost always happy. Except when she's sassy. But even then, it's a happy sass.

This is Claire's second season playing soccer. Her coach is the father of another girl on the team. He's never without the baseball cap bearing his alma mater's logo, and he needs to size up his T-shirt. When I look at him, the words *Dad bod* come to mind.

It's a perfect Spring morning, the kind I imagine people in cold climates fantasize about during the dark days of winter. In Phoenix there isn't a long winter, but that doesn't mean we don't appreciate a lovely March morning like this.

Claire's kicking the ball, dribbling like the coach showed her in practice last Tuesday, when something goes wrong. One cleat crosses over the other, and she goes down hard. My shoulders inch forward, but my feet stay planted as I wait for her to pop back up. I'm not too worried. Claire falls a lot. My dad says it's because her mind is so much faster than her feet.

This time, Claire doesn't get up. She rolls onto her right side and screams.

I'm by her side in seconds, crouching down. My dad and the coach arrive just after me, their voices blending as blood pounds in my ears.

Tears stream sideways down Claire's scrunched up face.

"Baby, what hurts?" My voice is panicked. I'm not good at calm. I could never be a first responder.

"My..." She's hyperventilating. Tiny, shaky gasps of air suck into her throat. "...arm."

My mind races, and my limbs feel like they've been hit with bolts of electricity. I'm trying to determine the next step. I'm the mother, I'm supposed to know what to do, but, *oh my God,* I don't.

I take a deep breath. "Mommy needs you to roll onto

your back, OK? I need to compare your arms to one another. Can you do that for me?"

She releases a fresh round of tears as she nods. With my hands on her back and bottom, I gently position her onto her back. She screams and grabs her left arm with her right hand. Adult hands crowd my vision, my dad's and the coach's, each automatically reaching out to help. I push their hands aside, my eyes finding the spot Claire has grabbed. *Her elbow.*

I don't have to look at her right elbow to know that her left elbow is already bigger than it should be. I meet my dad's eyes.

"The hospital's just a few blocks away. I'll go get the car." He jogs away.

I look back to Claire. She's quiet now, her cries soft, but that's going to end as soon as I pick her up. My insides twist, seeing my daughter in such pain and knowing that in order to get her help, I'm going to have to make it worse.

"I'm going to pick you up and take you to the hospital. Mommy loves you so much, and I'm going to make every-thing better."

Claire's gaze is frightened, but wide and trusting.

I'm gentle when I touch her. Gentle when I place one arm under her knees and another under her back. She whimpers the second I shift her. Using her right hand she keeps her left arm locked in place by her side and cries quietly.

With Claire secured to my front, I move through the crowd of concerned parents and children, delivering half-hearted promises to email them when we know the extent of the injury. I nod to the coach as we pass. He gives me a tight smile.

"Good luck," he calls out. He jogs back to the center of

the field, waving at the other little girls on the team to follow him.

Claire wails with every other step I take. "It hurts," she says through her tears. Somewhere in the back of my mind I appreciate the childlike ability to communicate pain. There is no holding back, no biting of the tongue.

"I know, baby, I know. I'm so sorry. I wish I had a magic wand so I could take away your pain. You're going to see a doctor, and he'll make you all better."

My dad waits on the curb, as close as he can be without driving onto the field. He jumps from the driver's seat and pulls open the back door. I slide in and keep Claire on my lap. She's keening, her grip still on her left arm. My dad's gaze flashes to her car seat, pausing there for a moment, then comes to rest on me.

I thought about it too, but there's no way to get her in there and buckled. I can't risk moving her elbow any more than I already have. "Just drive carefully." I close my eyes and rest my head against the headrest. "It's only half a mile." It makes me feel better to say this out loud. Nearly seventy percent of car accidents occur within ten miles of a person's home. Going in the direction of the hospital puts us roughly thirteen miles away from our house. Statistically, this is an acceptable risk.

Apparently my dad trusts me, because he runs back to the driver's seat and throws the car in drive.

Everything is going to be OK. It's probably a break. It's not as if something truly horrific happened. She's safe, she's not going anywhere.

When I open my eyes, Claire's eyes are on my face. Her lower lip quivers. I'm pushing all my love and good thoughts onto her, into those dark eyes that take me back to one hour nearly five years ago. Who knew sixty minutes of time spent with Isaac would produce the one thing I'd been missing my whole life?

Claire is my salvation. My saving grace. She came along and unknowingly gave me all the love I'd missed from my own mother. She gave me the opportunity to be in a mother/daughter relationship, even if I only know what it's like to be the mother.

My dad sends frequent, worried glances back at us in the rearview mirror. If we were driving any farther, I'd tell him to pay closer attention, but we're nearly there now.

I'm so lucky to have him. He's an incredible grandpa and an even better dad.

What would Isaac have done differently on that soccer field? I turn away from the thought. Claire has me, and I did my best.

THE HOUR-LONG WAIT in the emergency room feels like three. Claire stays on my lap and doesn't move. I haven't moved either, not since I adjusted myself without thinking and she cried. Since then both my feet have fallen asleep. Now they're numb.

I've never been to the emergency room. I've never broken or sprained anything. A cavity has never burrowed into one of my teeth, and not because Dad was vigilant about my oral care. Like most things, he assumed I had that covered.

So maybe my lack of experience waiting is why I'm fuming now. When we're finally taken back, we wait longer. The nurse comes back, I explain what happened, she takes Claire's vitals without jostling her, then she leaves. We wait *again*. It feels interminable.

"How much longer before she gets some kind of pain

medicine?" My question sails into the space and rustles the curtains hanging all around us. Distress, irritation, indignation, they all saturate my voice.

Dad has no answer.

With my free hand, I rub my eyes. Claire is cradled in my other arm, her lower half lying across my own. She's quiet but alert. It's only eleven in the morning. This day has already been forever. It might as well be eleven at night.

"I'm pissed too." My dad sends me an ironic smile over Claire's prone form. "Think we're alike?"

"Just a little." Despite my frustration, I allow a short laugh. When I was younger I'd pretend I was just like my mom. My Dad didn't put any sweetener in his tea, so I did, because that's probably what my mom would have done, and I was sure I was just like her. But ever since I became a parent, I see how much I'm like my father. And I also see how that's not a bad thing.

Finally, the nurse returns with a doctor.

"Hi, I'm Dr. Green." He extends his arm.

"Aubrey Reynolds." I do what I can not to jostle Claire while I shake his hand. "This is my dad, John."

Dr. Green shakes hands with my dad and looks at Claire. "And this is our tiny patient, huh?"

Claire looks at him with her big, brown eyes and nods. He bends down and shows her his stethoscope.

"I'm going to listen to your heart with this, OK?"

"I know what that is." Claire's little voice rings out. "I'm a big fan of stethoscopes."

I stifle a laugh. The doctor and nurse fall in love with Claire instantly, I see it in their eyes. It's the first Claire-like sentence she has spoken in hours.

Dr. Green smiles and asks Claire how she got hurt.

"I was playing soccer and my feet got tangled underneath me and I fell."

Listening to her talk about her injury makes my stomach ache. Dr. Green nods while she speaks, then he finishes examining her.

He tells Claire he's going to make her feel better and take some pictures of her arm. Turning to the nurse, he orders pain medicine and x-rays.

I lay Claire down on the bed, where she takes the medicine like a champ, but when we get to the x-ray room, she clings to me. Finally the x-ray techs give up trying to get me out of the room and drape a lead apron over me. I sit beside Claire, holding her good hand.

Once we're back in the emergency room bay, we wait some more. My dad takes out his phone and finds the PBS Kids app.

"WordGirl, please." Claire's request is so typical, it reminds me how constant children can be. All this drama, but she still loves what she loves.

Claire is on the bed, my Dad's phone propped up on a pillow that lies across her lap. Dad sits in the empty chair beside me.

"How're you holding up, Aubs?"

I groan under my breath, my eyes fixated on Claire. Blades of green grass stand out against the white bottoms of the cleats she's still wearing. Her soccer uniform is too big, the shorts folded over twice to fit her tiny waist. The hospital bed dwarfs her.

"I wish it were me." My eyes pinch as I try to maintain my composure. "She's only four. I'm twenty-six, and I have no idea what she's feeling right now. I hate knowing she's in pain."

"The worst thing for a parent is to watch their child suffer." He says it like he knows.

"And a grandparent, too, huh?" This can't be easy for him either. Grandpas are people who sneak you donuts when your parents aren't looking. He's that and more to Claire.

"Of course. But I was saying it from the perspective of a parent. Watching you suffer was hell on Earth."

My confusion pulls my attention from Claire and to my dad. "I've never injured myself. Did something happen I don't know about?"

His smile is sad. "Your mom. All your life I've watched you miss her, maybe less now that you have Claire. But so many times I saw the pain in your eyes, even though you never spoke a word of it. And there was nothing I could do to end your suffering." He shakes his head as if it's heavy, the white hair in his two-day-old stubble glinting in the fluorescent lights. "It's a hurt that lasts a lifetime. I'm sorry she did that to you. I'm even sorrier I couldn't give you pain medicine and make it better."

His words wash over me. This man, who stays quiet when most people talk, has just said more about my pain than I ever knew he understood. I lay my hand on his shoulder.

"It's OK, Dad. It wasn't your place to end my suffering. She should've never inflicted it. And you're right, I think about her less often since Claire was born."

Dad's hand covers mine, and he squeezes. Dr. Green pushes back the curtain and steps in, followed by a nurse. Dad and I stand.

"How are her x-rays?" I ask.

"It's a pretty bad break." He holds out a tablet with the images of the x-rays on the screen. "See this?" He points to a spot above her elbow, his finger moving along a line that cuts clean through it. "That's the break. It's called supracondylar, and it's going to require surgery." His gaze flicks to me. I think he's trying for sympathetic, but it doesn't resonate. This is just another day at the office for him.

"Surgery?" I look at my dad as if somehow he can make this all better.

"When?" my dad asks.

"ASAP. We're bringing in a doctor from another hospital now. He specializes in pediatric orthopedic surgeries. He's the best. No question."

"What happens next?" My dad asks the question that's in my head. My brain is still tripping over the idea of Claire's little body in a surgical setting. *Anesthesia... Iodine... Oxygen...*

A shudder snakes its way down my body. I take a breath and try to focus on what Dr. Green is saying instead of my own fear.

"We'll get an IV going, then she'll be moved over to surgery. They'll get her checked in and go over some things with you. Then the anesthesiologist and surgeon will tell you more." He looks at us expectantly, a canned smile on his face that isn't pleasant or unpleasant. Just a smile that says *my part of Claire's care is over.*

"OK." The tremble in my voice is impossible to hide. My Dad shakes hands with Dr. Green, I mutter a thank you, and he disappears back through the curtain.

Claire is still engrossed in her show. I sit beside her, one leg propped on the bed, the other dangling to the floor. "Sweetie, did you hear what Dr. Green said?" I press pause on the phone. Claire looks up.

"No. I was watchin' WordGirl."

Oh, my heart. She has all of it.

"The doctor said you're going to have surgery. You're

going to take medicine that will make you sleepy, and when you wake up, your arm will be fixed, OK?"

"I guess so." She shrugs, as if it doesn't matter one way or the other to her.

My eyes flash to the nurse setting up the IV. Dread sits like lead in my stomach. Like every child, Claire hates shots. She hasn't noticed what the nurse is doing, and just as I open my mouth to prepare her, the nurse says it's time.

The IV placement goes exactly like every immunization Claire has ever received. I hold her still and she cries loudly, even after the needle is out.

"Can I watch WordGirl again?" she asks when her sobs slow. The nurses eyes meet mine and we share a laugh.

"Sure," I say as I press a kiss to Claire's forehead. I hit play, and set the phone back on the pillow.

"I hope you weren't planning on using your phone anytime soon," I say to my dad as I settle myself next to him.

"Nobody needs me on a Saturday." He stretches out his legs, crossing his feet at the ankles, and leans back. "The only people who need to talk to me are here in this room."

"Thanks again, Dad. I'm glad I'm not doing this alone."

"Of course. Always."

He leans his head on the wall behind him and closes his eyes. Soon he's snoring softly. How the man can sleep right now, I don't know, but I'm envious. I settle in and find a spot on the wall to stare at.

Just when the wait begins to feel like it will never end, three nurses show up to take Claire to surgery. Claire, who fell asleep sometime after her third WordGirl episode, stays asleep the entire ride to the surgery floor.

My eyes never leave Claire. Not when the admissions person comes to ask me what feels like four hundred and sixty seven questions. Not when my dad comes in with bottled water and hands me one. What in the world did they put in her IV? She never sleeps through this much noise.

As if the nurse senses my concern, she informs me that a long nap is not uncommon. "Their little bodies are so good at doing what they need. Adults try to stay awake, but kids let their bodies lead."

I nod, appeased. I must look worried. I feel terrified. Like I've aged years since we arrived at the soccer field this morning.

Before the nurse steps out she turns back and says, "Dr. Cordova is almost here. He's a fantastic surgeon. Great with kids. I'll send him in to meet you as soon as he arrives."

I lift my eyes from Claire to watch the nurse leave, then get up to pull the curtain closed.

Dad sits in the corner, eyes closed again. Gently I settle into a seat on the end of Claire's bed and resume staring at my little girl.

This isn't a big deal. She'll be fine. This Cordova guy is supposed to be fantastic.

I keep going with my good thoughts, hoping positive vibes and prayers can keep the nausea at bay.

It works on my stomach but does nothing for the tears. They flow as I study my little girl's body. It's so perfect, so beautiful, so vital, so necessary to keeping my own heart beating.

The privacy curtain scrapes along the metal rod, and I turn to look at who's entering. A man in light green scrubs steps in, a smile on his face.

Our eyes meet, and his smile vanishes.

"Oh my God," I breathe the words, and the nausea I worked to contain fights to get out.

7

AUBREY

"You left the country." My first words are defensive. I'm already defending my choice, a choice he doesn't even know about.

Isaac swallows, his throat bobbing, and he nods once, slowly. "Yes. For eighteen months."

"You moved." I say it like it's an accusation.

"To a different place in Phoenix, yes."

We watch each other, two shocked expressions, two furiously beating hearts. Mine is anyway, and given his reaction, I can only imagine his heartbeats are keeping time with my own. The longer we stare, the more memories jump out of their hiding spots and dance between us.

My back pressed to his front door as his weight tumbled into me, his mouth on mine and the metallic sound of him fumbling to fit his key in the lock. How tangled his sheets became as we twisted in them. How we made the most of one hour.

His eyes are on me now, those deep, dark eyes.

Our daughter's eyes.

Oh no. *Our* daughter.

My daughter.

No no no. I'm doing this alone. Just me, Claire, and my dad. We're a team. Isaac doesn't know about Claire, and Claire doesn't know about Isaac. She's never even asked about her dad.

"It's nice to see you again, Aubrey." Isaac's voice is deep, full of something. I don't know what.

"You too, Isaac. Or should I call you...?"

"Dr. Cordova."

I nod, biting down hard on my tongue. The pain from it helps me calm down.

Isaac takes another step into the small space, closer to me. His eyes sweep my body. "Can I take a look at the patient?"

I look down at myself and see what he probably sees. Standing beside Claire's bed, my arms folded no less, I look like I'm trying to block access to her. *And I am, I suppose.* But right now, I can't. I have to let him in. Claire's arm is top priority.

I step aside, making it a point to look away from Isaac as I round the end of Claire's bed. As I pass him I feel the heat from his chest, remember what he looked like beneath me.

Briefly I meet my dad's eyes, ignoring the curiosity I see in them. Isaac steps up to Claire's bedside, and I suck in a breath.

She's yours, part of me wants to scream. Pictures of happy families flash through my head. But that could never be us. He's probably married by now.

He looks at her, and then back up to me. "She's your daughter?"

I nod, too afraid to speak.

"She's beautiful."

"Thanks." I whisper. He hasn't smiled since he stepped

in and saw me, and that's just one of many things that has my body tied up in knots right now.

"Dr. Cordova, I'm here. Traffic was awful, man." A man's loud voice fills the silence. We turn to it, and the man looks at Claire and winces. "Sorry. I didn't know she was asleep." He turns to me and sticks out a hand. "Dr. Main. I'm the anesthesiologist."

I take his hand. "I'm Aubrey Reynolds." My eyes flick to Isaac. He's watching me, his eyes lighting up when he hears my last name for the first time.

"I'm John Reynolds." My dad shakes hands with Dr. Main as Isaac walks around the end of the bed.

"Mr. Reynolds, I'm Dr. Cordova." Isaac's face is confused as his eyes move from me to my dad, like he's trying to understand who we are to each other.

It's not uncommon. My dad is young, very young to be a grandpa. We've been mistaken for a couple before, especially when Claire is with us, which is pretty much always.

They exchange pleasantries, and I wonder if Isaac is dying to ask if my dad is Claire's father. I'm dying inside too, trying to decide which to have a meltdown over first—my daughter's impending surgery or the fact that her surgeon is the man who fathered her and doesn't know it?

Of course I have to tell him, but I can't drop that bombshell on him right now. He's about to go into surgery. *With our daughter.* He needs to be focused and calm.

Isaac turns all business, and so does Dr. Main. "Claire has a supracondylar fracture. We're going to put two pins in her arm." Isaac focuses on me and my dad as he talks, and, using two fingers to represent the pins, shows us on his arm where they will enter Claire's. "We'll put on a temporary cast. I want to see her in ten days in my office for more x-rays and a hard cast."

"Mommy?"

I inhale sharply and turn to Claire. "Baby, you're awake. What do you need?"

"Have I had surgery yet?" Her voice is still sleepy. I run my hands over her hair and down her cheeks. "Not yet, love."

"Claire?" Isaac's voice is right behind me. It's smooth and strong and sends shivers down my back.

My hands shake so badly, I have to slip them into the back pockets of my jeans.

"Yes?" Claire turns her eyes on him.

"I'm Dr. Cordova. I'm going to fix your arm today. How does that sound?" His voice is soft, but not babyish. *It's just right.*

"Good. I tripped and fell playin' soccer." She smiles at him, and I see him in her face. He looks at me, his eyes questioning, and fear twists my stomach. Is he seeing himself in her too?

"Soccer?" He looks back to Claire. "I bet you're a great soccer player."

"I am," she says proudly.

He smiles at her. "Are you ready to get that arm fixed?"

"Yes." Her voice is unsteady now. Her lower lip trembles. "Can Mommy come with me?"

"You know what? This is an extra special room that only doctors and their brave patients can go to."

"I am pretty brave." Claire nods and purses her lips, like she's thinking. "OK, yeah, I can go. But not unless Mommy says OK. I'm not allowed to go places with people I don't know."

Isaac looks at me and smirks. "Safety first."

I allow a small smile, knowing he's thinking about the night we met and my open-drink policy.

Claire's head smells like last night's shampoo as I kiss it. "You can go, and I'll be there when you wake up."

Two nurses show up, and Dr. Main steps to the side of Claire's bed. He releases the bed's brake, and suddenly, it's all very real.

My baby is going under anesthesia, and the person who helped me create her is also the person who's going to fix her. It's too much for me to bear.

Tears roll down my cheeks as soon as the wheels on her bed start moving. "I love you, Claire." I'm trying to keep my voice under control, but it breaks anyway.

In three seconds she's past me, past the curtain, and heading down the hall. I feel sick watching her go.

"Everything's going to be OK, Aubs." My dad's tone is soothing, but it doesn't actually soothe.

"Aubrey, she's going to be OK. This surgery is a piece of cake. Honestly." Isaac still has that air about him, the one of total competence. It's a good thing for a doctor to have.

I swallow the lump in my throat, trusting him even though I hardly know him. Our eyes lock.

"I trust you." My voice is low. I don't know what it is about Isaac that made me trust him that night five years ago, and I don't know what it is that makes me trust him implicitly now. All I know is that I do.

Isaac and Dr. Main leave the bay. I hurry to the curtained exit and watch their backs, my hands steepled against my lips.

My dad steps in front of me. I didn't hear him walk up, but he's here now, his cheekbones pulled taut from his glare.

"You said his name was Mike."

. . .

"I JUST DON'T UNDERSTAND why you lied." My dad rearranges himself in the hard-back chair for the tenth time in as many minutes.

We were ushered to the waiting room mere seconds after my dad confronted me, and now we're trying to have a seriously private conversation in a very public setting. A very *quiet* public setting.

I rub my eyes and repeat the answer I gave him two minutes ago. "I don't want to talk about this right now. I'm scared and I'm freaking out and I don't know what to say."

Dad sighs and runs his hands through his hair.

I close my eyes, silently praying.

"What are you going to do now that he's back in the picture?"

My eyes fly open, and I turned to him. "Dad! Stop. Please." My whispered hisses don't go unnoticed, but the woman across from us looks away when our eyes meet. I can't blame her for being interested. It's not like there's much else to do right now.

Beside me, my dad's shaking his head. "I don't think I can, Aubs. It took everything in me not to blurt it out back there."

"Thank goodness you didn't. It's not your place."

He blows noisily through his nose and looks up at the ceiling.

My dad's a good ol' boy, the kind of man who does what's right. He'll do what he thinks is best or kill himself trying. There's no doubt in my mind he's going to insist I tell Isaac about Claire. And if I wait too long, he'll tell Isaac himself.

"I'll tell him, Dad. Don't worry."

"A child deserves two parents, Aubrey. Two." He holds up two fingers for emphasis.

"I'm painfully aware of that," I mutter.

"Then you should know more than anybody the right thing to do here." He's giving me his pointed look, the one he uses when he wants to convince me his way is the only way.

"I hear you." I hold up my hand to let him know to stop. "And I've already said I'll tell him. Let me just get my baby home and settled and take some time to understand what telling Isaac will mean for everybody."

"Don't wait too long. You're holding two lives in your hands."

"That's a little melodramatic."

He raises one eyebrow but keeps quiet. I look away and focus on the long hallway that runs parallel to where I'm sitting. I stay that way until Isaac appears at the wide entrance to the waiting room, a surgical cap on his head.

I jump out of my chair and rush to him.

"How is she?" The words fly from my mouth.

He grins his big Isaac smile. "She's perfect. Like I said, piece of cake. Someone will come get you and take you to her in recovery."

My dad's hand slides past me, palm out. "Thank you, Dr. Cordova."

"Just doing my job." He shakes hands with my dad.

"Aubrey." Isaac turns his attention to me. "As long as Claire comes out of anesthesia OK, she can go home today. They'll watch her for a while and make sure she doesn't fever, and then she'll be discharged. I want to see Claire in my office in ten days. We'll do x-rays and get her fitted for her next cast. My office information will be on her discharge papers."

"OK." I bite my lower lip, knowing there's no way my dad will let me go ten days before telling Isaac. Even right now I can feel him beside me, silently urging me to tell him this second.

I focus on those warm brown eyes I've seen in my dreams, and in my daughter's face, for five years. "See you soon, Isaac." I know I'll tell him. And I know I'll tell him soon. I just don't know what will happen after that.

I BARELY GOT a few bites of food into Claire after we got home. The discharge nurse warned me this would happen, but it still worries me. Usually Claire's appetite is voracious, the source of so many jokes about her being a teenage boy in a little girl's body. Begging her to take a third bite of applesauce took my already frazzled nerves and lit them on fire. She passed out as soon as I gave her pain medicine. Which was also something I was told to expect, but it was hard to watch.

I miss my little girl. Even though I've been with her all day, my little Claire has been absent. The wise nurse, who had clearly seen this plenty of times, also told me Claire would start acting like herself in a day or two. *Her body has been through a lot. And she probably doesn't understand most of it.*

As soon as I left Claire's room, I escaped to the front porch. Even though it faces the street, there's privacy. Ivy threaded trellises fill the space between the three brick posts that run the length of the porch. A large wooden swing hangs from the ceiling. My dad installed it last year, and when I questioned him about how securely it hung, he gave me a dirty look. I shut my mouth and fell in love with the damn thing, but every time Claire sits on it I feel nervous. I keep that feeling to myself though.

With one foot I push off the ground, letting the gentle

sway calm me. For the moment, hidden out here behind the wall of ivy, I can pretend like today didn't happen.

Of course, in order to forget, my mind would have to stop relentlessly throwing memories and what-if's at me. Right now, between the two adults living in this house, my dad is the only one allowing me to forget, and that's because he went mute the second we arrived home. I'm pretty sure he's mad at me for lying to him about Isaac's name. It was so long ago I don't even fully remember why I lied. Mostly I think it was to establish my distance from the fiasco that produced the best thing in my world.

The night is pitch black, but it's noisy. My neighbors are having a party. Judging by the giggles from girls and loud calls of *bro*, it's either the high-school son or older, college-age boy. Either way, it doesn't matter. It's a Saturday night. I'd care about the noise if Claire wasn't passed out harder than some of those partygoers will be later. And I certainly don't need quiet right now.

Taking a sip of wine, I push off the ground once more, sending the swing into the air. I breathe in a deep breath through my nose and blow it out loudly. The swing slows on its own, until it comes to a stop. With my face upturned and my eyes closed, I let out an audible groan.

"How did this happen?" The question slips out, joining the din next door. This whole day feels surreal. Maybe I'll wake up and find it was just a dream.

"That's what I'd like to know."

My eyes fly open.

Isaac is leaning against the brick post closest to me. He looks like Isaac from the night we first met. Jeans, a gray zip-up hoodie. His gaze is intense, and I find myself squirming beneath it.

"Mind if I sit down?" he asks, but he's already coming my way.

I shake my head and scoot over. The swing moves when he settles beside me.

"How did you find out where I live?" I concentrate on the intricate threading of ivy between the two posts. I can't bear to look in his eyes.

"I have a friend in admissions."

I nod, preparing myself for what I know is coming.

"I went there after the surgery. I wanted to know Claire's birthday." He speaks slowly, his tone resolute.

My breath sucks back into my throat and fills my lungs. If he hasn't already figured it out, he's right on the edge of knowing.

"February second," I whisper.

"And nine months before that was May. I don't know what you did for thirty out of thirty-one days that month, but I know what you did for one hour of it."

The nerves engulf my body. He deserves to know, I understand that, but what will happen once he does? I don't have the perfect family, but what I do have is my own tiny slice of heaven. Will he take that from me?

"Just ask the question you came here to ask." I can't take this. We need to get it over with so I can assess how much Isaac is going to threaten my way of life.

He shakes his head. "I knew the answer the first time I looked into her eyes. I went to admissions for confirmation. Between her birthday and the fact that you're the only parent listed on her paperwork, that was all I needed."

I look at him. He's facing me. I don't see anger on his face. His look is more...serene? No. Content? Maybe. More like pleased.

"I tried to find you." I feel the need to defend my actions, though he's accused me of nothing. "Two weeks after I got a positive test. I went to your apartment. You'd already moved. I knew you were long gone, to wherever it was you were going—"

"Africa."

"You went to Africa?"

"For a while, yes. Then I extended my trip and went to different areas in South America." He palms the stubble on his cheeks, throwing a glance at me. "I didn't think there was much for me here. And there, in the places I went to, the kids needed help. I learned a lot. It's why I was called today."

I don't know what to say. I'm beyond impressed, and in a way I feel like it's a good thing I left his place that night. All those children needed him to fix them, and back home there was one child who needed him in a different way.

"It's good to know you tried to find me." He says. "I didn't leave much of a trail, though."

The image of the man who answered the door at Isaac's old apartment flits through my mind. I shake my head and say, "I did what I could. After that, what was I supposed to do?"

Isaac's fists ball in his lap, then his fingers flex out. "I don't know... This situation is so messed up. This morning I got a call about a little girl who was going to need emergency surgery. And you know what? That's not uncommon. It's actually typical." He leans forward to rest his head in his hands. "But that's when everything typical ended. And what am I supposed to tell my fiancée?"

I knew it. I knew this was going to happen. He has a fiancée. He's a doctor with a fiancée and a perfect life and they're planning a beautiful wedding and he's going to take my little girl every other weekend and some holidays.

"You're engaged?" I don't know why it hurts, but in the middle of my chest, a twinge of pain creeps across my heart.

"We're getting married in June."

"That's only a few months away," I say, but he shakes his head.

"Next June. It's a long engagement." An odd look passes over his face. I can't place it for certain, but to me it looks like confusion. "She says there's a lot to do. Big affair. She's very traditional."

Of course she is. Ten bucks says she's blond. Long hair. Tall. Skin like porcelain. Face like a painting.

"Congratulations." I murmur. It's what I'm supposed to say.

Isaac looks down at the ground and laughs, but the sound is empty. "Thanks."

I curl my feet beneath me and scoot on the swing until I'm pressed against the far corner of it.

"So, what now?" I ask. Might as well get right to it. No need for pleasantries. No *what have you been up to in the past five years.*

"Can I see her?" Isaac asks, his face hopeful.

"Now, or always?"

"Both."

I nod and unfold my legs, standing. "She's asleep, but you can look in at her."

He follows me into the house. I lead him down the hall to Claire's room, which is across from mine. It used to be my dad's office, but he's never complained about the loss.

A big, oversize letter *C* hangs from a pink ribbon on her door. Gently I turn the handle and push, then step aside so Isaac can enter.

He pauses in the doorway and looks back at me. He reaches for my hand, pulling me until I'm beside him. His eyes find Claire in her bed, her broken arm propped up on an extra pillow. His face takes on a peaceful quality I know well. Looking at Claire does that to me, too.

He turns his head, and his eyes meet mine. He squeezes my hand. Our faces are only six inches apart, and even though I don't know Isaac any better than I did that night, I feel like I do.

I'm so conflicted right now. I know Isaac deserves to know his daughter. I know Claire deserves to know him. But I want to keep her all to myself in a place where I can protect her. I want all of her bedtime snuggles and Eskimo kisses.

And the tough reality is that she no longer belongs to only me.

8

ISAAC

I₅ I don't stop eating this ice cream, *caramel cookie* something or other, I'm going to be sick.

Doesn't really matter though. I'm a little sick right now anyway.

If Jenna wakes up and sees me with this tub in my hand, she's going to be appalled. My nervous eating bothers her.

But first I'd have to confess why I'm standing here in my kitchen with a half-gallon of ice cream in one hand and a spoon in the other.

Jenna, I have a daughter.

No, I didn't know about her. Not until today.

It happened five years ago. Right before I left for Africa. One night. One hour, actually.

One hour of Aubrey. Broken, sad Aubrey, who only wanted to forget about her pain.

I did that for her. Made her forget. I made her eyes roll back in her head, her back arch, her legs stiffen. Her dark hair fanned out on my white sheets, an incredible contrast. Her lips swollen, because I could hardly move my mouth from hers, even when I knew the clock was ticking. When I kissed Aubrey, my whole world felt *right*. And on that night, the night I found out everything I grew up believing was *wrong*, Aubrey filled a void.

But then she left an even bigger hole. I watched her go, and I wanted to stop her. We'd had an agreement, and she made her choice. I took from her, she took from me, and when I let her slip out my door, we had no idea what we'd created.

I'm not sure how Jenna's going to take it.

That's not true. I can make a pretty educated guess.

Jenna has a lot of expectations. She *expects* that everything will happen the way she plans it to. She *expects* that everyone will be just who she wants them to be. She *expects* problems will not arise, because she has created a world where problems do not exist.

I love her, I really do. She's been my friend since high school. When I ran into her two years ago at an industry event, it was like old times. We caught each other up on what's happened since we parted ways after graduation. She teased me for not being a part of social media and hiding from our friends. One date turned into two dates, and then we were dating. She didn't have any pain that needed healing, not like Aubrey. Jenna is a straight line. No fractures, no past wounds, just a whole body that's never been broken. I love her. I wouldn't be marrying her if I didn't love her. But I'd be lying if I said there isn't something missing.

That missing element was easy to ignore—until today when Aubrey came hurtling into my life again. Her breathing sped up, and mine did too. Her pupils dilated, and I didn't need a mirror to know mine did too. As a doctor I recognize the physical signs of excitement, but to feel them, to know the effect they have on the mind, is a different story. Right now those effects have me here in my kitchen, shoveling ice cream into my mouth and wondering if Jenna has ever made my pupils dilate.

I know the answer, but I'm telling myself I'm wrong.

What am I supposed to tell her? You don't excite me like a practical stranger does, but I still proposed? I was sure about you, but now I'm not? They're both true, but the second reason is more valid than the first. And it had nothing to do with Aubrey. When Jenna started buying Bride magazine, I started seeing things. Concerning things.

The wedding planning—that's when the veil was lifted, so to speak, when I finally saw just how many expectations Jenna has for her life.

Table settings, centerpieces, beribboned chairs, they're all just symptoms of the larger issue. This wedding is Jenna's life, in one flawless day. She has everything planned out, right down to our children's names. *Nothing trendy,* she told me. *Classic. Elizabeth and David.*

The name Claire shouldn't bother her then. But everything else about Claire will tear Jenna up.

Because I'm flawless too. Jenna's perfect surgeon fiancé.

Who has a lovechild from a one-*hour* stand five years ago.

Who eats ice cream from the carton in the middle of the night.

And, of course, there's that other thing that makes me imperfect, my invisible scar... Jenna doesn't know about that. Nobody outside my family does.

I shove another bite of ice cream in my mouth and toss the carton in the trash. Normally I would rinse the spoon and put it in the dishwasher and take out the trash—or at least bury the carton where she'd never find it. But not tonight.

In the morning I'm going to tell Jenna about Claire. She might as well know about the ice cream too.

"HEY, HANDSOME." Jenna's honeyed voice filters down to me. "Why are you on the couch? Did you sleep here?"

My sleepy eyes open to see her face hovering above me. She has white-blond hair, and it's long. *For the wedding*, she told me. After the wedding its *chop chop*. Those were her words, accompanied by a scissoring motion.

The bottom of her hair sweeps my shoulder as she brushes a kiss on my temple. Guilt parks itself in my core. I don't know why I feel guilty. I didn't do anything wrong. Maybe it's just because I know what I'm about to tell her and how it's going to affect her. Or maybe it's the fact that I woke up several times last night, and each time I thought about Aubrey.

I sit up and Jenna moves away, giving me space to stand. Instead I stay seated, reach for my T-shirt, and pull it over my head.

"I guess I fell asleep here." After I finished the ice cream last night, I sat on the couch to think. In truth, I was avoiding my bed, where Jenna lay peacefully, probably dreaming of invitations and exquisite floral arrangements.

Jenna smiles. "Sunday brunch? I haven't eaten since I got on the plane last night."

She travels for work, every week to a different city to visit different doctors. But she's always here on Sundays, the one day of the week we spend together. Soon she'll move her stuff in here, and this will be her home.

She's dressed in workout clothes, but I know she hasn't been to the gym. It's her regular Sunday attire.

"Jenna, we need to talk about something that happened to me at work yesterday." I look her in the eyes and wonder what her first words will be after she knows.

Confused wrinkles crease her forehead. "What happened?" She sinks down into a chair across from me.

"I was called to Mercy for an emergency surgery. A little girl." Claire's face comes to mind, her brown eyes so dark and deep. And those curls. I know where she got both of those things. The shock of seeing Aubrey made it harder to focus on Claire, and knowing I had to go into surgery kept me from delving any deeper. Questions darted around my brain, but I had to shut them down. My patient came first. *And my daughter. One and the same.*

"OK..." Jenna draws out the word.

I take a deep breath. "It turns out I know the mother. She's a woman I spent one night with a long time ago."

Jenna's top lip curls. "I get you have a past. We all do, but spare me the dirty details."

"Listen, please." I squeeze the back of my neck, trying to relieve the tension. When it doesn't immediately help, I drop my hand and say "I did the surgery, but something was bothering me. Afterwards I took another look at the patient's file." I keep my eyes on Jenna, because she deserves that much. Her chest rises slowly, she holds her breath for a long time, then slowly releases it. I think she knows what I'm about to say.

"So?" she asks, her voice shaky.

"Her birthday is nine months after the night I spent with this woman. The little girl is my daughter."

Jenna shakes her head vehemently. "It doesn't have to

mean that. It could be anybody. It doesn't have to be yours." Her breath draws in faster now, her chest heaving.

I despise what I'm doing to her. I've never seen Jenna anything less than poised. Her composure means everything to her.

"She's mine, Jenna. I confirmed it."

"How?" She bangs a fist onto her knee.

"Last night I went to see Aubrey."

Jenna's face pales. "The mother is Aubrey? Or the little girl? Where did you see her?"

"Aubrey is Claire's mother." I pause, letting Jenna have her reaction. She turns her head to the side like she wants to be sick.

I forge ahead. "I went to their house. The file listed their home address."

Jenna sets her eyes back on me. "While I was flying here to get to you, you were going to see your...your...baby mama?"

For a second I want to laugh. The words *baby mama* are so out of place coming from Jenna's mouth. The feeling dies fast.

"I needed to know for sure. I was already certain, but I needed to hear Aubrey say it."

"And she did?"

I nod.

"Well...uh...well," She falters for words, another thing that's very un-Jenna like. "She's probably lying. She's just found out her one night stand is a successful doctor and wants child support."

"Aubrey's not like that." I hear the defensiveness in my voice, and I know it's only going to make this worse.

"Oh, really? How would you know?" Jenna stands. She

crosses the living room, taking care to walk on the far side of the coffee table, away from me.

I'm up too, following her. She goes into the kitchen and opens the fridge, pushing stuff aside angrily. She slams the door shut, nothing in her hands. After moving on to the pantry, she stands in front of it, door open, fists balled at her sides.

"Aubrey didn't want to tell me about Claire. I think she would have preferred if I didn't know. She doesn't know me, and she doesn't know how I'm going to impact Claire's life. She's scared too." I walk to the open pantry door and stand behind Jenna. Her shoulders are lifted and tense, and I can't see her face. "Jenna, please. This is news to everybody—"

"Everybody except Aubrey." She whirls around. "Was she just saving this ace in her back pocket for the right time?"

"No, no, not at all." I rub my eyes, trying to figure out how to explain this to Jenna. "When Aubrey found out she was pregnant, she couldn't tell me. It happened right before I left for Africa. And…" I hesitate, embarrassment coming over me. "We didn't exchange a whole lot of information about each other that night. Including last names." My neck feels hot.

Jenna's jaw drops a few inches. "You had sex with someone whose last name you did not know?"

I don't say anything. I don't appreciate being judged, but right now isn't the time to point that out.

"Don't get hung up on that. It was a long time ago."

"Isaac—"

"Just understand, please. You're not perfect." But isn't she? Never a hair out of place. I'm not even allowed to touch her hair after a certain time of day. Does she have a fault? I'm not so sure. We never fight. Ever. Except right now. And it's not even a real fight. I'm basically just tossing shocking information at her, the equivalent of cold water, and telling her to deal with it.

She takes a deep breath. "OK. What now?" Her voice has returned to a normal volume, but the stress she's feeling strains it.

"I'm going to see Claire this afternoon. Aubrey said I could come over."

"What?" Jenna's face hardens. "Are you kidding? Sunday is our day. I leave again on Tuesday."

"Claire has school during the week. I'm lucky Aubrey is even letting me see her. She doesn't have to, you know. I have no right to her yet." But I will. It's something I'm going to see about.

I sigh and study my fiancée's face. The shock is still there in her dazed, bugged out eyes. I can't blame her for that, but shocked or not, I need to know where she stands. "Are you with me in this, Jenna? We need to be a team."

Jenna stares at me, her face only inches from mine. Her blue eyes are cold. It's terrible timing, but I can't control my thoughts, and right now I'm picturing Aubrey's eyes and how, even when she was revealing to me her ugly truth, her blue eyes remained warm.

"No." The surprise is gone from her face. Now her gaze is steady, a carefully placed mask of frosty calm. "I signed up to marry Isaac the brilliant orthopedic surgeon. Not Isaac the single dad." She steps away from me.

I silently repeat what she's said, just to make sure I understood. Her *no* is echoing in my mind. "Are you kidding me?" I have to ask, because what she just said is inconceivable to me. If the situation were reversed, I know where I would stand.

"Isaac, I love you. I want to build a life with you." She

takes another step away, her eyes on me. "I want kids, you know that. Just not somebody else's." She pivots and walks from the kitchen.

Like someone punched me in the gut, the air whooshes out of me. How could someone not want Claire? I hardly know her, and I want her more than I've ever wanted anything.

I stay there, in my kitchen, until Jenna comes back a minute later. Her roller bag is behind her, and I realize she was still packed from her trip.

"It's not fair of you to expect me to accept this." She stands straight, like she's up against a wall.

"I knew you'd be upset, but—"

"Stop. Don't tell me how I'm supposed to be a bigger person." She waves a stiff hand while she speaks. "Don't tell me how I'm supposed to be understanding. It's not fair for you to expect me to want this."

I'm not sure if I'm stunned or disappointed or both. "If you loved me, really loved me, you would find it in your heart to love what I created. She's a part of me. That will never change. And now that I know about her, I'm never going to be without her." I feel it so strongly that I wonder if, on some level, I knew there was a person out there with my DNA. The moment I spent in Claire's bedroom, watching her sleep, I felt whole.

Jenna stares at me, her face stoic. Between the empty expression and the white blond hair, she looks like an ice queen. With a heart to match.

She pivots and walks, the small plastic wheels on her roller bag making the only sound in the place.

Bump, bump, bump into the foyer.

Bump, bump, bump over the threshold.

The slam of the front door is like the exclamation point

on her noisy departure.

I could go after her. Make her see my side of this. Ask her to look at it differently. The seconds tick by and I stay frozen in place. After a minute, I know I've lost the chance.

Honestly, I don't know if I wanted it.

9

AUBREY

THE SWINGS WERE ALWAYS my favorite as a child, and they're Claire's favorite too. Seven times since she woke up this morning I've told her she won't be on the swings again for months. And just now makes the eighth time I've said it.

"But, Mom." She draws out the vowel so it sounds more like *Mo-om*.

"No, Claire," I say a little too sharply. Regret blossoms instantly.

"I'm sorry, baby." I pull her up against my side, careful not to touch her hurt arm. "I'm just a little out of sorts today. Forgive me?"

I feel the bob of her little head against my thigh.

"What *can* I do today?" She sighs and sits down carefully on the little pink-and-yellow striped chair with her name embroidered on the slipcover.

"We can play games. We can watch a movie. Just take it easy until you get your real cast." This isn't going to be simple. Claire is accident-prone, but she always bounced off whatever she collided with, including the ground. Before yesterday we joked she had rubber bands for bones.

"Hmph," she says, petulant. If she could cross her arms right now, she would. "I wish Grandpa was here."

My dad left early this morning. He didn't tell me where he was going, but it's his day off, so it's safe to assume he's trekking over some far-off mountain and he'll be gone all day. Hunting is his passion, and if he's not hunting, he's hiking.

"What if I told you you're going to have a visitor?" I try to smile, but trepidation might as well be my middle name right now. How am I ever going to tell her about Isaac?

She nods enthusiastically and bounces a couple times in her chair. I wince and put my hands out to settle her down.

"Aunt Britt?" she asks.

"No." I make a mental note to call Britt later. *Hi, Claire broke her elbow and had surgery and the surgeon turned out to be the guy who fathered her. K, bye.*

I attempt a nonchalant smile. "Dr. Cordova is going to stop by."

Claire sends me a questioning look. Even her four-year-old brain finds it odd. Our pediatrician has never visited our house.

I grab a book off the shelf and open it. It's a Magic Treehouse chapter book, one we've read a dozen times, but Claire loves it. Soon she's swept up in the story, and the swings and our impending visitor are forgotten.

We finish the book and start another. We finish that one, also, and one more. She hands me another, but I put it back on the shelf.

"I need a break. Mommy's mouth is getting tired." Besides, it's time for the next dose of pain medicine, and Isaac will be here soon.

She takes the medicine without a fuss and follows me to

our bathroom. Claire sits on the toilet lid while I make myself presentable.

"Can I have lipstick too?"

"It's lip balm. And yes, you can." Her tiny hand reaches for the tin. I hand it to her, forgetting for a moment that she can't do anything with it, thanks to her broken arm. Bending down next to her I take the tin, then hold it out so she can scoop a little balm on her finger and apply it. My breath catches in my throat when I watch her little hand work. Her mind is intelligent, her heart big, and her soul brave, but her finger is tiny.

She finishes smearing the cherry lip balm on her lips and smiles at me proudly. Using my pinky, I rub off what's beyond the lines of her lips and smile at her.

"Now I look just like you," she announces, her smile wide.

And she does...sort of. But after seeing Isaac yesterday, it's clear how much she resembles him.

Leaving the bathroom, we settle in the living room and play Candy Land. Every few minutes, my gaze strays to the clock.

"I won again!" Claire yells gleefully.

"How do you keep winning?" I ask, making a silly frown face. It's possible I stack the deck in her favor.

There's a knock at the door, and my heart moves into my throat. I stand, wiping my hands on my jeans as I walk, and run them through my long hair. With shoulders squared, I pull open the front door.

Oh, my heart... my poor, stupid, lonely heart.

Isaac has his trademark smile ready. His white T-shirt looks soft. I like the way it spreads out over his chest, how it hugs his biceps. His pecs are big enough that it causes a ripple in the shirt, like a plateau that suddenly drops off.

Don't even get me started on the tan of his skin against the stark white of his shirt.

"Aubrey?"

I finally look into his eyes, a blush warming my cheeks when I see the confusion in them.

"Yes, hi, I'm sorry." I stand aside to let him in. "Just nervous." *Is that what you want to call it?*

"Me too," he says, walking past me.

His scent swirls in the air. *Smoky wood and vanilla, mixed with something sweet.* It makes my legs feel weak and wobbly. I make good use of the open door by leaning against it and turning my head to gulp the fresh air flowing in.

He has a fiancée. Remember that.

"Hi, Claire. How are you?"

Isaac saying Claire's name brings me back to reality. I close the door and hurry into the living room, where Isaac is folding himself into a cross-legged seat beside Claire.

"Hi, Dr. Cordova." Claire smiles up at him, then resumes her gathering of all the Candy Land cards. She's turning them all face up and then putting them in piles by color. It's a process, especially one-handed, but she's determined.

"You can call me Isaac, if you'd like." He leans a cheek against a fisted hand and rests his elbow on his knee. The look on his face is unfathomable. I couldn't describe it if I wanted to.

"Mommy, what is Dr. Rialta's first name?" Claire doesn't look at me, too intent on her sorting.

"I don't remember. Why?" I settle myself on the floor, closer to Claire than to Isaac.

"Can I call Dr. Rialta by her first name too?"

I can't help but laugh. Isaac grins.

"No, honey. Dr. Rialta is just your doctor." I pause to look at Isaac. His eyes are on me, waiting for me to continue.

Emotion ripples across his face, and to me it looks like hope. "Dr. Cordova, I mean, Isaac... He's special, baby. More than just your surgeon."

My stomach knots. Am I going to tell her now? Is this the right time? And what will it even mean to her? She's a child. How will she make sense of this?

I take a deep breath. *Go into this without expectation. That's the best you can do.*

Isaac's gaze is still on me. I look into his eyes, trying to assess and understand what he wants me to do. He nods his head, only a little, but it's enough.

"Claire, can you take a break from what you're doing and look at me?"

She drops the cards and turns her wide, trusting face toward me. I gather her good hand in both of mine and wish desperately I could hold the other, too. But then if I could hold both her hands, none of this would be happening.

"Isaac is special because..." I freeze, swallow. The words are there, but they won't come out. I look to Isaac, eyes pleading. He scoots closer, until his crossed leg presses against my own. The smell of him fills my nostrils once more and makes this whole experience even more surreal.

He covers our bound hands with one of his. "Claire, I'm your dad."

Claire stares at him, her eyes narrowed as she mulls over what she has just heard. My breath sticks in my chest, waiting for her next words.

"Annabelle has a dad," she says slowly. "So does Walker. And Alexa. And Kohen. They all have dads." She falls quiet but keeps her eyes on Isaac. Then she looks at me. "I have a dad too?"

I will not cry. I will not cry. When the burning sensation behind my eyes passes, I say, "Yes. Isaac is your dad."

She looks back to him and nods her head. "OK. I liked you when I met you anyway."

Isaac and I laugh, and it cuts through the thick tension in the room.

"I brought my favorite patient a present." Isaac grabs a bag lying next to the couch. How had I not noticed him carrying it? Oh, right. I was gaping at his chest, then gasping for air.

Claire holds out her arm and grins excitedly. Isaac pulls a box wrapped in pink paper from the plastic bag and sets the gift on the floor. It's covered in loose, haphazard tissue paper, as if wrapped by a child. *He's made it easy for her to open.*

In seconds she has pulled off the thin sheet of paper. "What is this?" She asks, turning the box over and looking at the back.

Isaac sends me a disbelieving glance before he looks back at Claire. "LEGOs. Do you have any LEGO sets?"

"No." She positions the box between her legs and uses her thighs to hold it in place. With one hand, she tries to open the box. Isaac watches her with wonder on his face.

"Do you want some help opening that?" he asks.

Claire lets out a frustrated stream of air from her nose. "Yes."

"It's OK to need help," he says. "You're at a disadvantage with your broken arm." He looks up at me as he takes the box and opens it. "But it's good to see her figuring out how to manipulate objects. That's why kids don't need physical therapy the same way an adult would in this situation. Play will be her physical therapy."

I nod and gather the ripped tissue paper. I need something to do with my hands. I'm on my way to the garbage can in the kitchen when I turn back around.

"Would you like a drink, Isaac?"

He looks up from the piles of LEGOs he and Claire are dumping onto the floor. "Only if I can watch you open it. I don't accept open bottles from strangers." He winks at me.

I blush and look down even as a smile tugs on my lips. "One unopened bottle of water, coming right up."

I deposit the balled-up handful of paper into the recycling bin and grab two bottles of water, plus Claire's pink water bottle with the purple unicorns on it.

I step out into the living room and freeze. Isaac and Claire sit beside each other, LEGOs spread before them, bent over the instruction manual. Isaac points at a page, telling Claire what pieces they will need first, and then Claire puts her good hand on his knee, and he stops talking. She smiles up at him for a few seconds, then turns back to the pieces and begins rifling through them.

Isaac looks up, finds me watching. His eyes shine.

"Thank you," he mouths.

I don't know what he's thanking me for, and I don't ask. This moment is too beautiful to be interrupted by mere words. There's so much more happening here, so many emotions running as I watch these two people I've known but who didn't know each other. *Family,* I think, but the other *F* word comes screaming into my mind.

Fiancée.

I join Claire and Isaac in their building of a magical dragon and the elves who command it, but I keep reality closer to heart. There's no use dreaming of something I can never have.

Next summer Isaac will be married, Claire will have a stepmom, and we'll share custody.

I'll never have a happy little family, but is it really that big of a letdown? It's not like I ever thought I would.

10

ISAAC

I DREAMED about Aubrey last night. Her long, dark hair, my hands running through it. She was in my bed, but she was wearing pajamas. Sensible ones. My bedroom door opened, and Claire ran in and jumped into bed with us. She bounced and smiled and told us we were sleeping too late. She didn't have a cast on her arm.

I know why I had the dream. It's obvious. I spent the whole day with Aubrey and Claire. I stayed until John came home from a day spent scouting, which I learned was when you go to the place you're planning to hunt and look around to get a feel for the area. It's a foreign concept to me, scouting and hunting, but John made it sound interesting. My dad never does anything like that. His hobbies are gardening and golf.

I like talking to John. He has a slower way about him, like he's evaluating your words carefully before responding, instead of thinking about what he's going to say while you're talking. And I can't help but admire him for being a single dad. Aubrey hasn't mentioned her mom, or lack thereof, and Claire didn't reference a grandma.

I'm making the leap and assuming she's not in the picture.

Which I can't understand. I didn't understand it when Aubrey told me about her mom the night I met her, and I don't understand it now. How a parent just leaves a child... It's unimaginable to me. How can someone walk away from the child they created? How could someone walk away from Aubrey?

Kind, brave, gorgeous Aubrey... She wears her misfortune like a suit of armor. Her face stays so calm, stoic, not revealing anything. But her eyes say much more than her mouth ever could. Speaking of her mouth... She has the prettiest, pinkest lips that twitch when she holds back a smile, which is frequently.

I roll over and groan into my pillow. I've thought of Jenna a handful of times since she left. Considering I was going to marry her, I'd say that number should be a lot higher. But Aubrey? She has been rooted in place in my mind since I said goodbye to her last night.

I need to get my head straight before I go to work. When I work, there can be no Aubrey, no Jenna, no problems, no nothing. My focus must be singular. That's why I can't miss my workout today.

I jump out of bed, pull on running shorts and a T-shirt, grab my keys and phone, and head out. When my headphones are in place, I turn on something loud and frenetic.

Electronic music pounds in my head, and I pound the pavement. My route takes me a few blocks up and over, through a park, and, even though it's barely light outside, I think of Claire and whether she'd like it there. Don't all kids enjoy playing at parks?

I pass the swings and something that looks like it spins if pushed. Maybe in a few months, when her arm is healed, I can bring her here. There aren't very many kids in my neighborhood, but it's safe and clean and the few neighbors I've met are nice.

When I get home, I shower and eat breakfast. I have appointments all morning and a surgery this afternoon. Same goes for the next three days.

Scrubs on, I head for my car. My phone dings with a text message. I halt for a second when I see her name.

Claire is asking for you. Dinner tomorrow night?

I type out my response, pausing to finish before I get in my car and turn it on. I drive to work with a weird feeling in my stomach. I know I'm excited to see Claire, and I wonder if any of this excitement has to do with seeing her mother too.

I'M BEAT. It's late, I'm tired, and I want a shower. I'd also like to erase the images of the small child who needed surgery late this afternoon. Right as I finished up my scheduled surgery, a nurse came to tell me there was an emergency. She handed me the x-rays, the fracture in his leg easy to see. What wasn't so clear was how the injury occured. That's the part that has me feeling like I've been run over. I keep telling myself I did my job, and Child Protection Services will do their job now.

I need food, drink, shower, bed. In that order.

When I turn the corner of my neighborhood, I see my driveway isn't empty like it's supposed to be. Suddenly all those basic needs just got a whole lot further from my reach.

I park and get out, walking to the front door. Jenna leans against the wall. Her wary eyes watch me.

"What are you doing here?" I ask tersely, coming to a

stop in front of her. She made things perfectly clear on Sunday morning. She wants nothing to do with Claire.

"I think we should talk." Her face softens and she reaches for me, running a hand down my cheek. "You look tired."

I turn my head and her hands drops. "Shouldn't you be somewhere else right now? Portland, Dallas, Seattle?"

"Denver, actually." She exhales slowly. "I canceled my meeting. This is important. *We* are important."

"I thought you got everything off your chest yesterday."

Jenna glances out into the dark street. "Can we discuss this inside?"

Nobody is there, not that I know of anyway, but she's right. We don't need a public scene.

She follows me in, saying "I didn't want to use my key. Not after...yesterday. It didn't feel right."

I go straight for the kitchen and pull open the fridge. After pushing aside some stuff, I locate leftovers and begin to eat them cold.

"Do you want me to warm those up for you?" Jenna's watching me from the entrance.

"No thanks." I take another bite. Cold lasagna isn't good, but I'm too starved to care.

"Isaac, please. Look at me." She comes closer, stopping a few feet from me.

"Why are you here?" I set the plate on the counter and give her what she has asked for.

"To tell you that I want to try. I changed my mind." She folds her hands in front of herself. "I was in shock yesterday and I reacted badly. I'm sorry about what I said. Really."

She steps lightly until she's next to me. Her hand goes to my shoulder. "Isaac?"

"I heard you," I say.

"Then what do you think?"

Looking down at Jenna, I can't help but think about the mistakes people make. Everyone's allowed to have a bad reaction, right? I wasn't expecting it to be pretty, anyway.

Well, here goes nothing. Trial by fire.

"I'm having dinner with Claire and Aubrey tomorrow night. Do you want to come?"

11

AUBREY

I'm really happy Britt stopped by my desk this afternoon. I needed this drink. I didn't realize how wound up I was until I set my purse down and ordered my first fruity cocktail. With every sip of my pineapple mojito, it feels like my shoulders drop an inch from my ears. And it helps I don't have to worry about Claire. My dad picked her up from school and is probably letting her eat and watch whatever she wants.

"How was your date?" I ask Britt, smashing mint leaves into the bottom of my glass with my straw.

She finishes eating the cherry from her Dirty Shirley and looks at me, perplexed. "Which one?"

Britt dates for the both of us. That's our running joke anyway. She's weeding through the candidates so I don't have to. It's very pseudo-altruistic of her.

I laugh at her confusion. "The one you went on last week."

"Oh." Her face sours. "Awful. Terrible. He wore socks."

"And that's bad because...?"

"He was also wearing sandals."

My nose scrunches.

"Yep." Britt says, her voice grave.

"Do you think he has sex with his socks on?" My shoulders shake as I sip my drink.

Britt pretends to vomit in her mouth. "What if he has sex with his socks *and* sandals on?"

I shut my eyes and shake my head, hoping maybe that will make the vivid images fly from my mind.

"Let's stop talking about that guy." She puts a finger in her mouth and sticks out her tongue. "Tell me more about you. Tell me more about Claire. You sent me a message when you were in the emergency room with her, and then I didn't hear much else. How is she?"

"She's good. Really good. She went through her surgery and then... she's fine." I stall, taking a sip of my drink.

Britt gives me the kind of look someone who's being evasive should receive. "Feel free to tell me more than that. I'm her godmother. I sent her an obscenely huge cookie bouquet."

My eyes narrow. "Thanks for that. She can't do anything physical to release pent-up energy, and she's nearly bouncing off the walls from sugar overload. Between you and my dad, who can't seem to tell her no, I think she might combust."

"You. Are. Welcome." Britt tosses back the remainder of her drink. "I'm really sorry I couldn't be there for you. I was in San Diego and—"

"Don't be sorry. If you were in town I would've expected you, but you weren't. I had my dad. And..." I take a deep, noisy breath. Britt is going to lose her shit in about two seconds. "I had Claire's father."

"What!" Britt smacks her hand on the table. I don't need

to look around to confirm that people are staring. I can feel their interested gazes.

"You had Claire's father?" Her voice is opposite now. A shocked whisper.

"He was the surgeon who repaired her fracture." I fall quiet, giving the words time to sink in.

"Wha...What?" She shakes her head.

Saying it out loud makes it sound even crazier. "Apparently he specializes in pediatric orthopedic surgery. I didn't know it was a thing, but it is. Not all surgeons will work on children. But he does. So...yeah."

"So he showed up and you guys were like, *hey I know you*? Does he know about Claire?" Her voice turns lower, like it's a secret from the people around us.

"We recognized each other right away. He looks just like he did that night." *Maybe even better.* "And, yes, he knows Claire is his. He figured it out on his own." I recount the story of Isaac showing up at my house Saturday night, and his visit yesterday, all to the gasps and head-shakes of my best friend.

"Ho-ly shit." Britt tips her head to the ceiling and takes a deep breath.

"I know."

She levels her gaze back onto me. "What are you going to do?"

"I don't know. Go along with it. I'm sure he wants custody. Shared, probably. He's super into the idea of being a dad. He wants her." It was clearly visible on his face the day before. The way his eyes softened when he looked at her, the words he spoke to me when he left. *She's the best person I've ever met.* "Part of me feels bad, you know, because he missed out on the last four years. But I tried. I tried to find him. I just...it's not like there was much to go on."

"And how do you feel about all this?"

"Scared. Nervous." I stir the straw in my drink. "She's my everything. And I've never had to share her."

"Do you want to know what I think?"

"Sure."

Britt pushes aside her empty drink and levels her serious gaze on me. "You're an incredible mom. Even better than my own. And she's amazing. I know you're going to figure this out."

I give her a lopsided grin. "That's sweet but do you have anything more impactful? Like a how-to book?"

"I don't think there are instruction manuals on how to manage your baby daddy who didn't know he was one."

I groan. "Don't say baby daddy. It sounds vulgar. And Isaac is the opposite of the image those words conjure."

"Really?" Britt wiggles her eyebrows. "Do tell."

Images of Isaac in scrubs comes first, closely followed by the white T-shirt he wore yesterday. "If it's possible, he looks better. Aging five years agreed with him."

"It's hard to imagine Isaac looking *better*. He was delicious back then. Are you three going to become a happy little family?" She claps her hands together excitedly.

I shake my head. "He's getting married next year. June." The thought makes me sad, even though I have no right to be.

"That's a long time from now." She counts quickly on her fingers. "Fourteen months, to be exact. What did his fiancée have to say when she learned about you and Claire?"

"He didn't say. I don't know if he's told her yet. It's kind of a lot to tell a person."

"True. Do you know when you're going to see him again?"

"Tomorrow night. Claire asked to see him." Just the

thought of having dinner with Isaac sends my stomach into a tightly wound ball of nerves.

Britt taps her index finger on the center of her bottom lip. "Don't lose sight of your dream just yet, Aubrey. You may get that happily ever after."

"I don't dream of happily ever after, Britt. You know that. It's not in the cards for me. It never has been." Yearning for something impossible is foolish.

"You're ridiculous."

"I'm realistic."

"Is this where I'm supposed to say something like 'Open yourself up to love's possibilities'?"

"Please don't."

Britt studies me. Her lips pull and twitch like she wants to say something.

"What?"

"Of all the hospitals in all the towns, you walk into his..."

I throw up my hands. "No more Casablanca for you. And no more romanticizing this. It's coincidence. That's all. Make it into a math problem." I hold out my hands, gesturing with my left first. "In Phoenix there are x-number of orthopedic surgeons who do pediatrics and y-number of children who need surgery. Your answer is the likelihood each child has of ending up with each surgeon. Done."

"Call it a math problem if it helps you make sense of everything." She pats my shoulder. "Do what Aubrey needs to do to get through it."

"I need a subject change, please. This development in my life has been stuck on a loop in my mind, and I need to talk about something else."

We discuss Britt's parents and their move to a new house better suited for being empty nesters, but I'm only partially listening. Britt's words struck a nerve. *Do what Aubrey needs to do to get through it.*

Is there something else I'm supposed to be doing?

THE BUTTERFLIES in my stomach have increased throughout the day, growing and stretching, until I wonder if their wings are made of acid.

Work was hell. I sat at my desk and pictured all the disastrous endings this dinner will probably have.

I'm sure he's bringing his fiancée. He didn't mention it, but why wouldn't he? It has to happen one day.

Stopped at a red light, I poke my fingers through my gold hoop earrings, fiddle with the shoe strap around my ankle, check my lipstick in the rearview mirror, look back at Claire. We're almost to the restaurant.

Isaac called earlier this afternoon and offered to pick us up, but when I asked him if he had a car seat, he laughed.

"Right," he'd said. "I'd better get one of those."

Then he asked if Claire would like to go to an upscale arcade, a place with a bowling alley, billiards room, and restaurant.

When I asked him about her ability to play one-armed, he laughed again. Apparently, Isaac thinks this whole situation is great. He spends every moment of his life smiling or laughing. It baffles me.

I pull into a spot, get out, and unbuckle Claire. She hops out with a wide grin on her face.

"Is he here yet?" Her shiny eyes hold no reservation. She's one hundred percent excited, one hundred percent happy, one hundred percent into Isaac.

"Let's go find out." I offer her my hand and she takes it.

We find Isaac waiting out front for us. And he's *alone.*

"Hello, ladies." Isaac bends down and slaps a high five with Claire. He straightens and looks at me. His lips form a line until a slow opening in the center makes them peel apart. His eye dance with unspoken words.

What is he holding back?

"Thanks for inviting me out," he says, and I feel very certain that's not what he was thinking just now.

My weight shifts to my other foot. "Claire really wanted to see you again."

"Right." He nods. "Well, Claire, are you ready to have some fun?"

"Yeah!" she yells, one fist in the air.

"Can I have fun too?"

My head snaps around to the voice. A woman's voice. A tall, casually dressed but immaculately well-kept woman. Who has stopped at Isaac's side and woven her arm through his.

Isaac glances at me. I hope I've rearranged my expression into something that passes as kind. Whatever emotion was on there, it wasn't something I wanted him seeing.

"Aubrey and Claire, this is my friend Jenna."

Jenna smiles at us and waves hello, but keeps her position beside Isaac. Her posture is stiff, but looking at her face you'd think she's not at all nervous.

Isaac does his best to keep it from becoming more awkward than it already is. Thank god for Claire, who keeps us all from having to spend too much time faking conversation.

We follow her from game to game, watching. She squeals when she tries to smack the rodent that keeps popping up from different holes, and it's quickly apparent that one-handed basketball shooting is not where her talents lie. She wastes a majority of the tokens Isaac has given her to get candy from the machine with the grabber.

"I can't believe you've never brought her here," Isaac says as he hands our menus to the server after we've placed an order for food. Jenna sits across from Claire, leaving Isaac to sit opposite me.

I grab a rogue crayon from beneath our table and hand it back to Claire. She's wired from the four pieces of candy she gobbled before I took away the rest and hid it in my purse. Her coloring is more scribbling, as she uses the hand that sticks out from her cast to steady the paper and her good hand to draw a rainbow. Whenever her casted arm moves on the wooden table top, it makes a scratchy sound.

"Honestly, a place like this is full of germs." I take my little travel bottle of hand sanitizer from my purse and spritz it on Claire's hands, then rub it in for her.

"Safety first." Isaac smirks. Beside him Jenna has a frozen smile on her face. She has no idea what he's referencing.

I narrow my eyes. "Single mother, fewer sick days."

Isaac stares at me, his mouth a straight line. After a few seconds, he says, "What about John? Hasn't he been a big help?"

"My dad has been amazing. Without him, I can't imagine how I would've done it. And I'm sure if I asked him to, he would call in sick to work and take care of her. But I'd rather avoid having to ask by eliminating the possibility."

"When did you move in with him?" Isaac sits back, laying his arm across the top of the booth. Jenna sits back too, her posture relaxed for the first time all night.

"How do you know he doesn't live with me?" Eyebrows raised, I fish a piece of ice from my drink and pop it in my mouth.

Isaac gives me his own raised eyebrows. "So you chose the bear rug mounted on your wall?"

Isaac's right—the house is all Dad. "Is that what gave it away?"

"That and the sets of antlers on the shelf in the hallway."

"Oh?"

Isaac leans forward, his face playful. "I put it together with the bumper sticker on the back of his big truck. 'I'd rather be hunting.'"

"It was either that or 'I like big bucks and I cannot lie.'" I bite the tip of my finger to keep from laughing.

Isaac's eyebrows draw together. "A buck is a...?"

"Male deer."

"Of course." Isaac laughs when he says it, because he so clearly knows nothing about my dad's number-one pastime. Jenna laughs politely.

"To answer your question, I moved in with him shortly after I found out I was expecting Claire. The lease on my apartment was almost up, and I needed help. I had a year left of college and my job at the campus juice bar didn't quite leave me swimming in money."

"And now?"

"Now what?"

"Now what do you do? For a job, I mean."

My eyebrows pull together. Is this an interview? For what? Annoyance flares when I realize what he's doing. He's making sure Claire is well-cared for.

I tell myself it's a good thing he cares that much. But still, I'm offended. Claire's the gravity that keeps me in place, the only person capable of warming my cold heart. My body has been sore more times than I can count as I played the role of sentinel, keeping watch beside a sleeping Claire's crib, certain that at any moment she would stop breathing. I soldiered through my final semester, taking off only one week after delivering Claire, because I couldn't get a job without a college degree, and if I wanted to provide for Claire, I needed to graduate.

I want to tell Isaac I know what he's doing, and I intend to, but when I open my mouth, I remember the little girl beside me in the booth, listening to every word, her brain moving faster than ours. I can't ruin this night for her. I want her to think of Isaac and see butterflies and rainbows and whatever else symbolizes her happiness. She deserves that much.

"I'm an underwriter. At Bridgewater Insurance. Do you remember—?" I cut myself off when he starts laughing. "Did I miss the joke?" I glance at Jenna, but she looks as clueless as me.

His laughter fades, but the smirk is still there. "Your job... It's fitting. For you, I mean."

My head drops on one side. "How so?"

"Isaac, can you let me out please? I need to visit the ladies room." Jenna looks at him expectantly, her purse in her grip.

Isaac slides out and Jenna follows. He tries to say something to her but she sails away. He stares at her for a long moment before sitting back down.

"You evaluate risk for a living," he says, like the conversation never skipped a beat. "That's funny, considering your aversion to risk." He's even smiling while he's talking, like his lips only know how to form smiles, and smiles upon words, and smiles upon smiles, and smile smile smile smile smile.

To busy my hands and give me a reason to look away, I join Claire in her coloring. Glancing at our daughter, I say, "Apparently I'm not *that* risk averse."

"Do you check your weather app before you get dressed?" Isaac drums his fingertips on the tabletop.

My crayon stills as I watch the rhythm he creates. Those hands have been on me. Running through my hair, hastily unfastening my bra, digging into my hips. And those hands have performed surgery on my daughter. Pushed two pins into her arm, where they still are and will remain for the next eight weeks.

I put down the crayon and meet his gaze. Ignoring his question, I answer the one that started this whole conversation. The question he asked silently, using the other questions as a front. "I make enough at Bridgewater for Claire and I to live comfortably. I'm very lucky that my friend Britt's dad is a managing director there. He hired both of us right after graduation."

"Is that the same friend from that night? The one who made me text her?"

"The one and only." I grin, my mood lightened when I think of Britt.

Isaac glances at Claire, then back to me. "What was it like? Learning about Claire, I mean."

My lips twist, and I look at Claire too. She's focused on her coloring, her tongue poking out of the right side of her mouth, but I can't risk her hearing me. I pull up a game app and hand her my phone. With technology in front of her, she's as good as asleep.

When I'm confident she's immersed, I lean forward, my chest pressed to the table. Isaac mimics my movement, except when he does it, he takes up so much more of the table.

"My first thought was that there was no way it was happening to me. I went through both tests, then bought another pack. All positive." I take a deep breath as I think back on the final test, a result as positive as all the others. "I was scared, of course. Terrified, actually. But from the moment I was certain, I felt... whole."

As soon as the words leave my mouth I'm embarrassed. I've said too much. Isaac might as well be a stranger. But, of course, he's not a stranger. Not by a long shot.

Isaac reaches across the table and covers my hand with his own. His light squeeze tugs at my heart.

With pained eyes, he says, "I wish I'd known, Aubrey, so I could—"

"So you could've made an honest woman out of me?" I mean it as a joke, but Isaac's serious.

"Maybe. I don't know. But I mean, I would've helped. Financially. Physically. Emotionally. I would have been there." His words rush out, and he takes a deep breath to recover.

Would've, could've, should've. I'm filled with the same thoughts. *We could've exchanged last names. He should've brought his phone and then his number would've been in Britt's phone.* "That's not how it worked out. Sometimes, things don't go the way you imagine they will."

"Like ending up pregnant and not being able to tell the father?"

"Yeah, like that."

He squeezes my hand again, tighter this time. "I'm here now. And I'm going to be here as much as you'll let me. More, even." His eyes are bright, intense.

How is it that one person can want another person so much? I know, because I'm a mother. I carried Claire inside my body, fed her from my breast, and have never spent a night apart from her in five years.

But Isaac? He barely knows us. How is it that he can say he'll stay? That he *wants* to?

People leave. That's what I know. And I need to protect Claire. How much should I allow Isaac into our lives? But how can I possibly keep him out?

He looks like he means what he says. The planes of his face are fixed, strong. His eyes shine with conviction.

It's impossible not to remember her in this moment. My mother with her long, brown hair. Her soft laugh, spilling from her throat as she tipped her head back. How she would brush my hair and say *Fair Aubrey, the prettiest girl in all the land.* It's one of my only memories of her. One of the only good ones, anyway.

I know what leaving looks like. And it's my job to keep Claire from ever knowing how that feels.

"Aubrey?" Isaac's eyes search mine. "I'm not her. I'm not going anywhere. Ever."

My chest constricts. *He remembers.* Even though we haven't spoken about what sent me to the bar that night, have hardly spoken of that night at all, he remembers what I told him.

And I still don't know why he was there. But there was something, some reason he'd gone to a honky-tonk all alone.

The rough clearing of a throat breaks through our heavy conversation. Jenna stands next to the table. Her face is a mask of sculpted cheeks and rosy lips, but her eyes swim with emotion. She's looking down at the tabletop, at our intertwined fingers. It was innocent, a gesture to go along with Isaac's heartfelt declaration. He pulls away slowly, as if he knows that snatching his hand away will make it look like he was doing something wrong.

Isaac lets her in, his hand on her hip as though she needs the guidance, and right behind him is the arrival of our dinner. I turn my attention to Claire, to the temperature of her food, because I need something to take my mind off whatever the heck is happening across the booth.

When dinner is over we don't linger. I give the excuse of it being a school night, and quickly say goodbye. Claire hugs Isaac, but stays away from Jenna. She's obviously mad, and Claire has picked up on it.

Through bath time and story time, and all the way until I nod off to sleep, I think of Jenna and Isaac, and how I hadn't factored an evil step-mother into the equation. Until now.

12

ISAAC

I WISH I could use Claire as an escape, like Aubrey did as soon as dinner was over. The whole ride home Jenna was silent, seething in her seat, her body rigid. Now I'm sitting on my couch, just waiting for the pot to boil over.

She stalks around the kitchen, opening cabinets and closing them, accomplishing nothing.

At last, she says "You shouldn't have invited me tonight." Her tone is flat. Devoid of any emotion.

"I wouldn't have, if I'd known you were going to make it your mission to be awkward." I can see her in the reflection of the black TV screen. She leaves the kitchen and walks closer.

"I tried," she insists, coming to stand in front of the couch. "But then I saw how futile it was. How pointless it was for me to be there. You *like* her, Isaac. You have feelings for her."

My denial is automatic, even though her accusation is nothing but the truth. Liking Aubrey doesn't feel like a choice. I have no say in the matter. But that doesn't mean I have to follow those feelings. They don't need to make the decisions for me.

"Isaac, don't sit there and shake your head. I know what I saw."

"I wasn't holding her hand when you came back to the table. Not in a romantic way. I was telling her that I would've been there for her had I known about Claire." The downward spiral of this conversation is beginning. I know where this is all going, but I have to at least put up a fight. "That's all it was, Jenna."

She waves a hand, pushing aside my defense. "I don't care that you held Aubrey's hand. Not at all, actually. It was more..." She pauses, lips twisting in thought. "Your body language. You leaned into her every chance you got, and I don't think you even knew you were doing it. And the way you looked at her. It was like your eyes wanted to absorb every part of her." Her breath comes out in a short, irritated sound. "You've never looked at me like that."

"Jenna—"

"Don't bother." She stops me with an outstretched palm. "I tried, Isaac. I think I could've handled Claire, everything might have worked out if it was just her I had to accept." Her head moves slowly back and forth. "I won't watch you want Aubrey. I won't be the runner-up. And I won't fight a losing battle."

There are so many things I'm supposed to say right now. Half-hearted attempts to dissuade her stream through my mind. I let them all pass, because she's right.

She leaves quickly, taking only her purse. I get up to follow her out, to say good-bye, but she doesn't turn around.

I CAN'T BREATHE.

My mom's arms wrap around me, constricting my chest, until I croak out a reminder. "Mom."

"That's the best news ever," she says, releasing me.

I knew she was going to be happy, but she could hide her total elation at least a little. I give her my stern look.

"Sorry, sorry. What I meant to say was *I'm so sorry to hear the news. How are you holding up?*" She takes another step back, but she can't stop the smile that pulls at her lips. "I wish your father were home. He'd be happy about the news too." Turning abruptly, she says "Follow me to the kitchen."

She's walking away, and I've yet to move. There's still one more bombshell I need to drop on her, and I don't know if I should do it when she has knives at her disposal.

"Isaac, come on." She turns and sends me a questioning look from her spot seven feet away. When she sees me moving, she starts again.

Once we're in the kitchen she grabs a head of lettuce from the fridge and tosses it to me. I'm tearing it for a salad when I ask, "Aren't you going to ask why Jenna and I broke it off? We were engaged, you know." As if she needs the reminder.

My mom reaches past me and flicks on the faucet, so the water washes the leaves I've dropped into the colander.

"Never look a gift horse in the mouth." She snickers like she's just made the funniest joke ever.

I can't help but laugh. My mom liked Jenna well enough in high school, but when I ran back into her and brought her to my parents' house, I could tell right away Mom wasn't rekindling fond memories the way I was. Maybe it was the way Jenna asked for cream and sugar when my mom served her coffee. My mother is more of a double shot of espresso, no-nonsense lady. Love pours from her, even when she's pissed and cussing in Spanish and her black eyebrows are pulled so close together she starts looking like Frida Kahlo.

Mom managed to keep her opinion to herself, or at least from me, and I assumed she'd grown to like Jenna.

I guess I was wrong.

What I want to say is *Jenna left me because she thinks I have feelings for another woman. Who? Oh, just this girl I got pregnant five years ago. Now I have a daughter I found out about when I was her emergency surgeon.*

As priceless as the look on her face would be, I can't do that to her.

Shifting the lettuce in the colander, I start what is surely to be a long, painful, and possibly embarrassing conversation. "Jenna and I broke up because something I did in the past came back to the present."

My mom's hand stills, poised with a peeler pressed to a carrot.

"And what might that be?"

Her eyes are careful, as if she knows she's treading into dangerous waters.

I turn off the faucet and dry my hands on a kitchen towel, then toss it on the counter between us. "After that night, five years ago, the night that..."

"No reminder needed," she says softly. "Go on."

"I went to a bar. And I met a woman. Aubrey." Twenty-one-year-old Aubrey fills my head. She was so beautiful, but with an air of sadness. Maybe that was part of the instant attraction when I spotted her sitting alone at that table. The sadness in me saw her, needed her, wanted a person to hurt with.

"She was upset that night too. About her ex-boyfriend and her mother." Unwilling to air Aubrey's dirty laundry, I don't offer any more explanation than that. "We went back to my place." My cheeks heat, but thanks to my tanned skin, I don't redden.

Still, my mom somehow knows I'm flustered. "It's OK. Sex is normal. Besides, you're thirty-five." She winks at me. "So, you ran into Aubrey while you were with Jenna? That hardly seems like a reason to end an engagement."

"Jenna left because she couldn't handle what Aubrey and I created that night." *I really should just spit it out.* My mom's eyes narrow, the pieces of the puzzle shifting, so I put it out there. "Aubrey got pregnant that night, and she had no way to tell me. By the time she took a test, I was in Africa."

Fingers pressed to her lips, my mom drags in a shocked breath. "Did she have the baby?"

I nod. Despite the seriousness of our conversation, I smile.

"I'm a grandma?"

I nod again. Still smiling. And so is she.

"Oh my god." Her fingers curl away from her lips, except for one, which stays poised on her top lip. "I need to meet her. Or him?"

"Her. Claire."

"Now I really wish your dad were home. This is so exciting. I can't wait to meet Claire. When? She can come over here. I'll need..." She starts listing things, ticking her fingers up one at a time. "Toys. Dolls. Does she like dolls? Crayons and coloring books."

I place a hand on her shoulder. "Mom, slow down. This is new. Aubrey is..." I pause, thinking. What is Aubrey? Hesitant? Guarded? Defensive? Yes, yes, and yes. "This is a lot for her. She's been on her own with Claire. She's already been accommodating. I don't want to push her too hard."

I think my words bring my mom back down to reality.

"How are you handling this? Wait, how did you find out about Claire?"

I open my mouth to answer, but she cuts me off with another question.

"Are you going to file for custody? Shared, I'm sure."

It would be a lie to say I haven't thought a lot about it, but Aubrey's been flexible so far, and I don't want to burn any bridges.

"Not immediately. Eventually, we'll have to get the legal aspect figured out. But right now, I'm only interested in learning about Claire."

"What about Aubrey?"

"What about her?" I know what my mom's getting at, and it pulls up Jenna's words from my memory. *The way you looked at her. You've never looked at me like that.*

Aubrey's beautiful and strong. The moment I saw her again I felt that same pull in my chest as I had five years ago. Like there's a tether tying me to her. Pulling back that curtain and finding those blue eyes staring back at me, it was as if my heart was reaching out to hers. And then I'd managed to look past her, to the tiny patient in the big bed, and my heart had faltered.

"Think about it, Isaac. You and Aubrey have a one-night stand without enough information to find each other later, and then she shows up out of nowhere—"

"Not nowhere. At the hospital." I interject. "Claire broke her arm playing soccer, and yours truly was her surgeon."

She gasps, but then the sound keeps going so I'm not really sure what to call it. "Isaac, it's meant to be. Fated. Written in the stars." Her eyes are big, excited. It's all I can do not to roll mine.

"Mom, this isn't one of your telanovelas. It's real life." I point to my chest. "*My* life."

"Come on." She's not one to keep her eye rolls on the inside. "Maybe she's your person. *El que tu corazon desea.*"

I cross my arms, like maybe it will keep her words from affecting me any more than they already have.

"Jenna and I just broke up, Mom."

"You look devastated." Her tone is flat. Sarcastic.

"I am." It's a lie. I'm not. And the fact that I'm not says more about my feelings for Jenna than words ever could. Four days have passed since the dinner and she hasn't come to mind nearly as much as I would've thought. I'm defending my relationship with her because... well, isn't it what I'm supposed to do? Honestly, what I feel more than anything is guilt. Which only makes me feel guiltier.

My mom throws up her hands. "Fine. Whatever you say. Let's talk about Claire. When do I get to meet this grand-baby of mine?" She purses her lips and claps her hands quietly. Her excitement is back. She's somewhere up in the stars again, dreaming of running through meadows of wild-flowers with Claire by her side.

"Lucia?" My dad yells from the living room.

My mom hurries from the room, yelling "Paul," as she goes.

I walk after her, my pace slow. I'm not in a hurry to drop another bomb on someone today. If I even get to. My mom's probably too excited to wait for me.

I knew she'd be happy. She hasn't made it a secret she wishes for grandchildren. Or that she wants me to find the right woman. Who she obviously believed wasn't Jenna.

I'm thirty-five, and I still wish my mom weren't right all the time. And if she really is right all time, I have much bigger problems.

El que tu corazon desea. The one your heart desires.

Is that Aubrey?

. . .

A DARK APARTMENT is just what I need following an after-noon spent inundated by questions and thoughts and opinions, punctuated by my mom's random hand-tossing when her elation bubbled over. My sister arrived too, called in by my mother, and I knew I was in for it.

Lauren delighted in my news in a strange, competitive sibling way. She'd excused herself to the bathroom, and then my phone dinged with a message.

Lauren: Oh, how the mighty have fallen.

I ignored her.

Another one.

The sun doesn't shine out of your ass anymore.

And another.

Vacancy: Favorite wanted.

She came back from the bathroom grinning.

"Are you done?" I asked her.

"Almost. I just have to call you a man-whore, and then I'll be finished." She laughed at her own joke.

After dinner I told them I had to get up early tomorrow. It's mostly true. I'll set my alarm for six and go for a run, just to make it true.

Home sweet home, I think as I climb from my car.

Once my key is in the lock, I realize there's no need for it. My door is unlocked.

Unless I'm being burglarized, there's only one person who has a key to my place. I'm so sure I know who it is that I don't even turn around to look for her car.

"Hello," I say to her back when I find her. She's in my closet, pulling clothes from hangers.

Jenna startles, clutching her chest. "God, Isaac, you should wear a bell around your neck."

"And alert the cat burglar that the owner is home?"

She snakes a hand through her hair and grabs one of the shirts draped across her forearm. She folds it clumsily, which I know pisses her off. Shirts with crisp lines and sweaters with soft folds bring Jenna peace.

I grab the shirt from her and fold it. The guilt makes me want to help her. It's not her fault we're in this situation.

Her thank-you is reluctant. She's pissed.

When the other shirts have been placed in the duffle bag at her feet, I back out of the small space.

"Check the bathroom," I say. "There may be some things under the sink."

She goes in one direction and I go in another. When she emerges a few minutes later, I'm seated on the couch.

Jenna's eyes are red, and I find this more shocking than I did my unlocked door. In all the time I've known her, I've seen her cry three times. When her dog died, when her grandma Maggie passed, and at a homeless person who fell in the street.

"Did you get everything?" I ask.

She nods. "Let me know if you come across anything."

And that's it. She sets her key on the entry table and walks out.

It's quiet.

It's dark.

I sit for a long time.

Thinking of the cracks in my relationship with Jenna is pointless now, but hindsight is twenty/twenty and I'm seeing things clearly.

We were apart more than we were together.

When we were together, we were comfortable.

But guess who else I feel comfortable with? My mom. The people who work in my practice. The surgical team at the hospital. The barista I see on Monday mornings at the coffee shop down the street. Even the cashier at the grocery store I've been going to since I moved in here.

When two people are in love, when they've decided to get married, I don't think they should settle for *comfortable*.

I think maybe sometimes they should be *uncomfortable*.

Passion, in anger or in lust, should make them agitated.

Hurt feelings should touch them so deeply there's no way to keep from spilling over.

Desire should push them to the point of frenzy.

And they should be able to eat ice cream whenever they feel like it.

So I do. Armed with a spoon and a pint, I eat it on the couch.

And I think a lot, maybe even too much, about Aubrey.

13

AUBREY

MY HIP'S jammed against the kitchen sink as I stare at the man in front of me. He shuffles his feet, looking everywhere but at me.

It's not that I don't want this for my dad. I want him to meet someone. I really do. But that was an idea, a *maybe this will happen someday* thing.

Not tonight, like he has just informed me. I'm happy for him. It's just shocking, I guess. How many years has it been since he has been on a date?

To alleviate the awkwardness, I busy myself rinsing Claire's yogurt from her bowl. "Are you nervous?" I ask him.

"Nothing to be nervous about," he says, opening the fridge.

"Liar." I place the bowl in the dishwasher.

"Don't make a big deal about this. It's nothing." His tone is gruff.

"Fine. I won't." I hold up my hands, a dish towel dangling from my right hand. "It's nothing."

"Don't you have Claire's appointment today?" He closes the fridge and looks at me.

"Eleven. Are you going to come?" I'd like to have someone else in the room with me. Someone besides Claire. Isaac makes me feel... well, a lot of things. Things I'm not supposed to feel. Things that are asinine. Insane. Foolish. Things his fiancee wouldn't appreciate. It would be nice to have a buffer in the room. Someone with a different energy.

Dad shakes his head, zapping any hope I held. "I have to work."

"Why don't you want to go?" I ask, narrowing my eyes. It's ten o'clock. He never leaves our house this late.

"Don't give me that look." He frowns. "I'd go if I could, but I'm driving downtown for a meeting."

"I can call Greg." I warn. Besides my dad, Greg is the most trustworthy guy on their crew. He'll tell me if they're really working today.

"Call Greg." He lifts his chin in a challenge.

I consider him for a moment. I think my nerves are making me see things. It's not that my dad wants to leave me alone with Isaac. He really just can't go. "I trust you," I say slowly.

He laughs. "Sometimes I wonder who's the parent here."

"Both of us." I answer, grabbing my phone off the counter and slipping it into my back pocket. "I'm going to get Claire ready. Will you be here when we get home this afternoon?"

"Happy hour," he says around a mouthful of banana.

I pause, studying him.

"What?" He asks, his tone sharp.

"Nice beard. Very neat. Trimmed. But you're right. It's nothing." I turn and prance from the room as my dad grumbles something behind me.

· · ·

"HELLO, MS. REYNOLDS." The portly woman peers down at Claire through the glass window she pulled back when we walked in. "You must be Claire."

"I am," Claire announces, making the woman laugh.

"We've been expecting you." The woman winks at me.

"Wonderful," I murmur. Would Isaac have told this woman who we are?

Claire and I sit in the waiting room. I fill out paperwork while she draws on the little Boogie Board I brought with us.

When I return the paperwork to the woman, she beams at me. I wish she would stop smiling at me like that. It makes me uncomfortable. And embarrassed.

Claire's drawing a robot, one she says will pick up her dirty clothes off the floor. I check emails on my phone until our name is called.

I don't know why I thought it would be Isaac calling us in. I push the disappointment aside. With Claire's hand nestled in mine we walk to the young woman holding a clipboard.

She smiles, introduces herself as Nicole, and tells Claire she's going to take pictures of her arm.

"Do you mean x-rays?" Claire asks.

Nicole laughs. "Yep," she says, leading us to the x-ray room. We pass door after closed door, and inside one I hear a man's deep voice. *Isaac's?*

Inside the x-ray room, Nicole situates Claire and motions for me to stand behind a wall with her. She takes three x-rays, all with Claire's arm in different positions, then moves us to an exam room.

"Dr. Cordova will be right in." She closes the door behind her with a polite smile. It makes me feel better. Maybe he didn't announce who we are to his whole staff.

Less than a minute goes by before Isaac walks in. He's

holding an iPad in his hand. His scrub shirt is tucked into his pants, and his cell phone is clipped to his waist.

"How are you ladies doing?" He holds out an open palm to Claire. She slaps his hand as hard as she can. Grimacing, he shakes his hand and says, "Ow."

His eyes are on me. "Aubrey? How are you?"

"Good. Enjoying a morning off work."

"Me, too." Isaac laughs at his own joke. He sits down on the wheeled seat and rolls in front of Claire. "And you, Claire? How are you?"

"Good. Am I getting a cast today?"

"That depends. Do you want one?" He raises one eyebrow, a smile playing on his lips.

Her hair falls in her face with her vigorous nod.

"First let me talk with your mom about your x-rays, then we'll get you your cast. Start thinking about what color you want." Isaac brings the iPad to where I'm sitting and settles into the chair beside me. He leans over, holding the tablet in front of me. If I didn't want to see the x-rays so badly, I'd lean away.

Does he sit this close to all his patients?

"She's looking good," he says. His eyes are trained on the screen, fingers tracing the metal rods in her bone, objects that look out of place in an arm. "These are the pins."

My stomach flip-flops. I glance at Claire's arm in disbelief. I can't believe those are inside of her.

"We'll get a cast on her now, and then I'll see her back here in two weeks, and we'll do this all over again." He stands, opens the door, and leans out.

"Randall," he says, his voice raised. "Arm cast in six." He backs out of the open door and lets it close. "He'll be here in a second."

He looks at the seat beside me, but elects to lean back against the small counter where his iPad now lies.

"Are you OK?" he asks, squinting at me.

"Why wouldn't I be?" I didn't mean for it to come out that way. *Damn.* My teeth push into my bottom lip.

"You seem stiff." He crosses his arms. I feel like his eyes are digging into me.

"Do people in your office know about us?" I keep my voice low. Claire's drawing again, but she has ears. And they work just fine.

Isaac's face changes to concern. "Is that what this is about?"

"That woman up front—"

"Deirdre." Isaac interjects.

"*Deirdre* was very happy to see Claire."

"So?" Isaac shrugs.

"Too happy. Like she knew just who Claire was."

"And what if she did?" Isaac's eyes widen, a challenging look.

"It's none of her business," I hiss.

Isaac crosses the small space separating us and plants himself in the chair he previously occupied. He touches my chin, just one finger underneath, lifting it slightly.

"Lucky for you, I don't have a big mouth."

I watch the *mouth* he's referencing as it speaks the sentence. His lips caress the words, his tone stays low, his voice deep.

I move my head, a slight jerk, and his finger drops. "I don't think your fiancée would appreciate your behavior." It's another hissed whisper, this time accompanied by a disapproving look.

Isaac opens his mouth. At the same time the door flies open. Isaac jumps from the seat, his expression contrite.

The man who has stepped in is almost too tall for the doorway. He looks from Isaac to me, his eyebrows drawn together. Quickly he fixes his expression so he looks disinterested and mildly friendly.

"Dr. Cordova." He nods at him. "Hello," he says to me.

I return the greeting. Isaac introduces him to Claire.

Randall grins at her, and from his pockets he produces a few rolls of what appears to be colored tape. He holds them out to Claire, and she considers them, as though she's shopping for deli meat at the supermarket.

"Can I have two?" she asks.

"Anything for extra special patients like you." He winks at her.

She grins. "Purple with pink stripes."

Randall tosses the unchosen rolls onto the counter beside Isaac's iPad. He sits on the rolling seat and pulls up to Claire.

Isaac goes to the table to supervise the cast's placement. I leave my seat to sit on the table beside Claire. I would never know if Randall were doing anything right or wrong, but I want to be there.

I can feel Isaac looking at me. Tearing my eyes from Randall's work, I meet Isaac's gaze.

The only word I can think of to describe it is *heavy*. Like he's brimming with words. Things he can't say, won't say, isn't at liberty to say.

Randall finishes and gathers the only tool he brought in with him, a pair of angled scissors, and the rolls of what I now realize is fiberglass. I did an internet search right after Claire's break, so I knew the material they would use, but I wasn't expecting it to come in rolls.

He holds out a hand to me. "Nice to meet you, Aubrey." He turns to Claire. "And you too, little lady." And then, to

Isaac. "Man, this room is tense. You might want to air it out before your next patient comes in."

Isaac shakes his head at him. Randall laughs and heads out, the door swinging shut behind him.

I level narrowed eyes on the man who just told me his lips were sealed.

"He's my closest friend." He's giving me a *come on* look.

"Fine." I mutter. I can give him that one. Britt knows. It's the same thing.

Isaac's eyes light up. "Can I take Claire to the zoo this weekend?"

The word *no* springs to the tip of my tongue. *Claire on her own. At the zoo. Without me. No way.*

"Yes! Mommy, please? Can Isaac take me to the zoo?" Claire's eyelashes crawl up her brow bone as her eyes widen, her face excited and expectant.

"Isaac and I will talk about it." I smile at Claire, a competent *don't worry* kind of a smile. She looks back down to her drawing.

I grab my phone from the purse hanging across my body and type out a message. Isaac's pocket vibrates a second after I hit the send button.

He pulls out his phone and reads, nose scrunching on one side as he makes a disbelieving face.

His sigh is a slow, steady stream of air pushed through a slit in his lips. I stare behind him, at the sink, the cabinets below the counter, the iPad lying closed on the counter. I just don't want to look at him right now. I can't help the way I feel. My dad once told me that sometimes you have to piss people off to take care of your child, but I never knew just what he meant until right now.

A message pops up on my phone. *First do no harm. I took an oath.*

I can feel Isaac's gaze on me, imploring me to look at him. Under his scrutiny I type, then delete what I've written because it's too harsh, and type again.

Even doctors can be sickos.

Isaac reads the message and shakes his head. "Come with us." His voice is soft, a silk scarf wrapping over me.

The paper covering the exam table crinkles beneath my touch. Claire's hand has stopped moving across the board. Now she's singing. It's a song she learned last year in her three-year-old classroom.

I pick my phone back up and respond to Isaac. *Before I let you even further into Claire's life, I need to know you better. I need to see where you live. And yes, Claire and I will go to the zoo with you.*

He looks at his phone, waiting for the message to appear, and when it does, he reads it. I like the smile spreading across his face. Knowing I put it there makes me happy.

"Friday night," Isaac says, sliding his phone back into its clip. "After work. Come over and see for yourself that I have a normal home. You can even look through all my drawers."

I smirk. "Sounds great." Mollified, I slide off the table and load Claire onto my hip.

For a second Isaac slips back into Dr. Cordova as he gives me instructions on how to wash Claire with the cast. Just as quickly, he sheds the role.

He leans in to hug Claire, and I lean away to give him the space he needs.

Let's be honest, though. I'm giving me the space I need too.

"See you Friday night." He holds open the door for us.

I echo his words as I pass him. Claire stays planted on my hip as I walk down the long, white-walled hallway. I don't need to turn around to know Isaac is watching us leave.

THE SOUND of my dad's key in the lock takes me by surprise. It's too early for him to be home from his date.

He walks up behind the couch where I'm sitting. I turn off the TV and twist my upper half so I'm facing him.

"You're home early," I say cautiously. He's been an adult for a long time, but in dating years he's a toddler. My mother was his first serious girlfriend, and we know how that turned out.

"Yeah." He grips the back of the couch. "Didn't work out too well."

"What happened?"

"She wasn't my type."

My head tips to the side. "Do you have anything more to say than that?"

"No."

I throw my hands in the air and turn back around. He shuffles out, his boots giving away every step of his retreat.

I lean back on the couch and gaze at the picture on the side table. Me, my dad, and Claire, smiling. Two of the people in the picture are stunted, suspended by a moment in time. But the third has managed to escape damage. And she's the one I have to think of now.

14

ISAAC

IT's amazing how I can be calm in surgery, hands steady and certain of every slice through skin, every manipulation of bones until they fit back together. But knowing Aubrey's coming over tonight has me hyper.

My apartment couldn't be any cleaner. I could eat off the floor if I wanted to. My favorite carbonara, noodles twisted in a pile on the dark wooden planks, would be like eating off one of the shiny white plates from the set Jenna brought over to replace the colorful ones my mom gave me. *That's* how much I've cleaned since I got home late this afternoon.

Wait. Does it smell too much like cleaner?

I search the cabinets until I find candles. Also chosen by Jenna. I light one and place it in the center of the kitchen island. Far away from the edge where a child could grab it. *See, Aubrey, I can be trusted with Claire.*

Tonight is a big deal. Tonight I show Aubrey I can take care of Claire by myself. And for longer than a few hours. It's only been two weeks since Aubrey showed up out of nowhere, dark hair spilling down her back, her eyes fearful.

She was worried about Claire's break, sure, but then she saw me, and that's when the real fear took over.

I want to ask Aubrey what she's so afraid of. With the exception of the night we met, when whiskey and bitterness made the words pour from her lips, Aubrey keeps everything close to the vest.

If tonight goes well, I'm going to tell Aubrey about my parents. What I won't tell her is that my mother called three times yesterday asking when she's going meet her granddaughter. She also wanted to make sure I didn't get a wild hair and get back together with Jenna.

When she called the third time, Mom said "*Family is love. Blood means nothing.*"

I know that. Better than most. I let the comment pass, and we talked again about Claire and Aubrey and how this was going to change my life.

But it already has changed my life. From the very second I looked at Claire's papers after her surgery, my whole world shifted. There's gravity, then there's the gravity of Claire. Knowing she exists is what's keeping me here. Forget that job in Boston, the one with the big-name researcher at Mass General. It sounded good at first, but that was before Claire. I can invent a better way to fix an arm right where I am. No moving necessary.

That's what I mean about gravity. Being Claire's dad is heavier, more important, more impactful, than anything else. And now I want to be the very best dad to her. And that means taking responsibility of Claire. Aubrey's not in this alone anymore.

That's why I'm walking the length of my place one more time, doing a fifth check, hoping that one day it will be a second home to Claire.

Maybe I should calm down. I'm getting too excited.

Aubrey barely agreed to a zoo trip. She pulled out her phone right there in my office and sent a message asking if I'm a predator.

Aubrey is a cautious person, someone who anticipates the cracks in the road before she gets to them, but that's not going to scare me off. Claire is my daughter too, and I want her.

Family is love. All my life I've heard those words, but this is the first time I've experienced it from the perspective of a parent.

At the sound of the knock, I send a cursory glance over an apartment I know is beyond reproach.

I pull open the door. Aubrey looks at me expectantly. She shifts her feet. Her gaze descends to the floor and back up to me.

"Hi." Her mouth is soft, the word is soft, and it reminds me of Aubrey the woman, not Aubrey the mama bear.

"Come in." I step aside and motion with my arm.

Her perfume assaults my senses when she passes me. Would she wear perfume to see my place? Maybe it's not perfume. Maybe it's just Aubrey.

"Where's Claire?" I ask. I'd been looking forward to seeing her again.

"With my father." Aubrey glances to the living room. My leather couch faces the oversize flat-screen TV, which doesn't get much use unless it's football season. "I thought it best if I came alone."

"Just in case, huh?" I rock back on my heels, hands shoved in the pockets of my jeans.

Her arms cross. "So far your home is beautiful." She can't keep the annoyance out of her voice.

"I did a good job hiding all my drug paraphernalia." I snicker as she throws me a dirty look.

She stands still in the entryway, waiting for me to close the door.

I close the door *and* lock it. *Safety first, Aubrey.*

I take a step away from the door and realize how close I'm standing to her. She looks up at me, blue eyes piercing mine, splitting my chest in two. Her pink lips part, and they look so supple, so inviting. If I kissed her now, what would happen? Every cell in my body hurtles through me, alive, on fire, all because Aubrey looked at me and parted her lips.

She gulps and takes a step back. A big step back.

"Show me the rest of the place?" Her voice isn't soft anymore. More like someone making a request of their realtor.

"Yeah, sure." I turn away from her, the fireball cells in my body cooling like comets that finally realized they're just stars burning out.

I take her through the rest of the place. Kitchen, living room, office, extra bedrooms, two bathrooms. When we get to my bedroom, she looks everywhere but at the bed.

"It's not the same bed." I'm teasing her, and I feel a twinge of guilt. She's so serious, though.

"I know," she says hotly. She turns and leaves my room, but not before I catch the pink in her cheeks.

When I catch up to her, she's in the living room, looking at a large picture of a woman's chest dusted in silvery black glitter. *Art,* Jenna had called it when she'd proudly put it on the shelf. She'd called it edgy. I thought it was racy, but what did I care?

Aubrey's eyebrows lift. "Nice picture. I'm sure Claire will want to know why that woman has glitter on one of her private parts."

I look away from the *art.* "It's not mine."

Aubrey looks at me disbelievingly. "It's on a shelf. In your home."

"Jenna." I explain.

Aubrey nods. The tension in the air is thick, awkward.

"You don't like it?" I can't help the smile I feel spreading across my face.

"It's not that." Aubrey says quickly. "It's just..." She stops, looks around.

I look with her. I know what's there, but I want to see what she sees. Everything is black, white, and shades of gray. Lot's of glass. Silver vases so shiny they could be mirrors.

"It's very adult," she finishes.

I watch her lips twist. "You mean not kid-friendly." My heart sinks to somewhere between my knees. I want Aubrey to like what she sees.

"It's not that, not really. It would have been way less kid-friendly a few years ago." She reaches out, touches the tip of her finger to the corner of my media table. "Ninety degree angles? Not so kind to a toddling child's head. Or face." She closes her eyes and looks away, and I want to know what she's remembering. Is it a time when Claire got hurt? Or Aubrey?

"Are you saying I'm not a predator, then?" I can't help the indignation in my voice right now. I get where Aubrey is coming from, but it *feels* offensive. I want nothing more than to be a daddy to a little girl who needs one. End of story.

Aubrey sighs. "I'm sorry." She fingers the little gold *C* on the delicate chain around her neck. Her head jerks up suddenly. Her eyes are fiery. "Actually, I'm not sorry. Until now it has been me and Claire against the world. What kind of protector would I be if I dumped her into the hands of a man neither of us knows very well?"

"A gullible one, I suppose." I don't like admitting it, but she has a point. I also don't like admitting how impressed I am with her tenacity, especially since I'm the one coming up against it.

We stand, staring at one another, until the air is electric and I feel the charge running over my skin, sizzling and crackling.

"You should probably know that Jenna and I broke things off." My voice is rough. I drag my hand across the back of my neck and over my throat.

Aubrey pivots suddenly, hurrying to the front door. I stay rooted in place, watching her.

"We'll see you at the zoo this Saturday. I'm a member, so we can get in early. Meet us at nine?" Her lips part as she waits for my response.

I stare. Did she hear what I said?

It dawns on me that she's choosing to ignore what I've just told her. "Nine it is."

She leaves, the door falling shut behind her. I go to lock it, and when I turn around the glittery breast picture catches my eye. My stride across the room is purposeful. I want that picture out of sight. With one hand, I remove it and set it on the floor so it faces the wall. *Picture time-out.*

I fall back, letting the couch catch me, and lay my head against the back of it. Thoughts run amok in my brain. And they're all about one person. A girl with raven hair and eyes blue like an ocean.

Aubrey is a complex creature. Layered. And every moment I spend around her makes me want to spend more moments around her, until they become hours and days and years.

What the hell?

I barely know Aubrey. She might as well have warning

signs written all over her. Every movement of her body says to stay away. The pushed-out hip, the sharp angles of her arms that are almost always crossed in front of her. And those eyes. So guarded. But not dull. You'd think someone who spends her life keeping people at a distance would have lifeless eyes, but she doesn't. Every time I've seen Aubrey, her eyes are alight with some kind of fire. Like she's perpetually ready to fight, to defend, to protect. Herself. And Claire.

Aubrey is a fighter. The quiet kind. The kind that doesn't have to beat her chest to demonstrate her strength. She reminds me of my dad. I should consider myself lucky she's being so accommodating with Claire and leave it alone.

That's exactly what I'm going to do. It's what I have to do.

15

AUBREY

WHY CAN'T TEXT messages have a recall button? I should've kept my mouth shut like I did at his house, but no. I just had to lie down tonight and overthink and text. Because everyone knows texts sent after midnight are sensible.

About Jenna... Is it really over?

Ten excruciating minutes later: *So you did hear me.*

Me: *Was it about Claire? Is that why she broke up with you?*

Isaac: *Yes and no.*

Me: *Which one is it?*

Isaac: *Isn't this a conversation we should have face to face?*

Me: *No.*

Isaac: *It went far beyond Claire. But she was the impetus.*

I release a gigantic sigh of relief into my dark room. Now that I know that, I feel better.

Me: *Are you using fancy doctor words on me?*

Isaac: *???*

Me: *Your request to go to the zoo tomorrow was the impetus of this conversation.*

Isaac: *Are you using fancy doctor words on me?*

I can't stop the smile that spreads across my cheeks.

Me: *Nope. But if you're lucky I'll use some fancy insurance words on you.*

Isaac: *I look forward to it.*

Me: *See you tomorrow.*

Isaac: *Good night, mama bear.*

I set my phone on the nightstand. The temptation to keep talking to him is too strong. I don't even want to begin thinking about the fact that he's single now. Or that my daughter is the reason.

"ARE you sure you don't want to come with us today?" I ask my dad, whose back is to me. Spatula in hand, he pushes eggs around a pan on the stove.

"I have to work. Besides, you guys should spend some time alone. Just the three of you."

I make a face. "We're not a family," I say as I pick a raspberry from the bowl on the table and pop it into my mouth.

He twists at the waist, peering back at me with challenging eyes. "No?" He turns back to his task.

"No," I repeat, my tone firm.

"Then what *is* your idea of family?"

His back is still to me. Maybe that's why I feel free to say what's going through my head. "Family is a Thomas Kincaid picture."

The stiffening of his shoulders is my only indication he's heard me. After a moment, he asks, "What does a painting of a snowy cottage have to do with family?"

"It's not the snowy cottage." I already regret saying it. "It's what's inside."

"And what's that?"

I pick at the red nail polish on my pinkie. I wish this conversation weren't happening.

The scene is there, so realistic in my mind. I can see the fire blazing in the fireplace, feel the creamy pages of a book in my hands, smell the dinner in the oven. A meal prepared by my mother. The wood in the fireplace has been chopped by my father. All of this exists inside the snowy cabin.

"Come on, Aubs." My dad turns to face me, his voice gruff, but I know he's not mad. His tone comes from a place of uncertainty.

Gaze on my fingernail and the spot left bare by my peeling, I take a deep breath. I look up and recite the scene I've envisioned. My eyes never leave him. His expression never changes.

He only moves when it's time to grab plates. "I don't think what you're describing ever really existed. I think marketing companies created images of happy little families to drive you mad."

"It exists and I missed it," I mutter. Instantly I feel bad. I don't like telling my dad how I feel about it. It's not his fault she left.

"Sorry, Dad."

"Don't be sorry to me. I'm not the one who you're denying a family."

I blow out a short breath. "What's that supposed to mean?"

"Just what it sounds like. Claire's real father is in the picture now. He may not be family to you, but he is to her."

My dad doles out scrambled eggs onto plates and calls Claire. She skips in, smiling proudly. My eyes widen when I see why.

"You put on your own pants?" I go to her with my arms open. She nods and steps in. Her hair smells like the all-over baby wash I still use on her.

I pull back to look at her. "It's OK to ask for help while

your arm is in the cast, Claire. Mommy and Grandpa don't mind helping you dress."

"I like to do it myself." She climbs onto her chair and picks up her fork. Her pajama shirt is still on. She definitely cannot manage that on her own.

"I understand." I smile at her and eat my breakfast. Visions of Claire finagling her pants float through my head. While we're eating she tells my dad about every animal she plans to see today.

"Haven't you got that place memorized by now?" My dad laughs.

"Yes," Claire nods solemnly. "Are you coming too?"

"Not today, Claire Bear. Grandpa has a job to do." He gets up from the table and takes our empty plates with him to the sink. "Someone has to keep the lights on." I roll my eyes affectionately. It's his favorite joke. It's probably the favorite joke of every journeyman at every utility company that ever existed.

Leaving the dishes in the sink, he comes to the table and plants a kiss on each of our heads. "Have fun today, girls. Claire, tell your dad I said hello." He gives me a meaningful look over the top of her head and walks out.

Claire finishes her eggs, and with a tug of my hand says, "Let's go, Mommy!"

"We need to change your shirt first." I pinch one of the smiling moons on her nightshirt. She giggles and runs ahead to her room.

"Hurry! Daddy might already be there."

I freeze, palming the wall to steady myself. *Daddy?*

"Coming, baby," I choke out.

Daddy.

Daddy.

Daddy.

. . .

THE TWENTY-MINUTE DRIVE to the zoo has done nothing to untangle the knots in my stomach. Isaac has texted to let me know he's already there, waiting out front for us.

Claire and I walk from the car, and Isaac meets us halfway.

"I feel like an insider, getting into the zoo an hour before it opens to the public." He slaps a high-five with Claire.

She skips ahead to the bridge, where she can watch the ducks and turtles in the lake below.

"How's Claire's arm?" Isaac asks.

"Aren't you supposed to wait until her next check-up to ask me that question?" I tease. Or, at least I think I'm teasing. Isaac doesn't laugh.

He puts his hands in his jeans pockets. He clears his throat, and I watch his Adam's apple bob as he swallows. "I need to talk to you about something."

"OK." I draw out the word, but we can't keep talking, because we've reached the man waiting to take our tickets. I pull my membership card and ID from my wallet. He looks them over and hands me back my things. We step through the turnstile, and Claire runs ahead, snatching a map from the little brown stand. Isaac watches her, an amused smile on his face.

Claire surges forward, certain of where she's going. The zoo is nearly empty, so I'm comfortable with the lead she has on us. I can see her, and I know she'll stop at the giraffes. I can see one now, it's graceful neck bowing to pull food from the tall feeder.

"So that thing I wanted to talk to you about..." Isaac starts.

My heart beats faster. Bad things happen when conversations begin this way.

"I know you like living with your dad, but I was thinking maybe we could talk about one day giving Claire a home that both her parents live in."

I balk. "We—"

"Barely know each other."

"We're—"

"Practically strangers."

I fall quiet, miffed. We've caught up with Claire. She's leaning against the railing, her chin resting on her right hand. I hang back, taking a seat on one of the benches. Isaac sits next to me.

A giraffe strides across the expanse of grass. My eyes track its movements, but my mind is going haywire. "Why did you ask if you already knew my arguments?"

Isaac leans forward, elbows coming to rest on his knees. "Because you don't know mine."

"What are they?" The question has only been out of my mouth for three seconds and I already regret asking. I don't think I want to know.

He flicks his gaze over his left shoulder, so his eyes are on me. I don't like the determination I see in them. "We could get to know each other better. You've already been to my place. You know what it looks like. You've been to where I work. We've shared a meal. You know I don't like spinach."

I can't help but smile at that part. At the restaurant last week, he'd asked the server to leave the spinach off his sandwich, and when it came with spinach, he meticulously picked off every last piece.

"I know you don't like flowers." Isaac continues.

"I like flowers." I eye the large pink hibiscus blooms on a nearby bush.

"You don't like dates showing up with them."

I nod slowly. "Right." *He remembered.*

"Aubrey," he says, and the way he says my name makes me tear my eyes from Claire, who's peering through the metal telescope to the giraffes at the far side of the exhibit. "I'm trying to do what's right in an anything but typical situation."

"And you think moving in together is what's right?" I'm trying to understand his line of logic. Because it definitely wasn't mine.

"Yes. You'll have your own room, of course." He shakes his head. "I didn't mean to suggest something else. If that's what you're thinking."

"It wasn't." My words rush out. "I'm so surprised that I wasn't thinking much of anything."

Isaac stands, stuffing his hands inside his pockets. "I just wanted to put it out there. We don't have to talk about it again today."

Claire comes back to us, jumping like she's on a pogo stick. I'd like Isaac to put on his doctor cap and remind her she has a broken arm. Instead he laughs at her.

"Claire, please be careful. Your arm."

"Yes, Mommy. Flamingoes next!" She pivots, heading for the next exhibit.

"Her arm is safe inside that cast."

I throw a couple daggers at Isaac with my eyes. I'm not sure if it's for thinking I'm overprotective or for knowing me well enough to know how I was feeling. "I just want her to be careful."

"She's not doing anything careless. I've seen way worse, Aubrey. On a child even younger than her." He studies Claire for a moment before breaking into a jog.

He has a nice run. Graceful. Rhythmic.

When he catches up to her, he picks her up by the waist and twirls her around. She laughs and leans her head back, so trusting that the person who has her will never let her fall.

I walk slowly, catching up to Claire and Isaac at the flamingoes. They're both standing on one foot, imitating the smelly pink birds.

"You too," Claire points at me.

I stifle a groan and lift a foot off the ground. I'm not a silly person or a funny person. I never have been. But for Claire?

Anything for Claire.

"YOU KNOW YOU WANT IT..." The growl comes from low in Isaac's throat.

"OK, fine." I grin ruefully at the person behind the counter. "Brownie ice cream blast with chocolate sauce and sprinkles." I turn to Isaac. "Are you happy? I got the biggest, messiest thing on the menu."

"I'm ecstatic." He looks at the person waiting for him to order. "I'll pass. I think my friend here will be needing some help with hers."

I make a face. "Who said I'm sharing?"

"Sharing is caring, Mommy." Claire's eyebrows draw together as she gives me her serious look.

"You're right. I'll share."

"You don't want a time-out, do you?" She wags her pointer finger at me. Isaac laughs so hard he has to turn away.

"Nope, I don't. No time-outs for this mommy." I pick up Claire so she can see them making our order. Isaac goes to the register to pay.

"Thanks," I say when we're settled at a table outside. Soon it will be too hot to eat outdoors, but right now it's perfect.

"You're welcome. I owed you some ice cream." He winks at me and takes a big bite.

My cheeks heat like someone just lit them on fire. And Isaac doesn't miss it. His eyes tell me everything his mouth doesn't say.

As hard as it is, I tear my eyes from his. "Claire, what was your favorite part of today?"

"When the orangutan tried to kiss Mommy." She giggles, pink streaks of ice cream on either side of her mouth.

"What was that about?" Isaac asks. "In a past life, were you queen of the primates?"

I shake my head, confounded, and swallow the massive amount of sugar in my mouth. "He walked up to where I was standing, put his hands on the glass, and blew me a kiss." I laugh, remembering the big puckered lips. "It was shocking. To say the least."

"It was hilarious. I wish I'd been faster with my phone. Your face was priceless."

"I wish I'd thought to return the kiss." I pretend to blow a kiss at Claire.

"Ewww, Mommy. You can't kiss a monkey."

I shrug and take another bite of ice cream.

"What are your plans this week?" Isaac asks me.

"Typical week. Work. Claire will go to school. You?"

"Appointments. Surgeries. Typical week." He looks so nonchalant when he says it. Like surgery is no big deal. "I was wondering if I can tag along some time when you take Claire to school." He leans back in his seat and smiles at Claire.

"Yeah yeah yeah! Daddy can take me to school."

Claire's spoon goes right back into her bowl as if she hadn't said what she just said.

My mouth drops open. Isaac stares at Claire, dazed.

"Daddy?" His whisper is so low I barely hear him.

My loaded spoon drops back into the bowl. I've lost my desire for it. "She called you Daddy this morning too. Right before we left to meet you."

His eyes are shiny. "You guys have to move in with me. I need to be a dad, full-time." He swallows hard. "I can't be a part-time dad. I just can't."

"Isaac, it's too soon."

"Please think about it." He's looking at Claire, but his words are for me.

I nod. "I will."

Isaac is quiet while Claire finishes. I don't try to talk to him. Maybe he needs to think.

When she's done, he walks us to my car.

"Monday morning," he says, opening up the back door and swinging Claire into the air. She squeals. He sets her in her car seat and, after a few seconds studying the straps, buckles her in. I'm impressed. Five-point harnesses baffle most people.

"You want to come to school with us Monday morning?" I ask after he says goodbye to Claire and closes her door.

"Is that OK? I don't have patients until nine."

"I drop her off at 8:30. I have to be at work by nine too."

A small, ironic smile slips out the side of his mouth.

"What's so funny?"

"I still find it funny you're an underwriter."

I roll my eyes. "It's not exactly what I went to college for." I glance at Claire. She's paging through a book. "It was a desperate time, and I graduated college with an infant. I started as an assistant. Then I took my Series 7 and 63, and here I am." I put my hands in the air, palms up.

Isaac steps closer. The heat I felt when I went to his apartment starts up, like a push-to-start burner. "I love how you handled everything. How you took care of our girl. How you worked so hard."

I don't know how to work in any way but hard. I'm not a soft person. I don't wallow. Shit got tough, but I handled it. I hardly think that makes me special.

"It's what a decent human being would do. It's what we're hard-wired to do—care for our young. Most of us, anyway."

Isaac catches my hand and squeezes. "Most of us." He steps back, and my hand falls from his grip. "See you Monday morning. At your dad's house. Eight-fifteen."

"Eight-fifteen," I echo, watching him walk away.

"Mommy, let's go." Claire's impatient voice sounds from the backseat.

I climb in and drive home, my mind full.

How can I possibly say yes to Isaac? What about my dad? We have a rhythm. A routine. On Friday nights, I make tacos and he cleans up the kitchen. I fold all his laundry. He reads extra bedtime stories to Claire. He's not just my dad anymore. He's my friend.

Isaac's invitation plagues me all night, gnawing at my stomach and stealing my appetite. At dinner I attempt to eat but end up pushing the food around on my plate. My dad asks about our zoo trip, I give a perfunctory answer, and he scrutinizes me but stays quiet. By the time I lay down to sleep, my brain is exhausted.

I haven't decided one way or the other. All I know is that I have to do what's right for Claire. I'm just not sure what that is.

16

ISAAC

SHE CALLED ME DADDY.

Daddy.

My little girl called me Daddy.

Her tiny voice, thrilled at the idea of having me take her to school, so excited she called me Daddy. A second time, according to Aubrey. I knew right then they should come live with me. Screw the timing.

We barely know each other. Aubrey's right. Maybe we'll drive each other crazy. Maybe Aubrey is a slob. Maybe she leaves dishes on the counter. Maybe *I* leave dishes on the counter. Maybe all three of us will leave our damn dishes on the damn counter. Whatever. None of that matters.

Aubrey just needs time. She's a rational person, a person who evaluates risk for a living. She didn't understand why I was amused yesterday. How could something like that not be funny? Safety First Aubrey literally determines the riskiness of a business for a living. It's the perfect job for her.

I'm so stoked to take Claire to school that I woke up at five a.m., eyes popping wide open. Energy flowed through me like a river. I went to the gym and punched a bag until my arms burned. Unless there's an emergency, which could easily happen, I don't have a scheduled surgery for two more days. Enough time for me to eat some bananas and keep my arms from getting too sore.

It's only seven, but I'm dressed and ready. I wonder what Aubrey's doing right now? What's the morning routine? Claire's an independent child—I recognized that right away. So much like her mother. But with her broken arm, she needs help.

I look around at my place, picturing Claire here, needing me to make breakfast, tie her shoes, get her to pre-school.

I grab my bag, pat my pockets to check for my wallet and phone, and leave. I don't think Aubrey will mind if I'm early. Extra hands, right?

AUBREY MINDS. She's trying not to look annoyed, but her eyebrows keep pulling together. She answered the door with wet hair, one of those towels that looks like a turban in her hand. She's wearing light gray pajamas pants and a white tank top.

"You're early," she says tightly, smoothing back her hair with her free hand. The moisture makes it glisten. It has that messy look, the fresh from the shower tangles.

I clear my throat. It's hard to collect my wandering thoughts, but I do. "I thought maybe you'd like help getting Claire ready for school."

She opens her mouth, pauses, then closes it. I can guess what she was going to say. Something like *I've been doing it on my own and I can keep doing it on my own.* A comment like that would be part of Aubrey's armor.

"Sure." She walks ahead of me, using the small towel in her hand to squeeze water from her hair and catching it with the other end. "Claire's eating her breakfast." We walk into the kitchen, where Claire sits in a chair that dwarfs her. When she sees me, she hops down, nearly falls, rights herself, and runs to me.

"Daddy's here!" she yells, hugging my knees. Through the thin fabric of my scrubs I feel her cast digging into the back of my leg.

"Hey, little lady." I swoop her up into my arms and brush back a curtain of long brown hair that has fallen into her face. "How are you this morning?" Sparing a quick glance at her mother tell's me Aubrey's still not used to Claire calling me Daddy. Honestly, neither am I, but that doesn't mean I don't love it.

"Mommy made me pancakes this morning. With jelly. Strawberry jelly. Because I don't like syrup." She sticks out her tongue for effect.

It makes me laugh, and she bounces with the movement of my chest. I put her down and direct her back to her breakfast.

"Here," Aubrey hands me a cup of coffee. "Can you hang out with her? I need to blow-dry my hair."

"Definitely." I wink at Claire and she beams. Aubrey leaves us, a coffee cup in her hand also, and I take the seat across from Claire.

"Are you excited for school today?" I'm not sure what to ask her, but this seems like a good start.

"No. I saw mommy put broccoli in my lunch box. And I do *not* like broccoli." She shakes her head defiantly and stuffs two pieces of pancake in her mouth.

To keep from laughing, I take a sip of coffee. "What *do* you like?"

"Pancakes. And carrots, the purple ones with the yellow center. And grandpa's lasagna. And ice cream. And..." She goes on and on, using the same five fingers of her right hand over and over.

"Wow. You like a lot of things."

She pushes back her plate. "I'm done. Can you help me wash my hand?"

I stand quickly. I want to be put to use. Care for this child somehow. Together we walk to the kitchen sink and I lift her, holding her around the middle with one arm and washing her hand gently with soap from the dispenser next to the sink.

"Thanks," she says brightly when I've set her down and dried her hand. "Want to play LEGOs?"

"Um." I look toward the hall, knowing Aubrey is somewhere down there. The blow dryer turned off a few minutes ago. "Are you all ready for school?"

She nods.

"OK, then. Lead the way." I hold out my hand.

Claire takes me down the hall, to the very place I was afraid to venture. She pulls me into her room, where the LEGO dragon sits on her white dresser.

We're sitting on the floor, one of the Elves preparing to board the flying dragon, when Aubrey walks in. She's dressed in black slacks and a black and white polka dot button up shirt. It has fabric bunched at the the collar, a lanky bow falling into the valley her breasts create.

"Claire, you need to brush your teeth, baby. I put the toothpaste on the brush for you." Aubrey leans against the door frame.

Claire sighs in protest, but with my help she stands. When the sound of her electric toothbrush starts, Aubrey says, "I'm sorry I was short with you when you showed up. I was surprised you were here and a little embarrassed."

I get to my feet. With her heels on she's only a couple inches shorter than me.

"Embarrassed of what?"

She runs her fingers through her hair, eyes flicking off to the side. "I didn't want you to see me all wet-dog like that."

Wet-dog? That's the last thing I would've called her. Gorgeous, definitely. Tempting, absolutely. Maybe I can ask if we can screw all this nonsense and give in again? The words pile up inside me, heavy, but they stay there, an anvil on my chest.

"I wouldn't describe you as wet-dog," I mutter. It's the best I can do right now without terrifying her.

"And when...*if* you move in with me, you're going to have to get used to having wet hair in front of me. Among other things."

Aubrey shifts uncomfortably, her eyes guarded. We say nothing, then suddenly she straightens, like a puppet whose string was pulled. She looks back over her shoulder, to the bathroom across the hall. "Ready, love?" She throws her question across the few feet of space.

I don't hear Claire's answer, but I guess it was affirmative because Aubrey steps away. Claire walks out, a swipe of frothy toothpaste on her chin. With one thumb I wipe it off, realize I don't have easy access to a towel, and rub it into my scrubs. That's what I've seen parents in my office do, but it's not usually toothpaste. It's most often snot, followed by food crumbs. I thought it was gross, but now I get it. Although maybe I'll make it a point to buy more tissues. Snot might be a little too far for me.

I follow them to the living room, where Claire's backpack, lunchbox, and water bottle sit on the end of the couch.

Aubrey looks through her purse while I gather Claire's things. The family photo on the end table catches my eyes and makes me realize John hasn't made an appearance this morning.

"Where's your dad?" I ask on our way out the door.

"Hunting," Aubrey bites her bottom lip after she says it. Worry clouds her eyes for a brief moment.

"Is he retired?" I lay Claire's things next to her car seat while Aubrey straps her in. She leans over Claire, her hair swirling around her head.

"He's a journeyman. He worked this weekend, so he's off today and tomorrow. I think he left sometime around three this morning." She clicks the buckles into place and closes the door. I do the same, looking at her over the roof of her car.

"So your dad plays with electricity for a living and goes hunting? Is there anything else that could make him more of a badass?"

Aubrey smirks. "He was a Marine."

My hands fly into the air. "Of course he was. He probably thinks I'm some weakling trying to come in here and steal his family."

Aubrey snorts. "Hardly."

"He doesn't?" I raise my eyebrows, prodding.

"No."

"What is it he thinks, then?" I can tell she doesn't want to tell me, but this is something I need to know. John has more influence over Aubrey than anybody. Knowing his thoughts might help me.

Aubrey stares at me. The rest of her face is still, no emotion expressed, but I know there's a tornado smashing its way through her insides. Aubrey may be a statue sometimes, but she's not stone.

She breaks. Sighing, she mutters, "He supports your idea of us moving in. He thinks it would be best for Claire."

"Really?" I'm grinning. "And what do you think?"

"I'm still thinking about it." She peers into the window at Claire, then glances at the gold watch on her left arm. "We need to get going. Follow me?"

"See you there." I walk to my truck, resisting the urge to skip or dance or do something ridiculous to let out this excitement.

John supports me. That's huge.

Now all I have to do is make Aubrey see that Claire needs both her parents under the same roof.

WHEN MY PHONE rings at nine o'clock the next night, it startles me. After a morning full of patients, an emergency surgery, and dinner out with my office staff, I'm beat. The words in the book I'm reading were swimming together, and my head was growing heavy. Until my phone rang, anyway.

Now I'm awake. I splashed cold water on my face and changed my clothes. I'll be at Aubrey's house in a few minutes.

I don't live far, which is a good thing. As I drive, I think of what Aubrey said when I answered the phone.

"Claire is asking for you." Aubrey hesitated over her words. "I've tried putting her off, but she's in meltdown mode, and I really think she needs you." Even through the phone I felt how much Aubrey hated admitting it.

I arrive in record time, thanks to the late hour. Aubrey rises from the porch swing as I hurry up the path.

Disappointment falls over me. "Did she cry herself to sleep?" I wanted this moment. I want to be Claire's knight in shining armor.

Aubrey looks at the house as if she can see through the walls and straight to Claire's room. "No. She agreed to calm down when I told her you were coming. I needed a break from the wailing."

I try not to show my relief. "Can I go in?"

"Sure. I'll just wait out here." She sits back down and peers out into the darkness.

Quietly I slip through the house until I get to Claire's room.

"Claire," I whisper, tapping with two fingers on the partially open door.

"Daddy," she stage-whispers.

I push through and find her sitting up on her bed, smiling. She looks adorable in her yellow nightgown, her hair messy around her face.

"Your mom said you needed me," I say as I sit beside her on the bed.

"I needed to say good-night."

"Was that it?"

She gives me an offended look. "Yes."

"Your mom said you were really upset." I was expecting to walk into a tantrum like ones I've seen in public before, the kind where the parents look like they wish a sinkhole would suddenly open up below them.

She crosses her arms, as best she can, anyway. It's more of an awkward 'x' in front of her. "I told Mommy I wanted you to come here and say good-night, and she said we didn't need to. She said you were probably asleep."

"I see." I nod.

"Mommy said I could call you, but I said *no way, Jose.*" Her little head shakes, and I catch my laugh in my throat, where I keep it firmly in place.

"Well, I'm here now. What can I do for you?"

"I want you to do that thing you said your mom did when you were a little boy. When she called you a bug."

Ohhh. While Aubrey ordered Claire's lunch at the zoo I'd told Claire a story about how my mom put me to sleep at night. I never imagined it would lead us here, to a late night meltdown.

"OK, hop into bed." I hold back the covers far enough for her to slip inside. She wiggles down into them, and I pull them up to her chin. "You have a broken arm, so we're going to do a modified version. Your right arm can go under the blanket, but your left arm sticks out. Deal?"

"Deal," she nods excitedly.

I start down at her legs, tucking the comforter in on either side, working my way up until I'm around her right shoulder. "There," I say, leaning down to kiss her forehead. "Snug as a bug in a rug."

She giggles. "Good night, Daddy."

My heart lurches. "Good night, Claire."

Her eyes stay on me until I close her door. I leave the house and find Aubrey in the same position I left her in.

"Where's your dad?" I ask. His truck's in the driveway.

"Asleep. He has an early wake up tomorrow. He's going to Tucson for work."

I lean against one of the brick pillars that support the patio roof. "Does that mean he'll stay overnight? If so, you don't have to eat alone tomorrow night. I can take you and Claire out."

"That's very sweet, but it's only a day trip. He should be home by dinnertime." Aubrey shifts, her eyes on me. "How was Claire?"

The laugh I held back comes out now. "She said she told you *no way, Jose.*"

Aubrey laughs too. "We're going to have to work on her sass."

"She wanted me to tuck her in."

Aubrey rolls her eyes. "I know 'snug as a bug in a rug' as well as you."

I shrug. "What can I say? Yours must leave something to be desired."

She scoffs. "Hardly. I wouldn't have given in so quickly if my dad weren't sleeping."

"I'm glad you did. It's been killing me that I haven't seen her since yesterday morning." I look into her eyes as I say it. I need her to understand how serious I am. "I want to tuck her in. Every night."

"Isaac." Aubrey sighs. I can't help that it makes me think of the last time she said my name like that, thought the tone might have been different that night five years earlier.

"Give you time, I know. I get it." I push off the wall and head for my truck. When I get there, I turn and say loud enough for her to hear me, "If she wants me here tomorrow night, I'm here. OK?"

Aubrey nods. "OK."

My truck thunders to life, and when I pull away, I see Aubrey hasn't gone inside yet. Her head's tipped back, her hands cover her eyes. Is she crying?

I nearly stop the truck, but something tells me not to. Whatever Aubrey's feeling, she needs to feel it by herself.

CLAIRE ASKS for me the next night. And the night after that. Then the next two.

The first two nights Aubrey leaves me alone to say goodnight, but on the third night she sits on the end of Claire's bed while I read to her.

On the fourth night, Aubrey tells Claire a bedtime story about a girl named Natalie who lives in Africa.

When Claire falls asleep, Aubrey walks me out to my truck.

"Where did you get that bedtime story?"

She smiles shyly and taps her head.

"Seriously? That came from your imagination?" I lean a shoulder against the closed door of my truck.

She looks down and says nothing. Does my open admiration make her uncomfortable? I start to ask, but she grabs me and pulls me in for a hug. It takes me by surprise and lasts maybe three seconds. She pulls back but I can still feel the heat of her against my chest, as if I've been seared by her touch.

"Aubrey, I—" I stop. I can't tell her that the three seconds she just spent in my arms felt more right than anything I've ever felt. I can't scare her away. Not now. Not when I'm so close to convincing her to move in. "Never mind."

Relief floods her face. "So, um," she rocks back on her heels and presses her lips tightly together. "Thanks for coming over again tonight. To say good-night to Claire, I mean. Drive safe." She turns back and hurries up the sidewalk.

I climb into my truck for the fifth night in a row and pull away, my thoughts focused on Aubrey. What is she guarding inside that heart of hers? It must be extraordinary. Tonight, I caught a glimpse of it, and it felt like looking into the sun—blindingly bright in the moment with dazzling pulses of light to follow.

17

AUBREY

ONE OF THE benefits to working with my best friend is that I get to see her all the time. Sometimes, this positive becomes a negative. It's hard to hide from people who know your heart.

"Broker meeting should be interesting." Britt says when we get in my car at eleven. We're headed to a lunch meeting with an influential broker, the kind of person who can send us a lot of business.

"Um-hmm." I input the address of the restaurant into my phone's GPS and start driving. It's twenty-five minutes away, someplace in north Scottsdale with a view of a golf course.

"What's going on with you?" Britt rifles through her purse. She pulls out her travel make-up bag and flips open the visor mirror.

"Isaac asked us to move in." I glance at her. She's staring at me, lip gloss wand poised in mid-air.

"Are you kidding?"

"Do you think I'm kidding?"

"No." She touches-up her make-up in silence. I merge onto the freeway and wait.

She finishes and replaces the little teal pouch in her purse. "You should do it."

I groan. I knew that was going to be her response, but still.

"How about you tell me why you don't want to," she suggested, "and I'll compose valid arguments for each of your points."

"That sounds fun," I deadpan.

"I'm waiting." Her voice is serious.

"We don't know each other well enough, I don't want any drama, and I don't know if my dad can live alone." I say it all in one stream of air, then suck in a big breath.

Britt turns to face me and sticks out her hand, three fingers pointing up. "First point"—she grabs ahold of one finger—"how well does anybody really know anybody before they live together? And besides, you know him better than you think." She folds down a finger and grabs the second one, on the other side of her middle finger. "I'm skipping to your third point because I need to know more about your second one. As for your dad, he's an adult. He can live alone. He *likes* being alone. And you know that's a fact because he's hunting alone right now. Again. Like he has a hundred other times. All *alone* in the wilderness. Do you get my point?"

I nod, staring ahead, watching the cars around me. I worry about my dad hunting by himself. And this morning when I told Britt he was off on his own again, she rubbed my back and reminded me how capable he is. I stuff down my worry. "What do you need to know about my second point?"

She clears her throat in an obvious, look-at-me way. I

glance quickly over and snap my head back to attention, but I'm grinning. Britt has counted down so that only her middle finger is sticking up in the air. I bat her hand down, but we're laughing.

"Don't be juvenile."

"All jokes aside, why do you think there would be drama?"

I check my side mirror and move into the right lane. The GPS has informed me my exit is in two miles.

"What if something happens between us?"

"Is there something between you?"

"No...Yes. I don't know." That day, standing there in the foyer of his place, there was *something*. It was so intense, I had to physically remove myself.

"OK, let's just assume there's an attraction. Is that such a bad thing?"

"We're in this really awkward situation I thought only happened on daytime television. Adding to the emotion sounds like a bad idea. It's too much, too soon. Claire needs a mom and a dad. That's why he asked me to move in. He wants to give that to her. And I, of all people, should know how important that is." I exit the freeway and come to a red light, signaling a right turn. This conversation is getting heavy. Thank goodness it's just three more miles to the restaurant.

"Your second point is a front for what you're really afraid of."

I sink into my seat, defeated. Britt is right, and we both know it.

"You're scared out of your mind to trust Isaac. To let him in to your heart. Which might happen if you move in with him. But if you don't move in with him? What happens then? Claire doesn't get to have what you've always wished you could give her. The same thing life screwed you out of."

Britt's words are spot on. They fall perfectly in line with my truest thoughts and build on my dad's arguments to give Claire the father she needs. Her words coalesce in my mind and form the decision I always knew I would make.

CLAIRE FELL asleep in my bed tonight, and that's not something I usually allow her to do. I almost always make her fall asleep in her own bed, fearing the cultivation of a habit of nighttime waking I've heard other moms complain about.

Tonight I needed comfort. Broken arm propped on a pillow, Claire's little body tucked into my chest, we read book after book until her eyes grew heavy. She closed her eyes, and I closed the book. I held her, listened to her breathe, counted the seconds it took for her chest to fill with air and then decompress. I carried her to bed, situating her so the extra pillow from my bed kept her broken arm at the right angle. I kissed her face and went to double-check the door locks.

Lying in bed now, after a shower, I'm waiting for a return text from my dad. I haven't heard from him all day. Normally not hearing from my dad would have me worried out of my mind, but right now I'm filled with thoughts from my conversation with Britt.

My phone dings. I grab it, assuming it's my dad. It's Isaac.

My mom would like to have you and Claire over next weekend. She's dying to meet her. And you.

My eyes stay fixed on the screen. I take a deep breath and respond, then lay back on my pillow. I've seen Isaac's mother once, in that picture in his apartment, but I can't recall any details. I looked at the whole of the photo, the pretty picture it created, and not the parts. What will she think of me? I'm some girl who appeared out of nowhere, claiming her son is my daughter's father.

Panic makes my stomach turn, and I do everything I can to squash it. Isaac's mom can't be awful, right? She raised Isaac, and he's open and loving. That had to come from somewhere.

I knew this was coming, but the inevitability doesn't ease my trepidation. Claire has a whole family she doesn't know. A dad who wants her to live with him. And then there's me, her mother, the person who's supposed to manage it all as if she knows what's best. As if I know how this will all go. How it will all end.

I don't.

I'm Alice, falling down the hole. What will I find at the bottom?

Saturday afternoon. One p.m. That's the time set by Isaac's mother. Claire, my dad, and I went on a long walk after breakfast this morning. It helped me clear my head. It allowed Claire the chance to get out some energy. I'm not sure what it did for my dad, but he's the one who suggested it.

Claire walked between us, complaining that we couldn't swing her the way we usually do. "I hate this arm." She lifted her crooked arm, swathed in blue. At her appointment this week she'd picked a new color for her second cast.

"Hey," I say sharply, using my mom voice. "We don't hate."

"Fine. I *really* dislike it."

My dad smiles at me over Claire's head. He came

home from hunting late last Tuesday night and got an earful from me about checking in. "Who needs a wife with a daughter like you?" he'd griped. Then he stomped around the kitchen while he made himself dinner. I went to bed.

By the next morning we were fine. We hardly ever bicker. We're a team. Two halves of the same whole. Besides, I think our real problem is that we're afraid to live apart from each other.

Pretty soon, that's just what we're going to do. Because this thing with Isaac is bigger than me. Bigger than my fear.

I'm going to tell Isaac today, when I see him at his parents' house.

"I'm so excited, Mommy." Claire's bouncing in her car seat as we wave goodbye to my dad. He turns for the house, and I drive away, wishing he'd said yes when I invited him to come with us.

"Me too, baby." I hope she doesn't pick up on the hesitation in my voice. The nerves in my stomach have grown exponentially as the day has progressed. I'll consider myself lucky if I make it through the drive without hurling into the passenger seat.

"Harlow has a daddy, too. And a grandma and grandpa. Just like me."

I catch her face in the rearview, see the happy smile and bobbing head. What would it be like to live life like Claire? With a heart open wide?

Claire chatters to herself and to me. She informs me of the shape of the stop sign, makes sure I know a bird flew past our car at a stoplight, and softly sings a song about a chicken who couldn't lay an egg.

I follow the directions spouting from my phone until we pull up to the address Isaac sent me last night.

"Are we here?" Claire asks, kicking the back of my seat in an excited rhythm.

I peer out the windshield. The house is older, ranch style, with a big front yard. Mature citrus trees line the west perimeter of the lawn, creating a wall of deep green leaves. There isn't any fruit on them now, but I bet in winter they are bursting with vibrant color.

Isaac steps from the house and makes his way down the front walk. He's waving. Seeing him kicks me into action.

"Hi," I call, getting out of the car. I saw him last night for Claire's tuck in, just like every night, but he looked tired. I almost suggested he sleep on the sofa, but the words stuck in my throat. Despite what I'm going to tell him today, having him sleep at my dad's felt too close.

He jogs the last few feet to us, heading for Claire's door. "How are my girls doing?" His face is lit up.

My insides quiver. From happiness at being called his girl? Or just more nerves?

"We're good." I force a smile.

Isaac pulls Claire from the car and up into his arms, careful to put her on his left side, so her cast faces out. Claire wraps her good arm around his neck.

He knocks on her cast with two knuckles. "I'm glad you went with blue."

She beams at him. I stand there awkwardly, not sure what to do or say. Then I remember the gift I picked up for his mother and go to the passenger side, where I grab it from the floor.

"Ready?" Isaac asks.

I nod.

"My mom is probably hovering by the window watching us right now. She's been driving me nuts since I got here." He rolls his eyes and shakes his head, and I feel that familiar stab in my chest. What would it be like to have a mom to roll my eyes at?

He leads me to the house, Claire still in his arms, and the door opens before we get to it. A woman with shoulder-length dark hair stands on the threshold, a smile as big and ready as Isaac's on her face. *He must get it from her.*

Her shiny eyes are on Claire, fingertips pressed to her lips.

"Mom, this is Claire." Isaac steps to the right, so I'm fully in view. "And Aubrey. This is my mother, Lucia."

Lucia comes to life. She leaves her spot in the doorway and closes the few feet that separate us. Her arms are open, and she comes to me first.

Me.

Before I can register what's happening, she pulls me in. She's soft and warm, and she smells like honey and vanilla. My chest aches. When she pulls back, I feel sad.

"Aubrey, it's wonderful to meet you." Her face is inches from mine, her smile lovely. Genuine. She turns to Claire and Isaac.

"*Dios mio,* this baby." She holds her arms out. "May I?"

Claire pushes off from Isaac before I get a chance to answer.

"Be careful of her arm," Isaac warns, situating Claire on Lucia's left side. She gives him a brief reproachful look before returning her attention to Claire. "He thinks I don't know how to handle your special arm." Her voice is soft, admonishing. "He forgets how many bones he broke as a child."

"Daddy broke a bone too?" Claire's eyes are wide.

Lucia turns back to the house. Isaac steps aside, ushering me in before him.

"Oh yes," I hear her say. "An arm, a wrist, one in his foot,

I don't know how many toes, his collarbone." She glances back at Isaac and winks. "That's why he became an ortho-pedic surgeon. He was inspired by all that time he spent in a cast as a child."

I step inside and follow Lucia to the living room, where she sets Claire's feet down on the carpeted floor.

"Lauren. Paul." Lucia directs her yell off to her right. "They're here." She smiles at me, eyes dancing, and claps her hands together quietly.

I feel Isaac's breath on my ear, his chest against my upper back. "I should've warned you before, but my dad can be—"

"I have a joke for her," a man yells. "Do you think she likes jokes? Wait, is four too young for jokes?" The owner of the voice isn't visible yet, but his voice thunders down the hall. I can't make out the muffled response, but there's defi-nitely a second voice. Claire's hand grabs my knee from behind, an overgrown nail digging in.

Isaac's dad steps from the hallway, and he's nothing like I thought he would be. Average height, average face, and *blond*. Talk about brown being dominant. The Punnet Square called this one. Isaac looks just like his mother.

"Aubrey, so good to meet you." The man comes forward, his hand extended. He introduces himself as Paul.

The younger woman two steps behind him looks like an even split between the two parents. She has her father's blond hair, but her mother's big, brown eyes and high cheekbones.

"Hi, I'm Lauren, and I'm just going to hug you," she laughs as she wraps her arms around me.

"Hello," I say when Lauren steps back. Glancing down, I say "This is Claire."

Claire's hiding in my legs, her face pressed to the back of

my knees. Gently I use a hand to coax her out, sending an apologetic glance at Isaac's family.

"She's probably a bit overwhelmed." I explain.

Lucia nods knowingly. "Hmm... I wonder if Claire likes cupcakes? I have some that need frosting, but I'm not sure who can help me with that."

Claire's hair brushes my skin as her head peeks out from the side of my leg. Her eyes blink up at Lucia. "I do like cupcakes."

Lucia feigns surprise. "Well, then, I think you should be my helper." She holds out a hand. Claire takes it and looks at me. I nod, and they leave together.

Lauren bites her lip and glances my way. "Do you mind if I go with them? I want to talk to you more, but..."

"It's OK." I reassure her. "We can chat after you spend some time with Claire."

She hurries after them, sending a smile and an excited wave back at me.

Isaac rolls his eyes, but there's too much affection in them for the gesture to be negative. "She babysat all the time. And now she's a kindergarten teacher."

Even if Lauren didn't love little kids, I would get it. Claire is a person others want to be around. It's impossible not to love her immediately.

After watching her leave, Paul turns to me. "Aubrey, let's sit outside in the sunshine while you tell me more about yourself. Isaac, can you grab us some drinks? Your mother has something she's put together in the kitchen." Paul cups my shoulder and squeezes lightly. "This way." He walks past the couches and toward the back of the house.

As I follow him, I throw a glance back at Isaac, who hasn't moved. His gaze is fixed on me. I take a step, bump into something, and catch myself on the couch. Isaac's lips twitch, but he's not laughing. I get the feeling he's thinking really hard about something. Or maybe he's remembering.

I go after Paul, hurrying now that I've paused for so long. From the big windows, I see he's already outside, standing just beyond the patio door.

"Sorry," I mumble, when I arrive in the doorway.

"No problem. My son distract you?" He laughs.

"A little." My face is hot.

"Do you garden?" He leads me off the patio floor and onto a green lawn.

"No," I say, though I'm not sure he has heard me. Walking on large, flat pavers, we cross the backyard and around the side of the house.

"I think everyone should garden. It's good for the soul." Paul stops and steps aside.

The entire side yard, at least ten feet across and fifteen feet long, is filled with plants.

I walk around the raised beds, peering into them, as Paul talks about what fills each one.

I listen, watching his excitement as he regales me with the garden's history, how it almost wouldn't grow. He also tells me all the plants he cannot get to grow for the life of him.

His glasses slowly descend the slope of his nose because he talks with such animation. So different from my own father. My dad's words slide out of his mouth like they're facing resistance.

"Paul," Lucia's voice rings out.

"Better get going." He pulls his hands from the mint, a few stems in his grasp. "The boss is calling." He winks at me.

All afternoon I keep waiting for the questions to come. They must want to know the sordid details of how they have a family member they knew nothing about. At some point, will one of them demand a paternity test?

The questions never come. Not when we're eating lunch or enjoying the cupcakes. Not when we play catch with a football, or when Lauren tells me about her job. When Lucia asks me to help her in the kitchen, I think, *this is it*, but it doesn't happen. She hands me soapy dish after soapy dish, and I rinse and dry them, waiting for the accusations and questions to leave her lips. But they never come. Instead she talks about Isaac's job, how fortuitous it was that we ran into each other again, how happy they all are to have me and Claire in their lives now.

I knew it the moment I saw their smiling faces lying on top of the contents of a moving box. This family is perfect.

18

AUBREY

EVERYTHING CHANGED after the day at Isaac's parents' house. When Isaac walked us to my car that afternoon, I said what I'd been thinking. Instead of thinking about it *one more time,* I blurted out my decision.

And made Isaac the happiest man in the world. The consequences of my words are almost worth the joy of seeing him that happy. Almost.

Isaac doesn't waste time. That's one more thing I can say I've learned about him.

One week after telling him we'd move in, we're doing just that. I started packing two days ago. Claire's room first, and now mine.

Isaac's been busy this week, getting ready for us. Claire called him every night at bedtime to say good-night, placated only by the fact that we'd be moving in with him and soon she'll see him every night at bedtime *and* when she wakes in the morning. After Claire and Isaac finished their conversation each night, he waited on the line for me to finish my good-night with her. Every night, when I got back on the phone, he talked about what he'd accomplished that day. Aside from fixing broken bones, he also buys princess beds with canopies and constructs them. Because I guess he's not busy enough. Apparently, when Isaac puts his mind to something, there's no stopping him.

And now it's moving day.

"How's it coming along?"

My dad leans against the doorframe, arms crossed. He eyes the piles of clothing, the boxes, the stacks of books. I've never considered myself a packrat, but I'm starting to think maybe I have a tendency to hoard. A little less than five years ago, I moved back into the room that had been mine all my life, and in that time, I've managed to amass enough stuff to furnish a small village. The donate-pile is large. I stare at the item on top—my breast pump. It was a big purchase for me. Claire was an infant, and I had to work. If I wanted her exclusively breastfed, I was going to have to shell out for it. Setting the pump in the giveaway pile was hard, but what am I supposed to do with it now?

I swing my arm out to the room. "It's coming, I suppose."

Dad nods. He doesn't say anything, but he stays in his spot. He hasn't offered to help since I started packing, and I haven't asked for it.

I start loading all my books in a box.

"Aubs, that's going to be too heavy. Distribute the weight between a few boxes. Books first, maybe a quarter of the way up, then clothes on top. Something like that." Dad comes in my room, snatching an empty box as he walks by it. Together we pull the books out of the box they're in and re-pack them as he instructed.

"Thanks." I pick up stacks of clothes and place them on top.

"Anytime. Need help with anything else?"

I look around the room. "I think I've got it."

He heads for the door but pauses in the threshold. He keeps his back to me. "Now that you're moving out, I don't know if I want you to." His voice is reluctant, the words stuck in molasses.

The tears I've been holding back prickle my eyes. A few roll down my face. I clear my throat, as if somehow that will stop the tears. "I know, Dad. I'm scared too."

"It's all going to work out, Aubs." He disappears down the hall.

I want to yell after him, ask him how he can be so sure.

"Wow, Aubrey, I have to say it. I'm hurt." Britt stands in the front yard, one hand on her hip, the other lost in the bowels of a maroon foam finger. She pumps her arm like she's at a game and cheers silently.

"You can have it." I know perfectly well she threw hers away years ago. Britt doesn't keep things.

She playfully narrows her eyes at me and drops the giant hand. The pointed foam finger nearly touches the ground. "Can I please?"

"Britt, I have to get rid of stuff. I can't take that into Isaac's house."

"Fine, fine. Don't keep a memento of the game that launched our friendship." She fake cries.

I laugh. "OK. Put it in the save pile."

She pumps her arm and smacks herself a high five, shouting "Right next to the breast pump I rescued." She runs back into the house just as Isaac pulls up.

"Cordova moving service, here to help you," he says loudly from his open window, then grabs the bill of his baseball cap and tips his head. He gets out and comes around the front of his truck.

"I didn't know I hired a professional," I yell back before picking up a box from the patio where Britt has been setting them down. We have an assembly line going. My dad's keeping Claire occupied in the back yard.

Isaac strides across the yard and takes the box from my arms. "The pro can take it from here."

I frown. I don't need *that* much help.

He's already at the bed of his truck, sliding my box across. I pick up another box and hurry to my car, placing it in the trunk. When I turn around he's shaking his head at me.

"Well, well, well. We meet again."

We both turn to find Britt on the porch, setting down another box. She wipes her hands on her jeans and walks down the steps. Isaac meets her halfway, his hand extended, but Britt hugs him.

She steps back and surveys him, one eye closed from the sun's glare. "Five years ago I gave you the green light, but I didn't know you had super swimmers."

"Britt!" I smack the top of her arm.

Isaac laughs. Like always.

"What can I say? I eat a lot of protein." He shrugs, and now Britt's the one laughing.

I huff. "I'm glad you both find this so amusing."

Britt curls a hand around my shoulder. "Aw, we can joke now Aubrey. It's all over." She leans into me. "Or it's just getting started." Her whisper tickles my ear. I reach up to rub away the sensation.

She steps away. "Just a couple more boxes to go. Aubrey, come help me carry them out. I'm sure Isaac can load all that"—she tosses a thumb back at the stacks on the porch —"into his truck."

"On it." Isaac goes for the first box on the stack. I don't

miss the pull in the arms of his T-shirt when he lifts the box. And neither does Britt.

Once we're in the house and safely out of earshot, she grabs my arm and pretends to swoon. "Oh, my. Dr. Cordova just added about ten degrees to the outside temperature. And it's already almost sweltering."

"I know," I say under my breath, even though there's no way he can hear me. Through the open door I watch him cross the yard again, coming back to the porch for another box. I pull her down the hall to my room and say in my normal voice, "He's not lacking in the attractive department."

"No, he's not." She shakes her head. "Or in the personality department. Or the career department. Or the family one." She slides me a pointed look. "He's a dream come true. Literally. He's your dream of having a perfect family, come true." She goes to my closet and pulls open the door. "So why are you holding back?" She doesn't look at what's inside the closet, just at me. Obviously she already knows what I've left in there.

My sigh is deep, with a little groan thrown in. I don't know how to explain why I'm keeping extra clothes and shoes for me and Claire in there. Safeguards, maybe. My *just in case* pile. When you've spent your whole life protecting yourself, you don't just turn it off like a light switch. The night doesn't automatically give way to the day. It goes in stages. And I can't jump all-in with Isaac. I just... can't.

"We're becoming roommates for the sake of our daughter, Britt. We're not involved romantically. There is no 'holding back.'"

But there is, and she knows it.

And how could there not be? The instinct to defend is

primal, fundamental. And when you've been burned, the instinct only gets stronger.

Britt closes the closet and doesn't say another word about it.

"GOT IT ALL, AUBS?" My dad stands at the end of the driveway, arms crossed.

"Yes." I feel Britt's look, but I keep my gaze on my dad.

"I'm gonna get going," Dad says. "Someone spotted that lion from last weekend." He looks unsure of what to do next. He's ready to go on his short trip to whatever mountain range he's been called to, but he's hesitating. He won't be coming home to me and Claire, and I think we've both realized this is an effect of the move we hadn't considered.

"Be safe." I pull him in for a hug, blinking back tears. "Call me when you get in."

His neck moves with his gulp. He steps back. "Will do." He turns to Isaac. "You take care of my girls."

Isaac sticks out his hand. "Always, John."

They shake, and my dad moves to my car, tapping on Claire's partially rolled down window. He's already said goodbye to her, so he only waves.

He gets in his truck and backs out, throwing up a hand to the three of us in the driveway. I see him swipe the back of his palm across his eyes before putting it in drive.

"You ready?" Isaac asks.

I move my eyes off my dad's retreating truck, nodding.

Britt hugs me. "See you at work on Monday."

I echo her words. She gets in her car and pulls away from the curb. I watch her go, fighting the urge to run after her. They've really left me with him. And now I'm supposed to leave *here*. With him. The realness of this is finally hitting me.

"I think it's our turn." Isaac grabs my hand and runs his thumb across the top of it. His gentle touch soothes my nerves.

"Mommy! I'm bored." Claire yells from her car seat.

We chuckle and head for our cars. Isaac pauses at his open door.

"See you at home." The words put a smile on his face. He climbs in and shuts the door.

Those words... I wish they put a smile on my face. They strike fear in me. But also hope. Hope this all goes well. This thing we're doing, in the name of giving our daughter the very best.

19

AUBREY

"THAT'S ALL OF THEM." Isaac sets the final box on the floor beside my new bed. "I wasn't sure what kind of bedding you'd like. You can get something different if you don't like it."

I lean back on the bed, one hand supporting me, while my other hand trails along the stitching in the royal blue comforter. "You did a good job. It's lovely."

"I thought it might match your eyes." He bends, his gaze level with mine. Brown eyes penetrate me until my insides twist. "I was right," he whispers.

My breath feels hollow in my throat, and my chest feels like it's fumbling for heartbeats.

He doesn't move away, though by now I'm certain his check of my eye color versus the bedspread is complete. The seconds tick by, and I'm starting to notice things, like how Isaac's lower lip is a tiny bit bigger than his upper, and his gradual, barely there widow's peak. And the tiny freckle beside his nose.

I clear my throat, leaning away at the same time. I need distance. Now.

Isaac straightens and steps back. "I'll go make dinner." He pauses on his way out the door and looks back at me. "You don't care if we have ice cream for dessert, do you?"

"No." I shake my head slowly, a tad confused. I'm sure my face reflects it.

He puts his hands in the pockets of his jeans and shrugs. "Just checking." He starts to leave, then turns back quickly. "Lions don't live in Arizona."

I stare at him, perplexed. "Huh?"

"Your dad. He said someone spotted a lion from last weekend."

"Mountain lion. Not a *rawr* lion," I make claws with my hands and swipe the air.

Isaac grins. "Can you do that again?"

My arms cross, and I tuck my hands into my underarms. "No."

He chuckles and leaves. I listen to his retreat, then get up and go to Claire's room to start unpacking her clothes.

"WHAT DO WE DO NOW?" Claire gazes expectantly at Isaac. He pauses his gathering of the ice cream bowls, lips twisting as he considers her question.

"Um, I don't know. What do you normally do after dinner?"

"Play. Read. Take a bath."

Isaac finishes stacking the bowls and brings them to me at the sink, where I'm rinsing and loading the dishwasher.

"Do you ever play cards?" He goes back to the table and clears the remaining items.

"Nope. Never." Claire gives me an accusatory look.

"Whoa now." I hold up my hands, water dripping from

the spatula I was rinsing. "It's not like I was keeping them from you. I didn't think to introduce them."

Isaac comes up behind me, holding the dirty napkins and barbecue sauce from dinner. "Claire, I'm sure your mom would've showed you how to play a game of cards if she knew how."

I turn my head sharply to the side and glare playfully at him. "I know how."

"Oh, you do? Well then, you should join me and Claire for a wild game of Go Fish."

I walked right into that one. I was going to escape to the bedrooms to keep unpacking, and I think he knew that.

It's not that I don't want to play with them, but I'm getting overwhelmed by the events of the day and navigating our first afternoon and evening together. I don't know what to do next, and I'm not comfortable yet. Working on our rooms seemed like the best option.

"Come on, Mommy." Claire gets down from her chair and joins me at the sink.

I drop down, so we're eye to eye.

"You want me to play with you and your dad?"

She nods.

Behind Claire, Isaac watches us as he wipes his hands on a dish towel.

"OK, I'll play." I push some hair out of Claire's eyes.

She whoops and runs out of the kitchen. I stand and look at Isaac.

"This is a lot to take in—" I start to say.

At the same time, he says "I know this is an adjustment."

We laugh once, a bit of the tension melting away.

"Thanks for understanding." I take the dish towel he used to dry his hands and hang it from the oven handle.

"Thanks for not judging me when I had a second scoop of ice cream." Isaac pats his stomach.

His body will never show the effects of his love for ice cream, I'm certain of that. But there's no way that statement is leaving my lips.

I lean one hip against the counter. "You have a thing for ice cream, don't you?"

He laughs. "You've noticed?"

"That night, you told the cab driver to take us to an ice cream place."

"I did." He nods slowly. "But we never made it inside."

The air around us changes, igniting with a pulse of energy. It fills me, pushing into my chest and limbs, capturing my rational thoughts and turning them foolish.

He feels it too. I know it in the way his lips peel apart, how his eyes instantly look deeper, like they're holding more emotion than they were ten seconds ago.

"I'm ready to play cards," Claire yells from somewhere beyond the island.

I blink and look away, grateful for her interruption.

"So are we," Isaac yells into the open space. His voice is ragged.

We play cards until it's Claire's bedtime. She puts up a fuss about taking a bath, insisting I shut the bathroom door so Isaac can't see the garbage bag I've wrapped around her arm to keep her cast from getting wet.

I'd thought her protests had to do with modesty, but she told me she was embarrassed of the contraption.

"You know," I say, carefully leaning her head away from her hurt arm and pouring water over her soapy hair, "Your dad is the person who suggested we use this bag to bathe you. Remember at your first appointment?"

"Yes." Her voice is tiny.

"So why can't he see you like this?"

Her little shoulders shrug slowly. When her lower lip trembles, it nearly breaks my heart in two.

"What is it?" I ask, slicking her clean hair back over her head and squeezing out some of the excess water.

"Will Daddy leave? Will it just be me and you again? Will we have to go back to Grandpa's?"

My forehead creases with my surprise. I wasn't expecting such loaded questions.

For a second I contemplate lying, because it's easiest, but I can't. I don't believe in false hope, and I certainly won't set my daughter up to be disappointed. "I don't know the future, but I do know your Daddy loves you very much, and he won't ever be without you again." She seems satisfied with my answer, and I relax. She's pouring water from one cup to another when she asks, "Where did your mommy go?"

My hand, poised in the air to pour another bucket of water over her back, stills. I set the bucket down in the bath water and watch it tip over.

"I'm not sure, sweetie." It's the best I can manage when my brain cells are all falling over one another trying to process her question and the ramifications of answering it.

"Did she die?"

I gulp. Why has a seemingly normal bath time turned into a shock-Mommy marathon?

"Where did you learn about people dying?"

"Lincoln's grandma died. He told me at school yesterday."

"No, my mom didn't die." I pause, thinking. I guess I don't know that for sure. "She wasn't able to be a mommy anymore, and she had to leave me and Grandpa."

Claire's eyes are saucers, and I realize what I've done.

"No, no, no, Claire, don't worry. That will never happen to me. I'm meant to be your mommy. I'll always be capable of that job."

She nods, her eyes trusting me implicitly, and I think how amazing that would be. To trust someone like that. So childlike and naive. She has never been let down, and I'm dreading the day it happens.

"Are you ready to get this bag off your arm and let your dad tuck you in?"

Claire stands, and we work together to get her ready for bed. When we emerge from the bathroom Isaac is already there, waiting against the wall beside her bedroom door. I sit on the end of her bed while Isaac reads to her and situates her arm. We both say good-night and step out of her room, pulling the door shut.

He looks at me, face serene. "I know it's only been a month and a half since her break, but it feels like I've been waiting a long time for her."

I'm not sure what to say, so I smile. As we stand there, the awkwardness creeps back in until I finally think of something to say. "I'm going to bed too. It's been a busy day."

Isaac's expression goes from serene to sad. He looks like he wants to say something, maybe tell me how lame I am for a twenty-something, but all that comes out is, "OK."

Before the confusing energy between us can tidal-wave me to the ground again, I make my escape with a lousy *good-night*.

I'm in the safety of my new room when my phone chirps from the dresser.

Britt: Have a nice night. Hope things are going well for you.

I'm typing my response when another text comes in.

Isaac: Thank you for agreeing to move in here. I know it's not ideal for you, but knowing that tonight I'm going to sleep under the same roof as my daughter means everything to me.

My fingers move an inch above the keys as I contemplate what to say. After a moment, I settle on a response.

Me: It's best for Claire, and she's what matters.

I bite my lip and turn, my gaze caught by the gorgeous blue comforter he chose. The energy hits me, and he's not even here. I'm picturing Isaac in a store, standing in front of all the bedding, trying to find a comforter he hopes I'll like.

I feel cared for, and it's unsettling. I don't know how to handle the feeling. I want to grab it and push it away, but I also want to curl up with it, right onto the soft blue fabric covering my bed.

When I go to bed after responding to Britt, I battle warring emotions.

Isaac is the daylight, a rising sun, shooing away the pestering ghosts. Claire's questions invite the ghosts to peer over my shoulder and remind me with their wispy presence that they're still around.

Oddly, both make me feel the same way.

Terrified.

I SLEPT BETTER than I have in months, and I refuse to admit it had anything to do with the comforter I was wrapped in.

Before I walk out of my room, I listen at the door. I want to know what I'm getting myself into. When a few seconds of sleuthing yields no sound, I venture out.

And right into Isaac as he's walking past my room. His chest isn't a terrible place for my cheek to land. It's soft. And it smells good. All in all, there are worse places to be.

"Sorry," I whisper, pushing away from him.

"Come here." He takes my hand, leading me quietly past

Claire's room. He pulls me into the kitchen. "I have something for you."

"Oh, yeah?" I settle onto a barstool and lean my elbows on the island. "I hope it's a pony."

Suppressed laughter makes Isaac's shoulders bob, but he keeps his back turned, preparing the coffee. After a moment I hear the sound of liquid streaming from the complicated looking machine. "Unfortunately the store was fresh out of ponies." He turns, carrying a mug in his hand. "But, they did have this." He rounds the island and sets the cup in front of me.

I lift it, tilting it slightly to read the words.

I can't help my laugh. *I Mom So Hard* the mug announces in big block letters. I laugh again, but I like it. The recognition feels nice.

Isaac's at the machine, making a cup for himself. "I thought you might like to have your own coffee cup here." He comes to sit beside me.

"Yours doesn't say anything." I point to his plain white cup.

He brings it to his lips, nodding. "Maybe you can help me pick one out. What should mine say?"

"Baby Daddy?" I hold back my smile and raise my eyebrows. I still don't love the term, but it's annoyingly accurate.

He makes a face. "Try again."

"I Fix Broken Bones?"

"Boring." He sips again, eyeing me.

"World's Greatest Dad?"

He thinks for a moment. "A little cliché but I'll take it."

"We can go today. Find that new mug of yours. And then you can drink from a mug as cool as mine." I peer at him over the brim of my cup, and he smiles.

This thing we're doing right now... It's nice. We're loose, light, and airy, with none of the awkward tension I anticipated. It takes Claire another hour to wake up, and during that time, Isaac and I are crooked grins, friendly talk about work, and comfortable silences.

I don't think Isaac's even trying. He's only being himself. The man I met five years ago is still in there, bright and sunny, ready to take on the world with his anything-is-possible attitude.

Correction: the man I met five years ago is *here*. Right beside me, his elbow bumping mine. Claire came out of her room, and now she looks at home on his lap, tucked into the crook of his arm. And I'm six inches away, my insides swirling, feeling everything but tranquil.

It won't always be like this. Soon this will be your normal. This will pass.

ISAAC

"Dr. Cordova, you have a pharma rep in exam room three."

I lean forward in my chair, my interest piqued. "Thanks, Morgan. Do you know if—?"

The line clicks.

Never mind.

It's probably not her. What reason would she have to show up here?

I try to come up with answers as I leave my office and walk toward the room, but I have none. It's definitely not her.

Whoever it is, this won't take long. I'm meeting my sister for lunch in twenty minutes, and I can't be late. Lauren will be late, which means I need to be on time and order for us. I have surgery scheduled for three p.m.

Before entering the room I throw two quick knocks on the door, then press in.

I was wrong. It is her.

"Jenna, hello."

She stands across the small space, arms crossed. I'm relieved to feel nothing in my chest when I see her. Not that it surprises me. It's just good to know there aren't residual feelings lurking.

"Isaac," she nods curtly. "This isn't a professional visit, in case you're wondering."

"Unless you're suddenly in the business of selling metal pins, I didn't think it was." I tilt my head and wait for her to speak.

She barks an awkward laugh, fingering her silk collar. The Jenna I know doesn't fidget. The Jenna I know is never nervous. Then again, I'm beginning to think I never knew her very well.

Jenna brings her hand down to meet the other, fingers intertwining in front of her navy blue knee-length skirt. "I came here to talk some sense into you."

My chin raises a fraction of an inch, muscles tensing. Even though I already know what she's going to say, and I'm so confident of it that I'd bet my right thumb, I ask "About what?"

"Your choice to sacrifice your career."

Annoyance flares. "Your concern is touching. Now if you'll excuse me." I move to leave.

"Isaac, wait." Her hand goes out to stop me, although she's nowhere near touching me. "I'm here to help you see reason. God knows she won't. She probably has no idea what you're giving up for her. And her child."

My fists ball at my sides. "My child."

"Right, yes. Your child." Jenna's face screws up as if the words taste bad. "Isaac, I heard about your offer and I want you to think more about it. Saying no to Dr. Redmond is a bad idea. You could go so far with his help. A research position, Isaac. *Research.* That's huge."

Her words bounce around in my mind. To Jenna, this is

the ultimate step in a flourishing career. I can see where she's coming from.

"Jenna." I pause to take in her face. She looks like she always has. I wonder what she'll do when, inevitably, smile lines appear around her lips. "Sometimes, there are more important things than moving up in your career. And I hope you get to experience them." I step through the open door and pause in the doorway. "I'll see you around."

There's no point in sticking around to hear any other arguments she has prepared. She lifts her hand for a short wave, her face concerned, and I walk away.

I'm not worried about my choice. I know my priorities.

"HI, SORRY I'M LATE." Lauren slides into the seat across from me. "Did you order?"

I nod, checking the time on my watch. "I have a three o'clock surgery."

"Sorry, sorry," she mutters, hooking her purse strap on the back of her chair. She brushes her bangs from her eyes and blinks at me.

"Stop," I instruct as her eyes fill. "Nothing's changed."

"It feels different." She bites her lip, but she can't completely stop it from trembling.

"Did we go to see the Redwoods when you were eight? I tripped you, and you fell headfirst into a tree. Is that right?"

She nods.

"Did I chase your first date out of the house because he was a douchebag?"

A small smile moves her lips. "He was not a douchebag."

"He was and you're welcome." I bow dramatically until she's done laughing. Straightening, I grow serious. "My point is, everything's the same. You knowing doesn't change anything. Family is love."

She makes a grunting noise in the back of her throat and rolls her eyes. "Don't. I already heard those words from Mom. And now I understand why she's been saying them our whole lives."

The server drops off a basket of bread, and I thank him before he walks away. Lauren lays her napkin on her lap and tears a piece of bread in half. She pops it in her mouth and chews like the bite offended her.

"Give Mom a break." I take the other half of the bread and drop it on my plate. "I know it's new to you, but I dealt with it a long time ago."

"By going to a bar and making a baby."

"Best decision I ever made," I say around a bite of bread.

She smiles. "It was, wasn't it?"

I nod.

"How's it going living with Aubrey and Claire? It's been what, two weeks?" She sips her water.

She's changing the direction of our conversation, and I'm grateful. It's not a pleasant subject for me, despite the fact that I'm as over it as I can be.

I sit back in my seat, the tension melting from my shoulders. "It's going well, I think. Claire's adjusting. Honestly, she didn't need much adjusting." Claire's an easy kid. I've yet to see her throw a fit, though Aubrey assures me she's still on her best behavior, and it's just a matter of time.

"And Aubrey?" Lauren's gaze pins me. This question is more difficult to answer.

"Aubrey is..." I shift in my chair. "She's adjusting too."

"Why the hesitation?"

I sip my iced tea, thinking of how to answer Lauren's question. I don't know how things are going with Aubrey.

We have good conversation, she smiles and seems happy. Together, we put Claire to bed every night. But then she steps from Claire's room, mumbles good night, and practically runs to her room. It's as if she's reached max capacity and might implode.

"She seems happy, but I wonder if it's a front for Claire." The guilt I've been fighting creeps in. "I insisted she move in. I was so sure it was the right choice for Claire, but I didn't think much about Aubrey."

"Aubrey is an adult. She made the choice she thought was best."

"Yeah," I mumble, not because I agree but because it's easier not to argue with her. I check my watch under the table. Our food needs to arrive soon.

"Isaac, seriously." Lauren's voice is insistent. "Aubrey's a big girl. She's not anywhere she doesn't want to be." Her look is stern, eyebrows drawn together and chin cocked a few degrees to the left. It's the look my mother has given us a million times. I won't tell her that now, though. I know better.

Lunch comes to the table, and I eat like I haven't seen food in three days. I refuse to think about Aubrey any longer. For my sanity, and for the sake of my next patient, I need to start clearing my mind.

21

AUBREY

WHY?

Why?

I think I might be dying.

My body is too hot. I stretch across the short distance from my bed to my nightstand, reaching for my phone. My whole body screams in agony from the effort.

I check the time. Two forty-two a.m. I need water. Cold water.

After forcing one leg over the side of the bed, and then the other, I stand. Sort of. I'm bent at the waist. I shuffle out the door and down the hall, pausing twice. By the time I make it to the fridge, I've taken four breaks.

I'm overcome by the work it takes to remove the pitcher of water and get a cup while staying upright on shaky legs. My forehead meets the cool marble countertop for a quick rest.

"Aubrey?" Isaac is beside me.

"Hmmm?" The word reverberates against my lips. The marble feels so good even my lips are laid against it.

"Are you sick?" Concern presses into his voice.

Using my palms and every ounce of strength I have, I push up to my bent-standing position.

"I'm fine. I just... need... rest." It's hard to say so many words at once. "And water." I reach for the countertop to steady myself.

Isaac wraps one arm around my lower back and the other across my chest, from shoulder to shoulder. I release some of my weight. It feels nice not to be responsible for all of it right now.

"Let's get you to bed. I'll bring your water." Isaac's voice soothes me. "Have you checked your temperature?"

"Burning," I mumble. I don't need a thermometer to tell me I'm around 102. It's a mom thing.

We get to my room and Isaac helps me into bed. He pulls the covers around me and steps back. I watch him through hooded eyes.

"I'll be right back with the water. Do you need anything else?"

"I'll be fine," I croak, closing my eyes.

Every second blends into the next, and I don't know how long he takes. Eventually I feel a cold rag pressed to my forehead and hear the sound of a cup being placed on the nightstand.

I don't trust my body right now so I can't be certain, but I think I feel something brush my lips. Fingertips, maybe?

"Take a drink, Aubrey." His thumb pulls on my chin, willing me to open my mouth. His hand slips behind my neck, lifting my head for me. The glass is at my lips, and I sip three times. It's cold and possibly the best thing I've ever tasted.

Gently he lays my head on the pillow, his hand slipping away.

"Get some rest." His voice is soft.

I want to compliment his bedside manner, but I don't have the energy. Later I'll tell him.

I don't know if he's left yet, but my eyes are already fluttering closed.

ISAAC'S HEAD PEEKS IN. When he sees I'm awake, he says, "I'm taking Claire to school."

I roll over, try to lift myself up on my forearms, but they don't work. There isn't enough energy in my body to do that, let alone care for Claire.

"Thanks," I mumble, burying myself in my pillow. I don't want to know what I look like right now. And I definitely don't want Isaac to see me like this.

"Get some rest. I'll take care of everything."

"Isaac, wait." I turn my head so my lips are exposed. "Claire needs a lunch. And a morning snack. No peanut products, there's a student with an allergy."

"Aubrey, I got it. Promise."

I ignore him. How could he possibly know everything I know? "You have to write her name on the snack." I close my eyes. I'm exhausted.

Isaac laughs quietly. "OK. Lunch, sunflower butter and jelly sandwich. Snack with name written on it. Couldn't mess it up if I tried."

"Don't try." My voice is muffled by the pillow.

The door falls softly into the jamb. I turn my head and let out a long exhale. I feel weird. A weirdness that extends beyond this flu.

Uneasy.

Someone else is going to take care of Claire today. I'm always the one to do it. This is the sickest I've been in years. Today Isaac will do all the things I normally do. These things aren't difficult. They don't require any special training, but they're my job.

A chill sweeps over me, my limbs jerking from the suddenness of it. It takes every ounce of strength I have to get to my dresser and pull out a sweatshirt. Once I'm huddled in bed, my knees pulled into my chest, I close my eyes and pass out.

WHEN I WAKE AGAIN, it's from the sound of a soft knock.

Isaac must have come home early. Or I slept all day. My phone is lost somewhere in my sheets, so I can't check the time.

"Come in," I call quietly.

The door opens. Lucia stands in the doorway, her face etched with a concerned smile. The rust-colored skirt she's wearing reaches the ground, the sleeves of her jean jacket are rolled up, and a stack of gold bangles makes a tinkling sound as she sends me a small wave.

"Can I come in?" She steps in the room without waiting for my answer.

"Be careful, Lucia," I warn as I sit up, surprising myself with my strength. "I think I have the flu. I don't want to get you sick."

With her hand, she brushes away my protest. "Nonsense." She sits beside me on the bed, one leg tucked underneath her. "The flu, you say?"

I lift my arm, so I can talk into the crook of my elbow. "I think so. My body aches and I'm so cold. I had a fever during the night."

Lucia leans closer, and I shrink back. I do not want to be responsible for getting Isaac's mother sick. "Are you hungry?"

"Not really. I'm OK. I just need to rest." She frowns, so I decide to try again. "I'll eat some crackers after I take another nap. I promise." I feel bad. Lucia doesn't need to waste her time here. I can get myself crackers, for goodness sake.

She stands. "You rest. I'll just clean up a little, and, when you wake up, I will bring you crackers." She scoots from the room before I can tell her I can make do on my own.

Suddenly I'm very tired. Even that short conversation has exhausted me.

I hear the TV go on in the living room, but the sound doesn't bother me. I like knowing that beyond these walls, someone is out there who cares.

MY SECOND NAP of the day is interrupted by something less gentle than Lucia's knock on my bedroom door.

A loud, tinny sound barges through my sleep and continues while I pull myself from my groggy state. It stops, and a few moments later, my door opens. Lucia's eyes open wide when she sees me awake.

"I hope my cooking didn't wake you." She's wearing a green apron with flowers embroidered on the waist, just above the pockets.

"No, not at all." I smile weakly through my fib.

"I made you something I always make Isaac and Lauren when they're sick. I'll be right back with it."

She cooked for me. Something she makes for her own children. There's an odd feeling in my chest right now, and it's not related to my illness. It's heavy, but it's...happy.

Lucia comes back with a tray. I sit up, and she puts the tray across my lap. It has little legs that fold out so I don't have to balance it.

"Albondigas." Lucia grins proudly.

"Excuse me?" I say, confused.

She laughs, the sound musical. "The soup. It's called albondigas. Mexican meatball soup, basically."

The steam swirls up from the bowl, and I lean in, sniffing. "It smells like heaven."

"Tastes like it too."

Lucia's unabashed opinion of her own cooking makes me chuckle.

"What?" she asks, smiling, her hands lifting while her elbows stay at her waist. "I know how good it is."

I take my first bite and *oh, oh, oh* it's what heaven must taste like. I look at Lucia and nod my approval, then spoon more into my mouth.

Like a proud mama bird, she sits carefully on the end of my bed and watches me eat. The bowl is half empty when she leans back on her hands and opens her mouth. She closes it, opens it again.

"How are you, Aubrey? Aside from this temporary sickness."

I set my spoon on the tray and pick up the sparkling water. I take a long sip before I set it back down.

"I'm fine." I'm always fine. Always.

Lucia eyes me. "Are you sure? You've been through a lot in the past month. If I were in your position, I don't think I'd be fine."

I pick up the spoon and dip it into the bowl, picking up only the broth. I taste tomatoes, garlic, and onions, plus bits from the meatballs. I was wrong last night. This is the best thing I've ever had. The ice water doesn't even come close.

I swallow and pick up more. Lucia watches me intently, waiting for me to answer her question. She's not like my dad. She won't accept my *I'm fine*.

With a full spoon suspended over the bowl, I say "Technically, I'm OK. I have Claire, her arm is healing, we have a beautiful place to live, and she's happy. There isn't much more to it than that." I shrug, offering a small smile. I'm proud I can speak in long sentences again.

Lucia surveys me with shrewd eyes. "But what about you?"

"What about me? My job is to take care of Claire. And I'm doing that."

She shakes her head. "Who takes care of you?"

"I don't need taking care of." I learned that a very long time ago.

Lucia's face tells me just how much she disagrees with me. Her eyebrows rise and the corners of her mouth turn down.

I finish my soup and drink the water. The bubbles tickle my throat.

Lucia stands and takes the tray off my lap. She sets it on the nightstand and looks back at me. Her eyes are kind, but they're also concerned.

"Get some sleep." She leans down and kisses my forehead. My stomach tenses when her lips brush my skin. The heavy and happy feeling is back.

She retrieves the tray, looking back at me. "You know, everyone needs taking care of."

"Thank you for the soup." I've just realized I hadn't yet thanked her.

But Lucia shakes her head slowly, like I didn't understand her. "People need more than soup."

She leaves, and I lie down. I'm beat but my head is alive. Swirling and churning, conflicted feelings from a day spent being cared for by Isaac's mother. I'm a grown woman. I haven't needed anybody in a long time. I don't ask for help. I don't want it, and I've never thought I needed it.

Lucia came here today and didn't ask me what I needed. She knew. And it's clear she thinks I need more than soup.

I'M sick for three more days. Lucia comes every day to take care of me. She brings magazines to read with me and saltine crackers to munch on. I request her albondigas one more time. Isaac and Claire love the epicurean perks of living with an ill person. On the last day, when it's clear I'm almost back to normal, I go for a walk with Lucia. The coffee shop a few streets over is our goal. They have homemade red velvet whoopie pies that are so delicious, I swear my taste buds cry when I eat one.

We're quiet until we get out of Isaac's neighborhood and onto the main street.

"It's good to see you healthy again. Isaac was very worried about you."

"Why? It was just the flu." I shrug my shoulders. We reach the intersection, and I push the walk button.

Lucia waits until I look at her, then she rolls her eyes at me. Our past few days together have taught me a lot about Lucia. She loves telenovelas ("It connects me to my heritage."), she can't stand flies ("Do you know they throw up every time they land?"), and she rolls her eyes when she disagrees with you and doesn't want to say anything but really wants to make sure you know she disagrees.

"What?" The walk sign appears, and we cross.

"Nothing, nothing."

Lucia and I have become friends, I think. She's Claire's grandma, but it's more than that. We've bonded. In all of the craziness since Claire broke her arm, I didn't expect to gain a friend.

Lucia rolls her eyes again, but this time she cracks a smile.

I laugh at her. "Come on." I hold open the door to the coffee shop. "You can tell me exactly what you think after we sit."

The moment my butt is in the seat, she starts talking.

"I want you with Isaac."

My mouth falls slack around my big bite of whoopie pie. I chew and swallow, using my napkin to wipe the crimson crumbs I know must decorate the corners of my mouth.

"Lucia, Isaac and I have been over this. We're co-parents. That's it."

"But why? Why stop there?"

"This situation is hard enough. We don't need to complicate it with romance."

Lucia sits back and sips her coffee. I wait for the eye roll but it doesn't come.

"I get that," she says. "Really, I do. It's just... Isaac has put work first for so long. He was determined to be a doctor, then he became one. Now what? He's always wanted to be a dad, especially since..." She stops, coughs into a fist. Alarm widens her eyes the tiniest bit. She picks up like there was never a pause in her statement. "Since his dad is so amazing."

I let it pass.

Reaching across the table, I cover her hand with my own. She's so warm. "He's a dad now. I'm sorry it took him so long to become one. If I could've told him, I would have."

"I get it. Life is eventful. It has a way of racing forward without asking if you need to stop and take a breath." She tucks her hair behind her ears and smiles wistfully. "I've been married to Isaac and Lauren's father for thirty-six years, but I remember the beginning. The fear, and uncertainty. The should I's and shouldn't I's." She stares down into her coffee, her eyes far away.

Lucia is beautiful. Delicate lines border the corner of her eyes and make parentheses on either side of her mouth. She has an elegance to her. Maybe it's in the lift of her chin. Or in the confident way she talks, like she's a woman who knows. She gets it. Whatever *it* is. Lucia Cordova understands something I don't.

"Your son..." I pause, mulling over my next words. Lucia looks up, back from wherever she went a moment ago. "He's amazing, from what I can tell. But Isaac and I, we're in this awkward situation. We're parents to Claire, yet we've never been on a date." I feel the heat in my cheeks. "I mean, that night..." I look away. Mortification fills me. How can I talk about this with her?

"Aubrey, it's just sex." Lucia makes a noise with her tongue, an admonishing cluck. "Everyone has sex. Even me." She gestures with a hand to her chest, her laughter throaty.

"I'll make sure I don't mention that to Isaac," I say, laughing with her.

"Our family is very open. Though he might not want to hear about his mom and dad in that way."

It's hard enough to imagine my parents ever even knew each other, let alone did what they needed to do to make me.

"I am curious though..." Lucia's lips twist after she trails off.

"Ask away."

"That night... Did you two not use protection? I thought I'd had enough sex talks with Isaac when he was younger that he understood the importance of protection."

Beneath the table my hands fold together, my fingers intertwining. I take a deep breath.

"We did." Memories of that night come down on me like a curtain. Isaac, sexy as hell with his shirt off and his pants unbuttoned, leaning over me on his bed. We'd used protection. And yet... "I went over it in my head a hundred times after I got the positive result. I don't know what went wrong. I really don't." I shake my head, still as confounded today as I was that day in my bathroom, staring at the plus sign. "I don't think he made a mistake, but maybe our judgment was clouded. From alcohol and—" I purse my lips. I've said too much.

Lucia smirks. "Passion?" She raises her eyebrows.

I nod. Now I'm really embarrassed.

"So you and Isaac had passion? When you barely knew each other?" She makes the clucking sound again. "I wonder if you still have that fire between you?"

"Claire is between us now. She's our priority." I'm resolute about this. Claire needs two clearheaded, strong parents. There is no room for messy, dramatic romance.

Lucia watches me for two seconds, her eyes searching my statement for weakness. Then she rolls them.

It's her biggest eye roll yet.

22

AUBREY

Now that I'm pretty much healthy, I feel like I need to get reacquainted with Isaac's place. Four days confined to a bed has made me feel like a newcomer again.

I take a turn through his big, beautiful white kitchen. My fingers trail along the stainless-steel fridge, the island made of black wood, the marble countertops I needed so badly the first night I was sick. Part of me wants to spill red juice, just to see what it would look like in its marred perfection. The other part of me wants to never touch anything.

I'm in the pantry, rifling through boxes of crackers and bags of chips, when Isaac walks up behind me. He reaches over my head and pulls down a basket of oranges. I follow him to the counter and watch him peel one.

"You want?" He offers it to me.

I take it from his outstretched hand.

He peels a second orange and pops a segment into his mouth. I watch, transfixed. Something about the way Isaac chews is so manly. It's not annoying or gross. Shouldn't chewing be gross? Why isn't it for Isaac?

"Are you going to eat your orange?" He points at the fruit in my palm.

I look down at it. "I don't want to get any juice on your countertops. They're so..." I look around at them. "Clean."

He grabs a small plate from the cupboard and slips it under my hand.

"Not white?" I drop the orange onto the navy-blue plate and pull it apart.

"Huh?" Isaac grabs a bottle of red wine and pulls the cork.

"The plate. It's not white. Every time we've eaten, it's been on something white. I thought maybe white is your thing."

His back is to me as he takes two glasses from the cabinet, but I see his head shake.

"Not my thing." He turns around, meets my eyes, and looks back down.

"Do you miss her?"

"No. Not like I should, anyway." He shakes his head, like he's confused about something. "We'd known each other forever, and I think I proposed because it seemed like that was what I was supposed to do. I was taking a next step on a path that had ended." He shrugs. "But that's over now."

When he places my wine in front of me, I grab the glass and take a big drink.

"How did Claire go to sleep?" I ask. As excited as I was to be part of her nighttime routine again, I thought it prudent to wait one more day to make sure my illness is completely gone. I feel bad I haven't been well enough to help her to sleep. I was trying so hard to do everything just like I did when we were living with my dad, right down to the Eskimo kisses and twirly fingers at the door. I like to think my substitute can't possibly do it as well as I can.

"She wanted a Natalie story."

My eyes fly open. Natalie story? From someone other than me?

"Oh, really?" I try to play it cool.

"Yep. I'm getting pretty good at them." Isaac blows on his fingernails and wipes them on the front of his shirt.

I raise a palm. "All right, all right. Cool your jets. Starting tomorrow I can resume the Natalie stories."

Isaac winces. "I don't think so. Claire said my elephant noises are better than yours."

I make a face. "What? No, no, no. My Morabi is spot on." I've got the sounds of Natalie's pet elephant down, no question.

"Then do it."

"Um, no." I wouldn't be caught dead making elephant sounds in front of Isaac.

Isaac doesn't share my embarrassment. He raises an arm to his nose so it sticks straight out and up. A trumpeting noise comes from his throat, loud and frighteningly good.

I bend over and hold my stomach, the laughter competing for gulps of air. When I straighten, Isaac's twinkling eyes are on me.

"Do you want to hear an ugly truth?" he asks.

My laughter fades. "Are you finally going to tell me why you were in the bar that night?"

Something passes through his eyes, dulling their glimmer a fraction. "No." He goes to a lower cabinet and pulls it open, but I can't see what's in it because his body blocks my view. "My ugly truth is that I don't care for red wine."

I lean on the counter and press my chin to an open palm. "Then what do you like to drink, Dr. Cordova?"

He reaches into the cabinet. "Tequila." He comes away proudly holding up a bottle.

"Really?"

He laughs. "Well, yes. I am Mexican."

"Are you stereotyping yourself?"

"I guess. You want?" His eyes hold hope. He wants me to like what he likes.

"I've never had tequila." I know he's going to think I'm from another planet. Who has never had tequila?

"You're kidding?" He's excited now, grabbing a lime from the basket with the oranges and tossing it on the cutting board.

I shake my head. "I'm not."

"Well, then, I'm going to teach you something."

He cuts the lime into quarters and grabs a container of salt from a cabinet.

"Nope. No way." I shake my head. I know what he's doing.

"Fine. If you're happy with that boring red wine. Be my guest." He laughs. "Or my roommate. Be my roommate."

He rubs a lime on one quarter of the rim of the shot glass, rolls the glass around in the salt, and pours in the tequila. Eyes on me, he takes the shot and, without wincing, brings the lime to his mouth for a bite.

"Fine." I'm probably going to regret this, but in this moment I don't care. I'm finally not sick and being around Isaac makes me feel young, like I really am my age. Some days I feel so much older. I flash him a grin and point at his empty shot glass. "Teach me."

Isaac eyes me. "No more red wine?" He reaches over the counter to where my wine glass sits, abandoned. "You can't mix wine and tequila."

"No more red wine," I say with more confidence than I feel.

He pours it in the sink. I gulp. Why do I feel like I'm in over my head?

Isaac repeats the process, lining up the shot of tequila for me. "Lick the salt, take the shot, and bite into the lime. Simple as that."

"Right," I repeat. I'm nervous.

Isaac comes close so he's standing right beside me. "I've seen you do shots before."

I narrow my eyes at him. I remember that perfectly.

I do what he says, tasting the salt, grimacing at the tequila, and puckering when I bite the lime.

"Well?" He asks. I lift my eyes to his and find him grinning ear to ear.

Actually, it wasn't that terrible. I like salt. I like tart citrus. The sting of the tequila...well, I could get used to that.

"Not terrible."

He holds out his fist, and I bump it.

As I watch, he sets up a second round, and we take it together. There's a nice, warm feeling coming over me.

I turn around, the edge of the counter digging into my back as I let it support my weight. "You know, there's another stereotype about Latino men..."

Isaac gazes down at me. "And what would that be?"

I swallow. "They're incredibly passionate."

His eyes grow darker. "You tell me, Aubrey. Am I incredibly passionate?"

I lean my elbows behind me on the counter and look away. "Hard to say. It was a long time ago."

"I see. And there have been so many since me that I was swept to the back of your memory bank."

"Hardly."

"Not many? Was there someone special? Did some lucky guy get to spend time with you and my daughter?" Possession takes over in his voice.

"No. After you...well, I was pregnant. And then I was a mother to a baby. And things, you know, they, uh..." I look down at my midsection. "They don't really look the same after you have a baby." I run my hand over my stomach. It's mostly flat now, but there are telltale signs a life grew in there. My belly button isn't the same. It's bigger than it used to be. And the skin around it reminds me of a crepe dress my grandmother used to wear.

"Can I see?" His eyes are earnest. He leans forward.

"You want to see my stomach?" Did I hear him right? Maybe the tequila is clogging my ears.

"I want to see where Claire lived. I know it sounds crazy, but I missed seeing her in there. I missed out on seeing you with your belly swollen. I just... I don't know. I missed out on so much." He looks sad, so sad. I feel bad that I know what it was like and he doesn't. For a moment I wonder if somehow I could've tried harder to find him, but the thought dissipates. What more could I have done? Life dealt me the cards. All I could do was play them.

His sad eyes make me say yes. "Just remember, I'm not going to look like I did five years ago. Assuming you remember."

Using my hands, I hop to a seat on the counter and lean back on my elbows. Isaac steps in front of me, his hands pushing on my knees to split my legs. He steps between them and reaches for the hem of my shirt, eyes on mine.

My cheeks are warm. He's waiting for me to give him a green light, so I nod slightly.

The fabric glides against my abdomen, and the cool air

brushes my bare skin as he pushes up my shirt, past my belly button, coming to a stop just under my breasts.

I suck in a breath and turn my head. I don't want to see his face. What if he hates what he sees? He was with Jenna, perfection personified. I'm certain she doesn't have a dimple on her ass, let alone crepey skin on her stomach.

"Aubrey." He breathes my name and I look. His hand dangles out over my stomach. His eyebrows are raised, asking permission. I meet his gaze and nod. When his hand touches my stomach, I feel more than just it's warmth.

"You're as beautiful right now as you were the night we met." His hand runs in a circle, searing heat over my skin.

"Thank you." I sit up, and Isaac's hand drops from my stomach. My shirt falls back into place. Everything is as it was before. Except for Isaac. He hasn't moved. He's still between my legs.

I bite my lower lip and close my eyes. Isaac's nearness is almost too much to take. I can smell him, if I squeezed my thighs together I'd capture his waist.

With a gentle push, he lowers me back down on the counter. My eyes open when his hand releases the back of my head and I watch him lift my shirt again. He leans down, kisses my belly button, then branches out, working in a semi-circle. His fluttery kisses descend, until his mouth is at the top of my hipbone. He nips my skin and goosebumps cover my arms. His fingers meet the waistband of my pants, one finger running the length, from hip bone to hip bone.

My hands are in his hair, the urgent sound of my zipper competes for space with the sound of heavy breaths. I look down, and he looks up, the stubble on his chin grazing my tender skin. It's just like it was the last time, our only time. He stands, lifting my butt off the counter with one hand, then starts to ease my jeans off my hips. I wiggle to help him, and he smiles down to me.

A faraway yell pierces the thick, lusty kitchen air.

Everything pauses. My jeans, halfway down my hips, the peek of lavender lace, the rush of blood.

Isaac helps me up, then off the counter.

"I—" My hand comes to rest on his shoulder.

"It's OK. Go check on her." He adjusts himself through his shorts and clears his throat with a shallow, embarrassed sound.

When I reach Claire, she's already fallen back to sleep. Her rhythmic breath is deep, her lower lip slack. I lean in close to her face, feel the short stream of warm air touch my cheek, then back away so I don't disturb her.

I could go back out there. We could pick up where we left off.

The wall holds my weight as I sag against it. My heart thunders in my chest. I'm not sure if the adrenaline is from what I was doing with Isaac or from hurrying to Claire.

Either way, the spell has been broken.

I lie down beside Claire, careful not to jostle her casted arm. Streams of moonlight give off enough light that after a few moments of my eyes adjusting, I can see her profile. Her pert nose. Eyes the same color and shape as her father's.

Tears stream sideways into the pillow, and an ache starts behind my forehead. I don't know why I'm crying. It happens sometimes when I spend too long staring at my daughter. Maybe I should see a therapist again.

Or maybe I should go back out there and let Isaac be my therapy.

Instead, I close my eyes.

It's good things didn't go any further tonight. This is one relationship I can't afford to fuck up.

23

ISAAC

LAST NIGHT...

I roll over and close my eyes. I don't want to be awake yet. I want to envision what could have happened if Claire hadn't yelled out. If Aubrey hadn't fallen asleep in Claire's bed.

She was relaxed. Her walls were down. She was sweet and sensual. She wanted me.

I love seeing her like that. It's a welcome change from her usual front of self-possession.

She'll blame it on the tequila. I know she will. It's an easy target.

The sunlight peeks in through my curtains, and one of Aubrey's hairs shines on my sheets. It must have hitched a ride on my shirt, because she sure as hell wasn't in my bed. I pick it up, let it dangle from my fingertips before I drop it onto the floor. Outside my door I hear a giggle, then a shushing sound.

It's Saturday, but that means nothing to me. I don't sleep in. I throw back my covers and stand, ignoring the strain against the front of my shorts, and go turn on the shower.

When I get out, I feel more prepared for the day. Less affected by thoughts of last night.

"Hey girls," I say when I walk out to the living room. Claire's seated on the couch, her legs criss-crossed. Aubrey sits beside her, a book open between them.

"Hello," Aubrey says stiffly, briefly meeting my eyes. She looks back down to Claire's book, picking up where she left off.

She may have only looked at me for half a second, but I saw everything in her eyes. Regret, embarrassment, unease.

"Daddy, did you know sea scallops have one hundred eyes?" Claire blinks up at me. Aubrey's words trail off as Claire stops paying attention to the book. She tosses it on the empty couch cushion and gets up, walking to the kitchen. Even from ten feet away I can see the tension in her shoulders.

"I didn't know that." I smile down at the top of Claire's head. "Is your mom reading to you about sea scallops?" I head for the kitchen to get my dose of morning caffeine.

"Nope. My teacher told us yesterday at school." Claire's on my heels, carrying her book. I pick her up and swing her onto the counter. She sets the book beside her in exactly the same spot Aubrey was last night.

"Don't move a muscle," I tell Claire. I walk a few feet away to pour my coffee. Aubrey comes to stand by her, poking Claire on the nose as she leans against the counter. Claire giggles and Aubrey winks at her.

"What do you two want to do today?" I sip my coffee.

Aubrey tries to look everywhere but into my eyes. Finally she has no choice and has to look at me. Her cheeks color. She clears her throat. "I thought we'd visit my dad." She takes a strand of Claire's hair between her fingers and twists gently. "What do you say, Claire Bear? Do you want to see Grandpa?"

Claire nods her head vigorously. "I haven't seen him in ten years." Her eyes are wide, her voice somber.

I smash my lips together to keep from laughing.

Aubrey grins and points a thumb at Claire. "The exaggeration is strong with this one."

I laugh while I take the makings for French toast out of the fridge. "Am I allowed to tag along? I wouldn't mind seeing John." The guy fascinates me.

I pull back from the fridge in time to see the uncomfortable look is back on Aubrey's face. "I guess," she says.

"I guess?" I ask, dumping the ingredients on the counter and eyeing her.

"Sure." She shrugs.

"You can say no." I crack two eggs into a pie pan. Instead of looking at her I whisk the eggs. It's obvious she doesn't like to be put on the spot.

"It's OK, Isaac. You can come." She glances at me as soon as the words are out of her mouth.

I've caught the double entendre, and I'm guessing she wishes I hadn't. She flushes, and I can't help my smirk.

Even Aubrey can't maintain her stoicism. A smile tugs at the corner of her mouth.

Coughing, she turns away and asks "Do I have time for a shower before breakfast is ready?"

"Sure. Claire and I can hang out until you're ready."

Aubrey lifts Claire from the counter and sets her on her feet.

I wash and dry my hands at the sink, watching Aubrey go.

"Maybe take a cold shower," I say loudly after her.

She looks back at me over her right shoulder, running her middle finger down her cheek, a silent expletive statement.

Her spunkiness makes me smile. "I tried that last night. Didn't work out."

She exhales loudly and throws her hands in the air. But I know she's happy.

I COULD TALK to John all day. I'd be carrying the conversation, but still. John's not much for talking, but he'll answer any question asked of him. If he were a character in the movies, he'd be in one of those old westerns my dad used to watch on Saturdays, back before there were a million channels to choose from. John's character would have a cigarette dangling lazily from his lips, a constant frown, and be ready to kick ass at any moment. Now, in the present, he looks like he's still ready to kick ass at any moment.

"What was the scariest moment you've ever had hunting?" I ask him. We're sitting out back, watching Claire play in the sand box. I've warned her not to get sand in her cast, because there's no way to get it out until next week when she's ready for her final cast. Aubrey wanted to put a plastic bag over her arm and tie it off, but I talked her out of it. She's inside cleaning now. I think she wants to take care of her dad. And cleaning is how she does that.

John crosses a booted foot over one knee and leans back in his chair. "Once, I was bear-hunting with my friend David. We'd just gotten back to the truck, and it was nearly dark. I sat on my tailgate, and I was drinking a beer. I heard a rattle and said to David, "Do you hear that?" David said no, and I thought maybe I was just hearing things. A few moments later, I heard it again. I got down and shined a flashlight under my truck. Sure as shit, there was a rattlesnake under there. The damn thing had a rat in its mouth." John shakes his head. "Only reason it didn't bite me."

My mouth hangs open. Every rattlesnake I've ever seen has been behind an inch of protective glass. "That's crazy."

"I've done a lot and seen a lot, but that was the closest I've come to being badly hurt." He nods slowly. His voice is nonchalant, like the smooth surface of still water. No ripples from wind, no movement from a current. Still and steady.

John watches Claire pour sand through a sieve into another container. Inside I hear the banging of dishes. It's almost as loud as the Bob Seger music Aubrey turned on when she got started.

"Bob Seger, huh?" I say off-handedly. "Not what I would've expected from Aubrey."

At this, John smiles. "Aubs likes her Seger. *Old Time Rock n Roll* is her favorite. I played it when she was younger. Back when my old Chevy broke down every week and I'd spend Saturday's getting it running again. She sat on my toolbox and handed me tools. Usually the wrong ones." John's nostalgic grin reaches his ears. "She called them Chevy Days."

I chuckle, picturing Claire as a young Aubrey, handing me tools. I don't know how to fix trucks, so I've placed us in the OR. The tools probably have similar functions.

John leans forward, elbows on his knees. "Isaac, I hope you understand how special Aubrey is to me."

I mimic his posture. "Of course I do."

"And you know about her mother?" He meets my eyes. When I nod, he looks back to his hands.

"Aubrey doesn't let people in. Not readily, anyway. What she's doing with you goes against her nature."

"She's doing it for Claire, I think." It hurts even saying it, but I know it's true.

John nods. "Yeah, she is. But I think in time, she might come the point where she's doing it for herself too."

I don't say anything. I'm not sure what John's getting at. And I can only hope that he's right.

"What I need to know is if you asked them to move in just so you can be a full-time father to Claire. Did you?"

I sit back, my eyes on Claire. She brushes sand off her bare legs.

"Yes...and no. My goal is to be a father to Claire. But my hope..." I glance behind my shoulder, inside the house, but I don't see Aubrey. I lower my voice anyway. "My hope is that Aubrey will see we need to be a family. That we'd make a really, really good one. That we'd probably have been one this whole time if we'd exchanged last names five years ago."

John looks at me sharply. I'd like to look away, but I don't. He wants to stare me down for creating a baby with his daughter before I really knew her. I get it. Because I have a daughter of my own now.

His gaze stays on me for a few more seconds, then he goes back to watching Claire.

"Good luck." He says. "Aubrey's as tough as they come. She shoots from the hip and she doesn't play games."

I agree with John, but only to a point. I've seen Aubrey's softness. It may be well-hidden, but it's there, and she gives it freely to the people she loves. Her tough exterior is love-soluble. I've made a career out of fixing broken bones. And I know I can fix her broken heart.

"I understand." John is a lot like Aubrey. Or I guess

Aubrey is a lot like John. His exterior is more weathered than Aubrey's, but it functions the same.

"Dad." Aubrey steps from the house, one hand planted on her hip, the other holding out a grayish ball of...lint?

John's eyes flick over to her. When he sees what she's holding, his eyebrows squish together, and he looks away.

"Every time, Dad. You have to do it every time. I told you already. It's a fire hazard." Aubrey's exasperated. I'm still trying to understand what's happening.

"I will, Aubs." John reassures her, but he sounds a little petulant. Like a teenager being scolded by a mother. Or a husband nagged by his wife.

My back teeth clamp down on my cheek to keep from laughing. These two have the most unique relationship I've ever seen. And I thought my mom and I were different.

Aubrey thinks she and I are so dissimilar, but we're not. What has bonded her and John is the same thing that has bonded my mom and me. It goes beyond the normal and into the realm of shared brokenness.

"Claire, baby, come inside for a snack," Aubrey calls out. Claire stands up and comes to us, smiling. Always smiling.

She stops in front of John. "I made a castle with a moat. Because there's an army of monsters who want to get in. And the moat has alligators in it."

"That's a good way to keep the monsters out." John leans forward and lightly tugs on one of the braids I watched Aubrey weave into Claire's hair this morning.

Aubrey holds out a hand. "Let's go, little one. Your snack awaits you." They walk inside, and I hear Aubrey tell Claire to wash up before she eats.

John stands and I follow suit. He extends a hand.

As I'm shaking it, he says "Don't forget to clean out the

lint trap in the dryer, Isaac, or she'll come after you too." He laughs to himself and walks inside.

For me, the funny part is that I'm seriously considering forgetting, just so Aubrey will come after me. Because I want her to.

And that gives me an idea.

24

AUBREY

I KEEP TRYING NOT to think of last night, I keep telling myself it would've been just another hour. Meant nothing. But the problem is that I'm spending so much more than one hour thinking about it. I can still feel his five o'clock shadow scraping across my stomach, my body catching a fire of desire and urgency.

That's one of the reasons I felt relieved when we walked into my dad's house and I saw how messy it was. Putting myself to work helped me separate from my thoughts. The other reason was that it made me feel needed. It was nice to walk in and see the effect of us living apart.

Now we're back at Isaac's place. *Our* place. And I'm still cleaning because I have no idea what else to do. Why can't there be some kind of instruction manual for awkward situations like these?

I'm sitting cross-legged on my bed, folding Claire's laundry, when Isaac taps on my door. I know it's him because Claire's taking a nap. And because she hasn't yet mastered the fine art of knocking.

"Hey," I call out.

The door opens, and Isaac steps in. Immediately my neck feels hot. I don't know if he knows how incredibly good-looking he is. Is it the eyebrows? The chocolate eyes? Those full lips, the lower one in a perpetual pout. Or is it his smile?

It may be a mix of everything, but that smile has them all beat. I really, really like when he smiles.

"Are you running a covert operation in here?" he asks, his tone teasing. The door closes behind him, and he leans against it.

I lay a pair of shorts on the stack, ignoring the heat starting up in other places. "No, why?"

"Because you closed the door to fold laundry."

"I thought maybe you'd like some alone time. We spent the day at my dad's, so I just thought..." Doesn't everybody like alone time? The way Isaac's looking at me now, I'm guessing he doesn't.

"I'm good, Aubrey. I mean, I do like alone time." He comes forward, stopping when his knees are flush with the bed. He reaches over, one finger tracing my collarbone, which is exposed thanks to my tank top. "I like alone time that I spend with you."

I freeze, one of Claire's shirts in my clutch. My breath is shallow, desire slamming through me like a freight train. Swallowing hard, I force myself to knock it off. "Isaac, last night was—"

"Don't say it."

I take a deep breath and unfold my legs, rising so I'm on my knees on the bed. My movement knocks Isaac's magical finger off my skin, giving me the break I need. Distanced from his touch, I can think more clearly.

"A mistake." I finish my sentence anyway. "Our situation is messy enough without bringing sex into it." I have to focus to keep my thoughts from straying onto memories of how close it came to that. "And definitely no more tequila for me." I smile as I say it, trying to lighten my message.

Isaac nods slowly, his lips pushed out. "Right, the tequila. I thought you'd mention that part of it."

"It's kind of hard not to. We've slept together once, it almost happened last night, and both times there was alcohol involved." I look at him pointedly.

"Is that what you think this is? Beer goggles?"

"Beer goggles implies something else. Misguided level of attractiveness. This..." I gesture from me to him, and back again, realizing I have no idea how to categorize us. "That first hour we used like a Band-Aid. Last night... It was an itch. One we almost scratched. You wanted to see the body that housed your daughter. I wanted to recapture the feeling of being with a man."

Isaac's eyebrows lift. "That's it?"

"Yes." I say it with confidence I don't feel. A nagging feeling sits in my core, gnawing at me. It's best to ignore it. Caring for someone other than my dad, Britt, and Claire has only brought me sorrow.

"So, is that what you want us to be to one another? A collection of hours?" His lips twist as he reaches for me again, this time to brush my hair back from my face.

"One hour is not a collection." My argument is weakened by my voice. It's shaky, soft.

"I'm inclined to agree." He leans all the way over, wraps his arms around my waist, and drags me until I'm at the edge of the bed and pressed up against him. "But we can change that."

My heartbeats sound loud in my ears. The moisture in my mouth has dried up.

"I was hoping we could add more hours, and then more

hours, until they make a collection." His eyes shine with intensity. They're so close to mine that I could turn my head up just a little and stop him from saying more words I don't want to hear. "Aubrey, can I take you on a date tonight?"

I lean back, startled, and his fingers flex around my waist to hold me in place. "What?"

"Me. You. Date. You know, that thing we talked about doing years ago and then you walked out?"

I was *supposed* to walk out. That was our agreement. Technically, I mean. There was that second option. That thing he'd said about waiting until one hour was up to see if I wanted more from him. But he was headed out of the country and I was nursing a broken heart. What he'd said that night... Those were just empty words, weren't they?

What if they weren't?

Isaac deserves an explanation. "I didn't leave because I didn't like you." No, that wasn't the problem at all. "I left because... because..." How do I put the feeling into words? How can I explain how badly I needed to protect my heart?

"Shhh." Isaac leans his forehead to rest against mine. "You don't have to say anything more," he whispers. "I understand."

But how could he? How can this man with a flawless, intact family understand?

"OK," I whisper into the inches separating our lips.

"OK what?"

"OK I'll go on a date with you tonight."

Isaac pulls back, beaming. I wince, but only on the inside. I don't want him to think it's about him.

"You're going to have a good time. I promise." He squeezes his arms, still wrapped around my waist.

I don't doubt I'll have a good time. Not one bit.

And that's part of the problem.

. . .

LUCIA'S TRYING to keep her excitement from leaking out, but she's failing miserably. While she talks, she holds onto my arm.

"I was supposed to go to dinner with some women I know, but I cancelled. This is more important." Her eyes glimmer. "Do you know where he's taking you?"

"I didn't ask." My stomach has been tied up in knots since I agreed to go, and I think knowing our destination would only make me more nervous.

Lucia releases me and reaches for Claire. She pats her knee and Claire asks, "What are we going to do tonight while mommy and daddy are gone?"

"I'm going to keep you busier than a one-armed paper hanger."

I laugh, and Lucia looks proud of her joke. I don't tell her I'm not just laughing at her joke, I'm also laughing because my dad said the same thing soon after we arrived home from the hospital following Claire's accident.

Claire asks Lucia what's a one-armed paper hanger, a question I saw coming a mile away. While they talk, I go to the kitchen and start a pot of boiling water for Claire's dinner.

Isaac walks in and pulls open the fridge. "Got any plans tonight?" He pulls away with a water bottle and drinks it with his eyes on me.

I tap my chin and pretend to think. "This guy asked me on a date, but... I don't know."

"Not excited, huh?" He's smiling.

"I'm just kind of"—I shrug—"meh about it."

Isaac reaches past me to toss his bottle in the trash. His torso brushes my arm.

"Let's just see if we can get you the opposite of 'meh.'"
His deep voice reaches into me, stirring something deep
inside. I like the feeling—it's uncomfortable in a good way,
but automatically I want to fight it. How can I stop that?

Isaac pulls back, and the lid on the metal trash can
slams shut.

"I have to run out for something." He says. "Will you be
ready soon?"

"I can be. I need to finish Claire's pasta." The water is
just starting to boil. "What should I wear?"

Isaac's already on his way to the front door. "Casual." He
winks and walks out.

Dropping in the pasta, I mentally sift through my
clothes.

While I stir, I pair one thing with another and then
dismiss it until, finally, I think I've got it.

"Lucia," I call out. She and Claire are playing in the
living room. I'm spooning food into a pink plastic bowl
when they walk in. "Claire's dinner is ready. Do you need
me to do anything else?"

Lucia waves me away. "I could've made pasta, you
know."

"I know," I say quickly.

"You're still used to doing everything yourself." She hugs
around my shoulders. "You don't have to anymore."

I nod and thank her, leaving the room as fast as I can go
while still looking like I'm not rushing. I have to get away
from the motherly affection. Because I love it, but I love it
too much, and the force of it is too great.

When I get to my room I go straight for the bathroom
and splash cold water on my face. I'm almost done getting
ready when my phone chirps with a text message.

Isaac- Someone's at the front door. Can you answer it?

What?

I slip on my shoes and go to the front door, tossing a glance at Lucia and Claire on my way. Lucia glances up at me from the coloring book she and Claire are sharing. She's filling in Strawberry Shortcake's legs while Claire tackles her hair.

Why didn't Lucia get the door?

I pull it open. Isaac stands there, beaming. He extends a tub of ice cream with a note on the top.

Not flowers.

A tiny laugh escapes me, like a breath, then it's followed by more. I take the ice cream from him, it's chill giving me shivers, and turn it in my hands. How is it that he remembers his curbside declaration? It was so long ago.

"No death wrapped in tissue paper for Aubrey," he says, taking the ice cream from me and walking to the kitchen. Grabbing utensils from the drawer, he spoons out a bite for me. I reach for the handle of the spoon but he pulls back and raises his eyebrows. I roll my eyes and open my mouth, allowing him to feed me.

Claire and Lucia giggle, and Claire asks for her own bowl. "Big," she tells Isaac, her eyes serious.

He gives her twice the amount I would, but I don't say anything. Lucia's the one who will have to deal with her sugar-high and inevitable meltdown.

After ice cream kisses from Claire, we leave. Isaac locks the front door behind us, then pauses. He lifts a piece of hair and tucks it behind my ear. "That's how our first date would have started."

"It would have been a good first date."

He puts a curled finger beneath my chin and lifts it. "It *is* going to be a great first date." And then he gently presses his lips to mine.

25

AUBREY

LIKE A GENTLEMEN, Isaac opens the car door for me. Though I don't need it, he offers a hand. My first instinct is to ignore it and climb in without help. I could pretend not to see the gesture, and then it would be attributed to typical Aubrey behavior. But I don't.

I slip my hand in his. His other hand lands on the small of my back, guiding me into his truck. It's so proper. So... first date. Considering he had the milk before he purchased the cow, I'm surprised he's being so gallant.

Maybe the milk is different now. Maybe the cow has changed.

The slam of the passenger door brings me back to the moment.

Isaac slides into his seat and smiles at me across the space. He looks so happy, so present. So certain life will always be good to him. He turns on the truck, and I wince. The music blares through the speakers.

"Sorry," he yells, pushing a button on the steering wheel. The volume decreases until it's only background noise.

I stare at him. "Seriously?"

"About which part? The volume or..." His lips twist. "The selection?"

I keep the stare going a few more seconds. It won't hurt him to sweat a little. When his eyes widen, I break my silence. "My dog died," I croon, trying not to laugh. "My six-pack is warm," I sing off-key on purpose. "My lady just left me, but I'm country down to my roots and my boots."

Isaac throws me a disgusted look and puts it into reverse. I purse my lips, my muted laughter shaking my shoulders. We pass through the residential area and move into the commercial part of town.

"So..." I say, drawing out the word.

"Not all country music is about dogs, beer, and women." Isaac's voice is defensive. Not a lot, but just enough to tell me that he really likes it.

Still, I can't help myself. "What about boots?" I laugh when I say the last word. "Boots and roots?" This time I can't keep it in. I'm laughing so hard I might as well slap my knee.

"Oh, so now Aubrey is funny?"

I sober a little. "No, not usually. But that music... it really struck a chord with me." I bite my lower lip, my shoulders shaking again with contained laughter.

Now Isaac laughs too. "Fine." He takes one hand off the wheel and holds it in the air. "I have a thing for country music. There, I said it."

I tap his knee. "Admitting is the first step."

"What's the next step?" He stops at a red light and turns to meet my eyes. He's backlit by the lights of the cars driving the opposite direction.

Suddenly the cab of his truck feels full, the air thick. I drag in a breath, my chest expanding with the thickened air. How quickly we've gone from lighthearted teasing to whatever this is.

I don't have words for him. I don't have *next steps*. I have only me, and the jagged scars that tell the stories on my heart.

I don't know how it happened. I don't know who leaned in first. All I know are Isaac's lips on mine, his softness yielding, melting, until we're breathing the same air. So different from the chaste peck at the front door.

A car horn slams through the comfort our lips create. Isaac jerks back, regains control, and moves the car forward. I do not.

The seat back catches my slouched position, cradles my lower back, as I try to understand what happened.

"You OK over there?" Isaac asks. He flicks a wary look at me.

"Yeah," I whisper. I'm letting the tail lights of the car in front of us mesmerize me.

I am definitely not OK. I can blame last night on tequila. *Haha, remember that time you introduced me to tequila and we almost hooked up?*

Even the short kiss when we left tonight could be labeled friendly.

But not this. That kiss was us. Isaac and Aubrey.

And the hardest part, the part I can't stand to think of but won't stop racing through my mind, is how good, how very *right* it felt just now.

WHATEVER I FELT for Isaac on the drive here, it's gone now. It's just me, him, and this battle. He brought me to this place with games, and now he's paying the price.

I'm competitive. And not in your average, *winning is fun*, light-hearted way.

I play to win. Always. It's why Britt won't play games with me. She claims I suck all the fun out of it.

"All right, Cordova. Are you ready to be dealt the death-blow?" I'm also a shit-talker when I play games.

Truthfully, my hubris is a bit bloated right now. I'm blaming it on the kiss. My insides are still shaking. His lips were only on mine for a few seconds, but the effect of them lingers. My heart feels too soft right now, and it's making my outside more prickly than usual.

Isaac cocks an eyebrow from his place on the other side of the Cornhole game. His final bean bag just landed short of the hole, and all I have to do to clinch my victory is make this last shot.

Which I do. It sails through the air in a perfect arc and slips in the hole with almost no sound.

The cheering sounds coming from my cupped mouth are loud and probably annoying, but I don't care. "Aubrey for the win." I say in my best sportscaster voice.

Isaac's laughing and shaking his head. He reaches back to our table and hands me my drink. "To the victor go the spoils." The tinkling sound of our glasses sends a shiver down my spine.

"And what are the spoils?" I keep my eyes on him as I drink.

Isaac watches me, his eyes evaluating. He doesn't speak, so I ask my question again.

He steps closer, and the heat in my core starts up. It's a little annoying that my body does that every time. It would be a lot easier to keep him at arms' distance if my body would behave.

But with his chest so close to mine.... well, how much harder do I have to work? How much harder do I need to fight?

"To give you the spoils, I think I'll need about an hour of your time." His cheek rests against my temple, his words float down to my ear.

"One hour?" My voice squeaks.

I feel his nod. "Are you ready to go home?"

I want to tell him yes, that when his deep voice reverberates against me like that, I'm ready to go almost *anywhere* with him.

"Um-hmm," is all I manage to say. He pulls back, looks down at me, and I see what I saw that night in the country bar. A man in need of a woman. But this time, Isaac isn't in pain.

Am I? Certainly not like I was that night.

The pain is different now. A dull, unrelenting sort. Always there, never dealt with. My shadowy ghost. It beats a steady rhythm, much like my heartbeat.

Maybe I deserve a break from that. Just a brief respite where I can pretend to be whole.

I find my voice. "One hour." I don't squeak this time. I sound confident. "And Isaac?" I lift an eyebrow.

"Yeah?" His voice has grown deeper.

"No babies this time."

He laughs and curls a hand around my hipbone. "Agreed."

Is this the right decision? Probably not. But I'm tired.

Tired of hurting.

Tired of holding on.

Isaac takes my hand. As soon as we step away, a group of guys claim the bean bags we've left on the table. We walk out, Isaac in front, leading me through the crowd. His broad shoulders move with an easy confidence, giving me a feeling of peace and safety.

. . .

THE AIR around us changes the second the front door closes. After a long run-down of her evening with Claire, Lucia has finally left.

"You." Isaac walks toward me, his gait slow. The hungry gleam in his eyes is coming closer...closer...

I gulp. It's loud, and Isaac smirks.

He reaches me. His hand runs from my shoulder to my wrist, then he pulls back. Disappointment runs through me. "Our one hour starts the second we step foot in my bedroom."

When he talks, my thighs ache. "Then we'd better get back there." Lightly I push against his chest. He grins and takes my hand. His steps are steady and quick until we reach the entrance to his bedroom. He pauses, face earnest.

"Aubrey, I respect the hell out of you. I want you to know that. If you change your mind, it's OK. I'll understand."

Could he be any sweeter? Any more caring? My insides are feeling mushy again. "Isaac, stop talking. Seriously."

He opens his mouth, but before he can speak I wrap my hands around his neck and quiet him with my lips. His weight pushes me through his door. We swing around as one, so that my back closes the door for us. The lock clicks into place, and then his hands are on me, lifting me from the back of my thighs and carrying me to his bed.

Our kisses grow deeper, needier. His soft bed envelops my back, his hard front is deliciously heavy against me. He pulls away to undress me. I help him, lifting my hips, arching my back, until there's no clothing left on my body. It's my turn to help him, but instead of appreciating Isaac's beautiful skin, my fear tries to creep back in.

I ignore it and lay back down. Isaac covers me like a blanket. His lips once again meld to mine, and even though

I'm insanely attracted to him, some of my attention is diverted to giving my worry a swift kick in the ass.

"You with me, Aubrey?" he murmurs against my lips.

He knows me. Somehow, he knows the push and pull, the fear that keeps me running and the desire that brings me back. I'm strong and stubborn, but when it comes to Isaac, I lose all sense. I'm terrified to want him, but I'm even more scared not to have him.

"I'm with you Isaac." My words whisper against his lips.

Despite my assurance, I'm caught. Swaying, moving, this way and that, my heart and my brain in a tangle.

I'm a kite in a windstorm, and all I want is for Isaac to take me away, to the place we went to five years ago.

And he does. He wraps his arms around me, slides between my legs, and shows me once again how freeing it feels to fly.

26

AUBREY

MY FINGERTIPS SIT POISED on the keyboard, ready, but nothing comes out.

I should know this policy amendment so well I can write it in my sleep. And normally, I do. But right now, after that phone call from Lucia, I can't focus.

A mother-daughter brunch. This Sunday. To celebrate Mother's Day. *An annual event*, she'd said. She and Lauren have been attending since Lauren was a small child.

It's in the ballroom at the Fairmont Princess. *Daytime fancy*, she intoned. I Googled it. It's not a technical term, but I figured it out for myself. Skirt, nice blouse. Maybe a jacket that matches the skirt. Something frilly for Claire.

Good thing she chose a pink cast this time. Her previous cast would have clashed with everything. And this new cast isn't even dirty yet, although by Sunday it probably will be.

We'd gone to Isaac's office the day before. The front desk girl, the nurse, the x-ray technician, and the office manager —they all know who Claire is by now. I can only imagine the gossip when he told them. Suddenly the doctor they've worked with for two years has a daughter? His desk now holds a picture of a child when it never did before? Even if they're curious, they haven't asked me. They're nothing but kind when we're in there.

Watching Isaac work is amazing. The way his brows move when he studies the x-ray. He offered me the iPad the x-rays are on, using his fingers to zoom in on the break. The line is hardly visible anymore.

"We're almost through it." He'd smiled at me. It felt intimate. When Claire broke her elbow, I was a single parent, scared for my child. Now, nearing the end of this journey, I have a partner to shoulder this with me.

I wonder how Isaac is doing today? I could text him and ask.

Or I could write this amendment like I'm supposed to.

Britt stops at my desk, providing the distraction I need from my thoughts. The wording that was elusive comes to me now, and while I'm talking with her I type out the amendment. I forward it on to the underwriting assistant with my approval to increase the limits of the policy.

"Lunch?" Britt asks when I hit send on the email.

"Can we go to the mall? I need to do some speed shopping." I pick up my purse.

"You want to go shopping?" She raises her eyebrows and follows me out to the elevator. I'm not a shopper. I order online.

On the way down to my car, I explain the situation.

"Are you ready for something like that? Have you thought about what that room is going to look like?" Britt's forehead creases as she looks at me from the passenger seat.

"Yes, of course." I start the car and put it in drive. "That huge ballroom will be full of mothers and daughters and—"

"Full-grown mothers and daughters, too. Not just young girls and their mommies. It won't be like dropping Claire off at pre-school. There will be women your age. With their mothers. And probably some of those mothers will have their mothers with them." Worry soaks Britt's words. "I just... I don't know how to say this."

"Say it." We're almost to the parking structure. The mall is only a few minutes away, making it perfect for a lunchtime eat and shop. "Please," I add, in case she thinks I'm angry.

"You've come so far. Since you had Claire, I mean. She gave you something to focus on besides *you know who*. I'm afraid this brunch will cause undue pain." She shrugs apologetically. "Sorry. I evaluate risk for a living."

"So do I." I sigh and rub my eyes at a red light.

"Which is why I find it so interesting you agreed to go."

"You aren't the only one wondering what I was thinking."

"You must have a reason?"

"It felt like the right thing to do. Lucia asked. I didn't want to tell her no. And Claire might enjoy it. Maybe this is a tradition I can start with her."

"At the expense of your feelings?"

I get what Britt is trying to say. But what she doesn't understand is that everything I do is at the expense of my feelings. I'm bombarded with reminders of my mother's absence. Last week I watched a movie, and the credits showed the actress and her mother sitting on a couch, and the mom was talking about the actress as a child. One of the mothers of a child in Claire's class got caught in traffic yesterday, and she couldn't make it to pick-up in time. Guess who bailed her out? This morning at drop-off she gushed about how *amazing* it is to have a mom, and the other women standing around started saying things like, *I couldn't live without my mom* and *my mom is my best friend*. Me standing there and chatting with these women was at the expense of my own feelings, and the crazy part is that I never know just when the hits will come. Willingly subjecting myself to this brunch won't be any different. If anything, at least I'll be prepared.

I drive through the now green light and pull into the parking garage. "I appreciate your concern. But don't worry, I'll be—"

"Fine?" Britt's lips twist in an ironic smile.

I park and climb out, shooting her a look over the top of my car. "Yes. Now can you please help me pick out something daytime fancy? Or do I need to go it alone?"

"God, no, don't go it alone." She shudders playfully.

Our heels snap against the concrete floor as we switch into power shopping mode. If anybody can get me daytime fancy in forty-five minutes, it's my best friend.

I'M READY.

I think, anyway.

Maybe prepared is a better word. I'm *prepared* to be hit over the head with mother-daughter love.

It's not just the brunch I needed to prepare for. All week long, it's been a gluttony of maternal love and praise. This time of year always is.

I walk out of my room, Claire's rose gold patent leather flats dangling from one hand. Isaac and Claire are in the living room, sitting on the couch. He's running a brush through her hair. She sits poised, eyes wide, and Isaac looks like he's concentrating. It makes me smile.

Isaac catches sight of me and whispers loudly down to Claire. "Look at Mommy. Doesn't she look pretty?"

Claire giggles, one hand over her mouth. "I like your skirt, Mommy."

I twirl, and she and Isaac laugh.

"There." Isaac smooths Claire's hair. "All the tangles are gone."

Claire scrambles off the couch. "I need my headband." She runs from the room.

When she's disappeared down the hall, Isaac turns to me, eyebrows creased. "Aubrey, while we have a second alone, I just wanted to make sure this brunch is OK with you."

His concern makes me feel warm inside.

When I don't answer right away, he takes my hand and turns it over, fingertips trailing across the skin. "You can tell her you changed your mind. My mom won't be mad. She'd understand."

I swallow, fighting off the tingling sensation starting up in my thighs. He's so close, and he smells so good. Does he know? Does he know what his nearness is doing to me? I can't focus on anything right now. He's waiting for me to answer him, imploring me with his eyes.

"Um, yeah. I don't think that's necessary. I'll be all right." I withdraw my hand. It's for the best that we break physical contact. Hurt shadows the brightness in his eyes. Knowing I put it there makes me feel bad.

"You know what's best." His frown turns to a smile.

Since our first date last weekend, we've spent four more hours together. Each hour amazing, each hour fulfilling, each hour giving me so much more than I deserve. I wish I could say all this, but thinking the words and actually releasing them are two different things.

"Did my dad call you back yet?" I ask, searching through my purse for my lipstick.

"He's meeting us for lunch."

"Technically it's brunch." I raise an eyebrow while I apply the lipstick.

He gives me a look. "Do you think your dad goes to brunch?"

"Hah. Good call."

Isaac fingers the hem of my skirt. It's modest, falling just above the knee.

"I like this on you."

"Are you about to tell me you'd like it better on the floor?"

"Hmm maybe." His hand slips under my skirt, fingers blazing a trail up my thigh.

"Isaac." My voice is a warning. I cross my legs. Access denied.

"I know, I know," he sighs. His fingers retrace their steps, appearing out from under my skirt. I uncross my legs and stand normally again.

"You need to get your game face on." I can hear Claire coming from her room, and Isaac still has his hooded gaze on me.

He rubs his eyes and blinks twice. "I'm back," he says, bouncing his shoulders a few times.

Claire walks in and rests her arms over the back of the couch, her pink cast standing out against the fabric. I double check my skirt, just to be sure. We spend a few minutes saying goodbye, and Isaac reminds me how to get where I'm going.

I don't need the directions, but it's Isaac's nature. He's a caretaker.

"Good luck with my dad," I say, walking out with Claire in tow.

"Good luck with my mom and Lauren. They're a little at

odds right now." Isaac frowns as he says it. "I wouldn't advise asking them about it either."

"Thanks for the heads up," I say just as the door swings shut.

I'm happy to stay far away from whatever is going on with Lucia and Lauren. I don't want anything to do with any mother-daughter dissension.

Claire holds my hand and attempts to skip all the way to the car, and I try to keep up, without twisting my ankle.

LUCIA IS WAITING for us at the fountain near the entrance. When she sees us, she rushes forward.

"You both look lovely. I'm so glad you decided to come." Her hat bumps my forehead when we hug. She bends down so she's on Claire's level.

"Look at that pretty dress."

Claire nods with happiness and runs a hand down her stomach. She hasn't stopped touching the soft fabric since I put it on her.

Lucia straightens. "Lauren should be here any minute." She checks the gold watch on her wrist. "She's always late. Operates on Lauren Standard Time." There's annoyance in her voice.

We wait a few more minutes before Lucia decides she's done waiting.

"Come on. Lauren can join us when she arrives." She leads us away. "No use missing out on fresh mimosas!" She links an arm through mine.

The Princess is a local treasure. It's lush greenery and opulent accommodations have been featured in magazines, so I know what I'm about to see. We walk through just a fraction of the grounds until we come to a big building with massive doors. Lucia pulls on one of the ornate iron door handles and ushers us in.

The ballroom carries a cacophony of ladies' voices. White-linen-dressed tables take up the center of the room, while long rectangular tables laden with trays of food and carving stations flank the edges. At the front is a platform stage with a microphone.

"We're at table three," Lucia says, passing me. We weave our way through the tables until we arrive at ours. A shallow bowl filled with white roses serves as the centerpiece, and each place is set with silverware.

As soon as we settle into our seats, a man comes over and hands Lucia and me a mimosa. Claire receives a pink lemonade.

We're the first at our table. As the others join us, Lucia makes introductions. Everyone knows each other, it seems, and this event is a ritual. Each person asks the same question: How do you know Lucia? And then they have the same aghast reaction: Lucia, you have a granddaughter? Since when? Lucia smiles gracefully each time. *Life can be so interesting, don't you think? The important thing now is that we have Aubrey and Claire.* She moves on, telling them about Claire's arm, and then Claire takes the floor. She informs everybody of what grade she's in and who her friends are.

Their hungry eyes tell me they're all dying for something juicier, but Lucia either doesn't see or is a fantastic pretender.

Lauren arrives then, and I'm grateful. It takes the heat off me. Her cheeks are rosy, like she's fresh from a workout. I'm not the only person who notices.

"Did you get to the gym today?" Lucia lifts a section of Lauren's hair. It's still wet underneath.

"Before you get upset with me, you should know that I'm

training for a 5k." She gives Lucia a pointed look. "I want to do well. And by *do well* I mean *not die*."

Lucia's frown turns into a resolute smile. "I'm proud of you. And I'd rather you not die, too."

Lauren barks a laugh, but it's enough to cut through the tense moment. She greets the women around the table and makes small talk with them. Like the proud mother she is, Lucia announces why Lauren was late.

Maybe Isaac's wrong about there being an issue with Lucia and Lauren. That seemed more like general irritation, not being *at odds*.

The ladies ask question after question about Lauren's training regimen. Claire grows bored, so I give her a coloring book and crayons from my purse.

A tall, blond woman takes the stage. She introduces herself as the chairperson of the mom's organization and talks for a while about the group and what they do in the community. She ends her speech by asking if there is anybody celebrating a birthday today or tomorrow. "Mother's Day birthdays are extra special!"

A dampness springs up on my palms. My knee bounces. I look down, willing my leg to stop, but it doesn't work, and now I'm queasy.

"Mommy?" Claire whisper-yells.

"What?" I whisper back, my voice strained.

"Your birthday is in May."

I look from Claire and into Lucia's curious eyes. My smile is shaky. "End of May," I clarify. I feel bad for lying to her.

She looks relieved. I can practically read her thoughts. *Of all people, Aubrey couldn't possibly have a birthday that falls around Mother's Day. That would be too cruel.*

Except I do.

Mother's Day is always the second Sunday in May. And my birthday is May tenth.

The irony isn't lost on me, and it wasn't lost on Lucia just now either. Luckily Claire doesn't remember my actual birthday, and now Lucia thinks I was shown some mercy.

The moment passes, lunch is served, and just when I think I might make it out of here with only that tiny incident, the woman directly across from me clears her throat and says my name.

"Yes?" I smile at her. She has a pinched face, the kind that looks judgy all the time.

"Your mother couldn't make it today? Does she live out of state?" Her eyebrows draw together, but the concern looks fake.

My fork is paused mid-air, and I grip it tighter.

"She was unable to attend. It's just me and Claire today." My cheerful tone sounds as false as the woman's concern. I set down the utensil and use my now empty hand to wrap an arm around Claire's shoulder.

"Well, I don't know what could be more important than a mother-daughter brunch. Especially when you have a grand-baby as sweet as Claire." She smiles at Claire.

I don't respond. I'm too busy using my napkin to meticulously wipe the chicken salad off Claire's face. *See how busy I am cleaning my child's face? Way too busy to realize you are even speaking.*

"I couldn't agree with you more, Astrid." Lucia speaks up. "Where in the world are Grace and those little munchkins of hers?"

With a lot of irritation and hand flapping, Astrid (if I ever had to pick a name for someone with a face as pinched as hers, Astrid would be it) explains that her daughter and their family are in Washington DC for the weekend.

Some of my irritation dissipates. Obviously her questions were really meant for her own daughter. I was just the lucky recipient.

I jump a little when my knee is squeezed under the table. I look to the hand, then up to the person it's attached to.

Lauren offers a small, lopsided smile.

"I'm OK," I say quietly. In a normal voice, I ask her about work. I don't want to talk about my absentee mother or the fielding of insensitive questions.

We spend the next ten minutes talking about three difficult children in her class, until a dessert tower is placed on our table. Claire's eye's gleam, making Lauren laugh.

"Just like Isaac," she says, grinning.

I nod and chuckle. Isaac's excitement over sweets is cute. The way his mouth forms a small 'o' and then he says, "Ohhhh". Chocolate is his favorite, so I guess the stereotype is wrong. Men can love chocolate too.

Lauren grabs a cupcake from the bottom tier and extends it across me to Claire. "Did I guess correctly?" She asks her.

Claire nods vigorously, reaching out. She licks some frosting off the top.

"Mmmm," she smacks her lips.

I peel the wrapper off for her and help her eat it one-handed. Lucia sneaks her another when she thinks I'm not looking and they giggle together. When Lucia catches my gaze, she winks and laughs. I return the smile, but my insides feel like jelly. Claire has a loving, doting grandmother, a fun aunt, and a mother who loves her with ferocity. She's beyond lucky, and she doesn't even know it.

After a closing speech from someone else on the

committee, including a very obvious call-to-action, the brunch is over.

And me? I am so done too.

I want to go home.

The thought doesn't put me at ease, though, because when I think about home, I realize I've pictured Isaac's place. Not my dad's house.

And I've put Isaac right in the middle of the picture.

27

ISAAC

FOUR MONTHS AGO, if somebody had told me this would be happening to me, I would have laughed in his face.

Daughter? *I don't have any kids.*

Girlfriend? *Her name is Jenna.*

Job? *It just so happens I'm being considered for something in Boston.*

Fast forward to now. Completely different answers.

I wouldn't say Aubrey and I are dating. She's too skittish for that. When our hours are up, we leave each other alone. Every day since the night I took her out almost two weeks ago, we've spent an hour together. It's the reason for her nickname.

"Hey, Sixty," I say when she walks into the kitchen.

She smirks and sits at the table with her coffee. "Hello, Doctor Cowboy."

I think she really liked discovering my soft spot for country twang. She hasn't let me forget it since.

"Good morning, Claire Bear. Are you excited for today?" Aubrey tickles Claire's side.

"Yes," Claire says through her giggles.

I come from the kitchen with Claire's scrambled eggs. "Today is a big day." I wink at her and set the plate in front of her. She digs in. It's going to be different to see her with two working arms. I've only seen her arm once, when I was performing surgery on it. At the time I didn't know she was mine. If I'd known, would I have stared at her arm a little harder, knowing that it would be a few months before I could see it again? Would I have been able to do the surgery at all?

A thought comes to me. "What do you say we celebrate?" I'm looking at Aubrey.

"Ice cream!" Claire yells. The child definitely has my affinity for sweets.

"Actually," I say, "I was thinking of a weekend trip. Somewhere wooded. A little cooler. We can do an easy hike, and Claire can use *both* her arms to explore. What do you think?" My eyes haven't left Aubrey.

Just a moment ago, she was so excited for Claire. Now she looks guarded. Wary.

"I want to go to the woods and hike." Claire's grinning. "Please, Mom?"

Aubrey hesitates. I point to her coffee cup. She looks down at the words on it and does a quick eye-roll.

I mouth the words to her. *I Mom So Hard.*

"Hiking and nature exploration sound like the perfect way to start using that arm again." She smiles at Claire "If you're finished, please go get your backpack. It's almost time to leave."

Claire runs toward her room. Aubrey turns her worried eyes on me.

"Is this a good idea?"

Knowing Aubrey, she's drawing up a risk analysis in her head. She's back to being careful Aubrey, but last night...

"Is it a good idea to skip breakfast?" I challenge her. I've discovered she needs it. The challenge, I mean. She's competitive. Challenging her to something is the most effective way of getting her to open up.

"Typically, no." She narrows her eyes. "Why?"

"You worked up an appetite last night, Sixty. I thought you'd be hungry this morning." I take Claire's empty plate and walk away, laughing to myself.

Claire returns, backpack dragging behind her.

Aubrey swoops it onto her shoulder. "We'll see you in a couple hours." Claire marches in front of Aubrey, so she can't see her mother when she sticks her tongue out at me.

I say goodbye to Claire and watch them leave. I feel like celebrating. Not only did I get Aubrey to agree to a weekend away, but I won something else too. One more brick removed from Aubrey's wall. Another chink in her armor. She's a beautiful bronze statue covered in cement, and I'm the guy with the hammer and chisel, breaking apart the heavy burdens laid upon her.

I LOVE SEEING Aubrey like this.

She has her hair piled on top of her head in a messy ball, and on her face is the most carefree smile I've ever seen. After ninety minutes of driving, she put her bare feet up on the dash. Red-polished toenails wiggling, she'd asked if I minded.

I told her no. What I kept to myself was the fact that everything about her, including her cute feet, was making it harder to concentrate. But, seeing as how my whole life is in my truck right now, I focused on the road.

Claire fell asleep after a bathroom break fifteen minutes ago, her head slumped against the side of her car seat. She has her left arm bent across her body, as if it's still in a cast.

Aubrey looks back at her. "Do you think she's comfortable?"

I shrug. "Comfortable enough to fall asleep."

"But her arm..." Aubrey bites her lip. I think about telling her to stop.

She faces front. "That skin was so gross."

Perfect. The switch to that subject is *exactly* what I need right now.

"I should have warned you. Sorry." I don't think of it as gross anymore. Aubrey, however... She was shocked when the cast came off.

"What's that?" She'd asked with alarmed eyes, pointing at the dead skin covering Claire's arm.

I felt bad. Normally I tell my patients ahead of time, but I keep forgetting Claire and Aubrey are my patients.

Aubrey shudders lightly, as if she's remembering with me. "It's OK. It's common sense. Anyway, I brought the vitamin E oil. She's been trying to scratch it."

I open my mouth, but Aubrey holds up a hand. "I know, Doctor Cowboy. Don't let her scratch it." She laughs and settles back into her seat. I shake my head.

"Tell me more about the day I went to the brunch with your mom. I just can't picture my dad hanging out with your dad." She makes a sound like a disbelieving exhale.

"It was...good. Interesting." I tap my fingers on the wheel, thinking of the day my dad and I met John for *lunch*.

"You said that already." Aubrey reminds me.

"That's about all there is to it. Your dad was quiet. My dad attempted to talk about sports. Your dad made no attempt to talk about sports. I remembered they both like animals, even though one of them prefers to hunt them, and finally they had something to talk about."

Aubrey sighs. "They could not be more different."

I nod, but inside I know the truth. Those two men are more alike than anybody knows.

"Your mom and Lauren aren't at odds, by the way." She says it off-handedly while she stares out her window.

"No?" The last time I saw Lauren she was angry. Hurt. And she had a right to be. Everything she knew was upended, just like it was for me. Of course, it was worse for me because it was *about* me. "Well, good." I sneak a quick glance at Aubrey. Her head's tipped back while she yawns.

"Go to sleep," I tell her.

"I just might," she says, yawning again, but bigger this time.

She uses the remainder of the drive to take a nap. Every once in a while, I peek at her from the corner of my eye. Her lips are parted, her arms crossed at her waist.

Five years ago, I was immediately attracted to her. Physically, yes, but also mentally. She was smart. The pain in me reached out to the pain in her. That night she was like a mirror, reflecting exactly what I was feeling on the inside.

Maybe it's time to tell her my ugly truth. The real reason I was at the bar that night.

The problem is that my ugly truth does not belong to only me.

I can't be totally honest with Aubrey until I get the green light from *her*.

28

AUBREY

It's possible this is the cutest town I've ever been to. Although that might not be saying much. I'm not exactly well-traveled. My dad likes to stick to the surrounding geography.

Sugar Creek, Arizona. Population... I don't know. Not much, I'm guessing, based on the quaint main street. There are off-shoots, streets that lead away and have some businesses on them. The businesses look like homes, though. We haven't stepped from the truck yet, but I'm certain there's an unhurried pace in this town. What could there possibly be to rush to? Or from?

Isaac props a piece of paper on the steering wheel. There are only four directions on it, and he's glanced down at it so many times he probably has it memorized. The directions scrawled on paper is old-school, but that's because the place we're going to doesn't have an address.

Yep, that's right. *The Lost Place.* Literally. That's the name of the cabin. It has a name, but not an address.

I balked when Isaac told me. *How will help get to us if we don't have an address to give?*

Are you planning on needing help? Isaac asked.

That's when I told him what an emergency is, as defined by my profession. *A state of need for help or relief, created by an unexpected event, requiring immediate action.*

Isaac laughed and reminded me he *is* an emergency responder.

I could've kept going and told him about all the emergencies he is not the best fit for responding to. Instead, I shut my mouth. Because he was excited. Because he was smiling, and his eyes were smiling too. And in three days, it's very unlikely that anything could go wrong.

Now that I see the little town, I feel better. It looks like something from a pop-up book, a small expanse of brick buildings and sidewalks, storefronts with hand-painted signs. No traces of the desert we've left behind. It's all pine and green leaves.

I glance at the paper on the steering wheel and look up just in time to spot the final direction. "There's the bakery she mentioned." I point as we come upon it. Mrs. Iams, the owner of the cabin, said we'd know where to turn once we saw the bakery. I peer closer at the quaint store window. It's painted with a coffee cup, steam rising from it, and a blueberry muffin.

Isaac follows the direction of my finger. "Mrs. Iams said we have to go there. And to get there early, because apparently these blueberry muffins are to die for, and they sell out every day."

I don't tell him how much I hate blueberry muffins. No need to ruin the mood.

We roll until we find the next left. Isaac takes it and follows the road until the only structure in the area comes into view.

The wildflowers are the first thing I notice. Lemon

yellows, hot pinks, royal purples—they all shoot out from the grass that surrounds the cabin. Swinging from a post is a wooden sign. *The Lost Place*. Maybe *that* is what you would tell 9-1-1 if you had to call them.

I turn around to Claire. "Wake up, baby." I say, my voice coaxing.

She blinks, her eyes heavy, and looks outside. "We're here!" she yells.

Isaac laughs and gets out of the truck. I follow, opening the backdoor to get Claire. Behind me I hear clang of the tailgate as it's lowered. As I unlatch Claire, I look back through the rear window. Isaac leans forward, his hips pressed to the edge of the tailgate, reaching for our bags. Suddenly my throat is dry. Memories of two nights ago flood me. His hands, his mouth, his caresses on my hot skin. And then when he left my room, he'd whispered, "Good night, Sixty." I fell asleep smiling.

"Mommy, come on." Claire's complaint brings me back to the present.

"Sorry, sorry. Mommy was daydreaming." I finish unbuckling her and tap her on the nose.

She's in no mood for playfulness. She pushes against me, urging me out of the truck. I back out, keeping my hand on the door so she can climb down safely. Once her feet hit the ground, she's off. In mere seconds she's on her knees at the base of a pine tree, pawing through pinecones and brush. Watching her use both arms fills me happiness, enough to not care that by the end of the weekend, she'll have dirt so far underneath her fingernails I'll have no hope of digging it out.

Isaac comes from the cabin, drawing my attention away from Claire. He strides to where I stand at the back of the truck. Just when I think he's going to reach for me, he slides his arms past me and pulls on the handle of an ice chest. It makes a dull scraping sound as it slides on the truck bed.

"The ice chest was a good idea," he says, opening it and reaching in. He produces two bottles of beer and the dishtowel I used to wrap the bottle opener.

"When you said there was a kitchen, I thought it made sense to have *food* to go in the kitchen." I smirk. Isaac hadn't thought that far ahead, and when I suggested the ice chest he was confused. *Leave everything to the girl who has spent more than her fair share of time hunting, camping, and scouting,* I'd said. I didn't know what this place had for grocery stores, and now I'm glad I insisted on the cooler. It's a damn good thing I put steaks in a bag to marinate. I highly doubt Isaac planned to spend the first night of our celebratory weekend foraging for food.

Isaac laughs as he takes the tops off the beers. "I still can't believe you went hunting with your dad."

I grimace. "Not my favorite memories. It wasn't my thing, but there wasn't a lot he could do. No sitter, no second parent, and ..." I shrug, "Aubrey goes hunting."

"I bet he has some good stories."

I shake my head. "Not gonna happen. And don't even think of asking."

Isaac tips his beer against mine. "Wouldn't dream of it, Sixty."

A shiver runs down me. I love that he has a nickname for me. Sixty... sixty whole minutes when I get to be open and free.

We sip, watching Claire, until she calls Isaac over and asks him to help her spell out her name in pinecones.

"You have to start with a C," she intones as he approaches, her eyes serious.

"Thanks for telling me." He bends down and begins gathering pinecones. "I was going to use a Z."

"Da-ddy." Claire gives him an admonishing look.

While they do that, I go inside. The place seems bigger inside than it did from the outside. It smells like the wood it's made out of, but there's another smell. Dust? Not bad, but not great either. To clear it out, I open the back doors. My eyebrows raise in surprise at the sound of running water. I follow it, down the three steps and out twenty feet until I'm at the edge of an embankment. Just a few yards out, a steady stream runs past. I sit, enjoying the fluidity of sound and the peace the water creates, until Claire calls for me.

Before I go back in, I pause on the top step and listen for the watery lyrics. Now the name of this place is starting to make sense. In the middle of nowhere lies a dwelling with no address, and a creek that sings.

If I wanted to get lost, this would be the place.

29

AUBREY

I'M BACK out at the stream. The second I woke up my first thought was of coming out here to experience it in the morning hours. The smell of water and dirt, of bark and leaves, for some reason, it calls to me. Maybe it's because I live in a desert. Something about the lack of natural water in my everyday life makes me want to be near the flow, and the nature that inevitably goes with it.

"I can't believe she's still asleep." Isaac's voice reaches me from across the space between the cabin and the embankment I'm sitting on. On slow and steady feet he walks to me, two coffee mugs in his grip.

He settles beside me and extends a mug, the steam swirling up into the air. I take it with a grateful smile and wrap my hands around it, letting the warmth sink into my hands. It's practically summer, but the mountains haven't received the memo.

Taking a sip, I say "I snuck out of our room on tiptoe. She needs her rest after staying up so late last night."

"You don't have to sleep with her, you know." Isaac rubs his shoulder against mine.

My heel pushes into the wet-looking pebbles that start just beyond where we're sitting. "Isaac—"

"I'm just saying." He stares out at the water and sips from his mug.

It would be so easy to stay with him. To sleep, our arms intertwined, our legs tangled. To wake up to the stubble that appears on his chin every morning. Would he kiss me awake?

We finish our coffee without saying anything more. It's not uncomfortable, our silence, but it's not without tension. I know what Isaac wants. I just can't give it to him.

"You know what?" I stand and brush off the seat of my jeans. "I think Claire would really like to wake up to some blueberry muffins. I'm going to that bakery Mrs. Iams mentioned. Do you mind?"

Isaac gets to his feet. "I can run there."

"Are you afraid to let me drive your truck? I promise not to change the radio station." I elbow his ribs lightly.

He chuckles, places his hand on the small of my back, and guides me to the cabin. When we get inside, he reaches for the keys he left on the kitchen counter.

"Just wait. You're going to be a cowgirl before you know it." He drops the keys into my outstretched palm.

I smirk and turn my attention to jamming my feet in my shoes.

"Aubrey?"

"Hmm?" I straighten and look at him.

He's suddenly right next to me, hands on either side of my face. He kisses me until there's no air left in my lungs.

"What was that for?" I ask when he lets me go.

"No reason. I just wanted to kiss you."

"But," I cough, trying to regain my composure, "I don't have time for an hour with you right now." As though my stomach can understand me, it lets out a loud growl.

Isaac stares at me for a long moment. Finally, he says, "That wasn't what I was after."

"Oh. OK." Embarrassed, I hurry through the front door and to the truck. It takes me a minute to figure out how to adjust the seat to fit me. Carefully, I back up. He's probably watching me. While I retrace yesterday's drive, my brain mulls over this morning with Isaac.

We didn't actually talk about it, but the agreement seemed unspoken, the parameters set up by our behavior.

We had hours.

And outside of those hours, we were co-parents.

I rub my eyes. I can't think about it anymore.

And it doesn't matter anyway, because I'm here. I pull the truck into an open spot a couple businesses down from the bakery and climb out.

I really hope this place makes more than just blueberry muffins.

FOLKS. That's what I would call the people in the bakery. I've never used that word in my life, but these people seem like people that should be referred to as *folks*.

The smells of the bakery assault me in the very best way. Sugar, vanilla, cinnamon, swarming into an aroma that makes my mouth moist and my stomach yell.

Two glass cases flank the cash register. Inside are muffins in every flavor, chocolate croissants, bagels, cookies, cupcakes, baklava, and more.

Are there enough people in this town to eat all this food? It would appear so, because every seat in this place is taken.

I'm the third person in line. The man in front of me talks

to his wife about going somewhere to get a paper. She tells him they can't spend all day at Hatcher's, because she has gardening to do before the sun is beating down on her.

I try to tune them out, but it's hard because they're loud talkers.

"Jane here today?" The man asks the young girl at the register when it's his turn to order.

I bristle automatically at the name. Like blueberry muffins, the name Jane sends up a flare in my brain.

"Of course," the girls says, pulling their order from the case. "She's finishing up the final batch of muffins in the back."

They finish their transaction, and I step up to the counter.

"Hi. What can I get for you?" The girl asks, her voice chipper.

"Hello." I smile. She has bad acne but a very warm smile. "I'd like four blueberry and two spice. Muffins, I mean."

"Sure." She grabs a white paper bag and moves to the case on the left. "I've never seen you before. Are you visiting?" She ducks down, pulls the muffins from the case, and places them in the bag.

"We're renting a little cabin for the weekend." I pull cash from my wallet and hand it to her.

"The Lost Place?" She asks, at the same time the swinging door leading to the back opens. Her eyes are on her hands as she pulls my change from her drawer.

I shouldn't be surprised she knows it. I'm opening my mouth to respond when a woman comes through the doors, back-end first. She pivots, a tray at her chest. Her eyes meet mine for the briefest second, then she bends at the waist, sliding the tray into the case.

"The Lost Place is great." Her voice comes up over the

case. "I stayed there for a while when I first came to town. That was a long time ago, though."

She's adjusting the tray, so she doesn't look at me when she speaks.

But I don't need her to look at me.

Her face, her voice, it's forever burned into my soul. She's fire, and I'm her charred remains.

My mom.

What do I do?

What do I say?

The thoughts in my head, they smack against one another, but nothing comes together. I'm tangled, jumbled, and the woman is arranging the fucking muffins like her life depends on it.

My shaky fingers snatch the bag from the counter. I turn around and run. Behind me the girl yells out something about my change.

I don't slow down until I'm at the truck. I climb in quickly, afraid she might be right behind me. My eyes squeeze tight until the strain hurts my nostrils. Any moment she's going to tap on the window. In my head I count.

One...

Two...

Three...

All the way to thirty.

And then ten more because I'm sure she's going to come after me.

Nothing happens, and I'm not counting anymore. Maybe she's just standing there, right outside my window, waiting for me to open my eyes.

I dare a peek.

Nothing. Nobody.

My head tips back. Now my eyes are open wide, looking at but not seeing the car's ceiling.

I push the start button, and the truck roars to life. In my left hand is the bag of muffins. I relax my grip and drop it onto my lap.

As I back out of the space, I give myself instructions.

Don't look over there. You don't need to know if she's looking for you.

But I do.

I look. Because I'm weak. Because I want to see her face, twisted with distress, sick with guilt.

She's there, in the window, but she's not looking for me. She's talking to someone seated at a table. She's smiling. She's still beautiful.

I've never hated blueberry muffins more.

30

ISAAC

DOCTORS ARE KNOWN for being egotistical, especially surgeons. I've always gone easy on the self-congratulations, fearing the accusation of having a God-complex. But today, on this Saturday morning filled with towering pine trees and chirping birds, I allow some inner praise.

Aubrey loves the cabin. I startled her this morning when she was staring at the stream. *What was she was thinking?* I'd give anything for a glimpse into her thoughts. I know they're complicated, but I'm a fixer. If she would just let me, I'm sure I could make everything better.

Claire woke up a few minutes after Aubrey left. She went directly for the toy suitcase and chose a pediatrician Barbie. We've been playing ever since.

"It's time for my check-up, Dr. Claire." My voice is high-pitched, my best impersonation of a young girl's voice. I shift my weight and unfold a leg. The ground isn't exactly comfortable.

Claire manipulates Barbie's hands, using an otoscope to look in the ears of the little doll I'm holding.

She pauses, looks at me, her right eye still closed from

looking through the tiny instrument. "I'm Dr. Cordova. Like you." She resumes her examination.

"Sounds good," I say in my own voice.

I've thought about that. Making Claire mine in a legal capacity. I thought about it more when I first found out about her, when I wasn't sure how much of a fight I was in for. But then Aubrey turned out to be agreeable, and now... I haven't given it much thought. It's an eventuality though. It has to be.

I hear my truck tires crunching leaves and sticks. The engine cuts off.

Claire looks at the door at the same time that I say, "Mommy's home and she has a surprise for you."

"Muffins," she whoops, running to the front door. Aubrey opens it just as Claire gets there.

I can't describe the look on Aubrey's face. Aghast? Overwhelmed? Stricken? Maybe she hit an animal and feels bad. Or a car and doesn't want to have to tell me. In this tiny, quaint town, what else could it possibly be?

"Thanks, Mommy." Claire's already pulled one from the bag Aubrey's still holding. Even as I'm staring at Aubrey, trying to read the hollowness in her eyes, the scent of the muffins registers in my brain. I swallow the pool of saliva in my mouth and ignore my growling stomach.

Mechanically Aubrey walks to the kitchen and drops her purse and the brown bag. It's crinkled to hell on the bottom half.

Claire, not noticing her mother's wooden demeanor, has taken her breakfast back to her dolls. My steps toward Aubrey are slow and cautious, evenly paced. She's not looking at me. She's turned away, her stomach leaning against the sink, her gaze fixed on something she sees through the small window over the sink. Maybe she's looking at nothing. Maybe she sees something visible only to her.

I don't know what to say, so I reach for the bag.

At the bottom are two, maybe even three, crumpled muffins. Crumbs fill the space, except for the big lumps where they have stuck together and formed a ball.

I want to help Aubrey. Hold her. Take away whatever the hell happened to make her react this way. I'd also like to know what this is all about.

"Aubrey," I say softly, coming up behind her, but from the side, so she can see me in her peripheral vision. No need to scare her, if she really is that lost in her thoughts. "Are you hurt?"

She turns, her eyes on me. They grow wide in surprise, as though she's only just now realized I've been in the room. "Physically?" She makes a weird sound in the back of her throat. My chest constricts as I think of the possibility that Aubrey is injured... Or worse.

"No," she says, looking back down at the sink.

The relief I feel is overwhelming. "What is it then?" I take a step closer. I can see into the sink now, to her hands. If Aubrey's posture is wooden, then her hands are leaves, shaking in the wind. Her fingers beat a soft cadence on the metal.

I need to make this right. Whatever it is. I need to put Aubrey back together.

I take her hands from the sink and hold them in mine. My thumbs rub the tops of her hands, as though maybe she's shaking from cold and not shock.

Her eyes are dark, fathomless. I squint into them. "Sixty?"

She breaks. Her eyes flash. A rush of air escapes her mouth, like she's been holding her breath for too long.

"Put on a movie for Claire and come to my room." She pivots without warning. Her long hair snaps me on the chin. I watch her hurry away. No more wood. More like lightning.

I do as I'm told, and Claire is only too happy. Aubrey monitors her screen-time, so there's no way Claire will question an unexpected movie.

Before I leave Claire, I lock the front door, double check the lock on the back door, and give her a cup of water.

"I'll be right back. I'm just going to talk to Mommy."

She doesn't respond. The movie has already taken Claire to the land of make-believe.

Firmly rooted in reality, I walk to Aubrey's room. Staying calm under pressure is a necessity for my career, but right now I'm struggling. Suddenly I think about the Titanic and the unshakeable Molly Brown. That would be Aubrey. Unshakeable. Until today, anyway.

I tap on her door with two knuckles.

"Come in."

I push open the door and find Aubrey standing in front of her dresser. She's wearing the same red bra and black leggings I peeled off her last night. What's missing is the oversized sweatshirt she'd had on a few minutes ago.

She strides right up to me, reaching behind me to shut the door. Her breasts graze my chest, and in the back of my mind I register the sound of the lock turning.

"Don't you want to talk about what upset you?" It takes a lot of willpower to ask this question. Aubrey's rarely this brave. I like it. But then it reminds me that her bravery is clearly tied to whatever has upset her, and that changes it.

"Not right now I don't." Her lips are on my neck, tongue fluttering over the hollow at the base of my throat, and I'm having a hard time concentrating.

"You'll feel better if you talk." My voice is garbled. It won't take long before I give up. I can only take so much.

She steps back, it's only a foot, but instantly I miss her heat.

Her eyes flash like they did just a few minutes ago in the kitchen.

"Talking won't make me *feel* better. What I need now is to *not* talk. I need you to push me up against the wall and make me forget my name." She steps back toward me, her hands slipping under my shirt. She traces a design across my chest with her flattened palms. "Make me forget what's inside my chest right now."

She leans back so she can stare at me, pleading eyes on mine. I can feel the edge I'm teetering on. Shouldn't I be a gentleman? Refuse her? But this is Aubrey. Aubrey knows what she wants. Aubrey doesn't speak words she doesn't mean.

"If you're expecting me to be gallant and refuse you, this is your very last chance to tell me." My willpower is worn down to a nub.

She shakes her head. "No white knights allowed in here right now."

I do as she asks. With my hand over her mouth, I push her until the wall stops us, and I give her some time to live outside of whatever is inside her chest.

31

AUBREY

IT WORKED. But then time was up, and it was over, and I'm right where I was before I asked him to take me out of my mind.

I've got to leave this bathroom, go out to the living room, and tell Isaac what happened. And that's when it hits me.

She was here.

I'd been too busy feeling the splintering of my chest. I didn't stop to think about her *here*.

My fingers trace my reflection in the mirror above the counter. Did she look in this same mirror? Did she stare at herself, wonder how she could have left? Did she almost change her mind, run back to us, envision how she would pull me into her arms and smell my hair? Or did she stand tall and congratulate herself on a job well done?

I walk out, and with every step, I wonder if I'm placing my foot in a spot her weight pressed upon. The cabin is new to me now. I'm looking through her eyes.

A lot of this has probably been updated at least once in the past eighteen years. But not that fireplace. And not the stream. Maybe that's where she did her reflecting. She's a mother who left her child behind. She had to have reflected on that. She's not a monster.

I can see her in the bakery. Carefree smile. Not an ounce of regret in those eyes. She should have sad eyes.

Just the thought of Claire starting kindergarten in August sends me into full blown ugly cry. How could she not be upset by the idea of never seeing me again?

Isaac stands in the kitchen. He's drinking from a bottle of water, but his eyes are on me.

Just a few minutes ago, he was everything I needed. He filled me in all the ways I needed. I think, if I let him, he'd do that every day. Not just the physical part, but in the other ways. He'd slip in, occupy my heart, try to fix what's broken.

Claire's movie is still on. There was no hour for us today. It was fast, visceral, and raw. Just what I asked for.

"Hi," I say softly, approaching him. My stomach feels queasy. It's the dread. I don't want to say the words. To tell him what, *who,* I saw.

"Are you ready to tell me what happened?" He tosses the empty plastic bottle onto the counter, where it rolls until it bumps into the brown bag of muffins.

The muffins that started everything.

I glance at Claire. I want to be sure she can't hear. When I'm certain she's engrossed in her movie, I turn back to Isaac.

"The owner of the bakery... Those glorious muffins everyone raves about." I curl my lip at the bag. The mere sight of it is offensive. "The person who bakes those is my mother." The last word is a whisper.

Isaac does all the things a person in shock should do. His eyes widen, his head snaps back in disbelief, and his mouth falls slack, causing his lips to part.

My stomach is sick. Just saying the words makes me feel like I've taken a fist to my gut.

Isaac finds his voice. "Are you...sure? It's been a long time. Maybe you got it wrong?"

"No doubt." My eyes close, and her image appears behind them. The slope of her shoulders as she came from the back, tray in hand. They were down, away from her ears. Not the scrunched shoulders of someone holding a dark secret. "All this time, I pictured her somewhere depressing. She was supposed to be atoning for her sin with a sad, hard life. Regretting every step she took away from me." My cheeks are wet. "But she's not." I open my eyes. Isaac is closer now, his face inches from me. I see the pain in his eyes, as though he's feeling this hurt with me. "She's...happy."

Isaac touches my shoulders, grips them, squeezing once. He loosens his grip, and his hands slide down my arms until he reaches the end. When my fingers weave through his, he leans his forehead on mine. I close my eyes, because the world seems nicer when I can't see.

"She's not happy. No matter what you saw." His breath is warm on my face. He smells like cinnamon and nutmeg, and I want to cry in relief. He chose the spice muffin. "Nobody could ever be happy after knowing you and never seeing you again. *I* couldn't. Now that I know you, I don't want there to ever be a time when I don't."

I'm afraid to look at him. I don't know how to hear these kind words. Like rubber, they bounce off me. I'm not porous. I don't absorb love like this.

Is that what this even is? Love?

He didn't say that word.

But I did.

It doesn't matter, though. None of it does.

Her happiness, her ease, her content, they all form the confirmation I've been searching for my whole life.

She didn't want me enough to stay.

DESPITE ISAAC'S offer to leave, we stayed the rest of the weekend. I couldn't let her ghost win. This was my weekend getaway with my makeshift, unconventional family, and she wasn't going to take that from me too.

Now we're back to real life. I'm at work, Claire is in school. I was a wreck when I dropped her off this morning. She's wearing a sling, just for the next two weeks while she's at school. Isaac said it's a good reminder for her classmates, so they don't grab her elbow. To me the sling is nothing. No barrier between her tiny bones and the thousands of things I've imagined her falling on. Twice already I've called the school.

She's fine, Ms. Reynolds. The assurances from her teacher don't do much to alleviate my concern. I'll feel better when I can see her myself.

Britt wants me to join her and a few other people for lunch. I ignore her email. I don't want to go. I want to sit at my desk and bury my nose in a pile of work, forcing the day to go by faster. Britt comes to find me.

"Teppan yaki," she whispers into the space between my ear and my hairline. She knows it's my favorite.

"I think I'll just stay here." I give her a reassuring smile. At least, that's what it's supposed to do.

It doesn't work. She frowns, her eyes suspicious. "What's going on with you today?" She comes around my chair, leaning her backside against the edge of my desk.

I haven't told her about my mom. I'm afraid of what Britt will do. She has a protective side, and that protection extends to people she considers family. *Me.* If I tell her where my mother is, it's possible Britt will jump in her car and hunt my mother down.

Not that the thought hadn't crossed my mind. I'd been thinking of little else since I saw her forty-eight hours ago. Dreaming up our dialogue. Or, more accurately, my cutting take-down of her actions.

"I had a bit of a rough weekend." Lame excuse.

"Not the good kind of rough weekend, I take it?" She's making a joke, but her eyes don't hold any laughter.

I look up at her, and suddenly my chest feels tight. My lower lip twitches, maybe I'd even call it a tremble, but I refuse to cry at work.

"Oh, God, this is bad." Britt looks horrified. She picks up my cell phone, fingers pressing the screen, then she puts it to her ear.

"Hi," she says after a few seconds. I watch and listen. She orders two sandwiches and salads from the place on the first floor of our building.

"What about your teppan yaki?"

She waves a hand in the air as if the promise of freshly prepared Japanese food is long forgotten.

"Let's go." She hands me my purse.

We're quiet until we get outside with our lunch. Britt has found us a little table off the entrance to the building, and she's already unwrapping her sandwich.

"So, this weekend's family trip wasn't a hit?" She takes a bite. A few strands of julienned lettuce fall onto the table.

"No, that wasn't it," I open my sandwich and pick out the onions. Britt takes them from me and hands me her pickles. "Actually, that part was great. Isaac is..." I think back to our weekend. "He's kind of amazing." My voice is soft. It feels like an admittance, something I'm not supposed to say out loud.

Britt's head bobs. Normally she would be hounding me for more information, but she knows there's more to the story.

"And?"

I set down my food, trading my sandwich for the coral and gold bib necklace I'm wearing. My fingers bump alone the stones. "The town he took us to... Sugar Creek. Their resident blueberry muffin baker—" I stop when Britt's mouth opens wide.

"No," she gasps. She knows how, and why, I abhor the baked treat. Her head moves back and forth, slowly. "It's not possible."

My lips twist. "I'm afraid so."

"Please tell me you confronted her. Please tell me you demanded to know what the fuck she's been doing all these years." Her fist slams down on the table. She's half-standing, leaning toward me over the table.

I want to tell her that of course I was brave and strong. Like she would be. I saw the women who broke my heart and demanded answers. But, no.

I was a coward.

Her indignation over, Britt lowers herself until she's back in her seat. She looks as if she's in pain. *Like Isaac did.*

"You didn't say anything to her, did you?" Her voice is full of pity. Because I did nothing? Or because it was done to me in the first place?

I look at my hands. They're in my lap now.

"Did she see you?"

I shrug, meeting Britt's eyes. "I'm not sure. She was carrying a tray of muffins. But she spoke to me. She said she stayed at the same cabin when she came to town eighteen years ago."

Britt makes a disgusted, grunting sound in the back of her throat.

"I ran out. She must've watched me go." I chew my lip, trying to see myself through her eyes. Or the eyes of the girl at the register. What had I looked like, running away like that? Did I make any noise? Cause a commotion? I was there, I lived it, but for some reason I can't remember it.

"And she didn't go after you?"

My eyes close for a long moment. "No." In hindsight, I'm mad at myself. If only I were stronger. If only I could have spoken her name, forced her to look at me, waited for her to realize who I was. Why couldn't I do that?

Britt comes to my side of the table, sliding across the bench until she's beside me. "I'm sorry, Aubrey."

I want to ask her what she's sorry about. Is it my inability to speak up? The fact that I've just found the woman who abandoned me as a small child? Or that I've lost her again?

I choose to stay quiet. I let my best friend's hug warm my chilled center.

Her love feels much nicer than my anger.

"Have you told your dad?"

My Dad. Somehow I'm going to have to tell him. I don't know what it will do to him, but he deserves to know.

"Not yet."

"Soon?"

I nod. I'm dreading it, but I can't use that as my reason to keep this to myself.

Lunch is over. We go back upstairs to our separate desks. I feel better now, less heavy. I still feel like someone has punched me in the stomach, like it's one long gasp for air, but it's not so sharp.

I send Isaac a text.

I need to see my dad tonight. Can you handle Claire?

It takes Isaac two hours to respond, which I expect. His scheduled surgeries are in the afternoons.

A smile pulls up the corners of my mouth. Isaac the fixer. The man who accepts me.

I'm incredibly lucky.

32

AUBREY

"DO YOU WANT TO SIT OUTSIDE?" My dad walks ahead of me, leading the way, even though I haven't said yes.

It's hot, and I'd rather be inside in the air conditioning, but considering what I'm about to tell him, I can acquiesce.

He settles in a seat that's in direct sun. It's like he runs on a different thermostat than most people. He loves the heat.

I grab the chair opposite him that's in partial sun and pull my legs into myself.

My dad aims his gaze at me. "What's going on, Aubs?" A little grin plays at the corners of his mouth. I'm not sure what he finds amusing, and now there's guilt in my stomach because I'm about to change that.

I open my mouth, but he speaks first. "Before you say anything, I want you to know you have my support. I really like Isaac, and I'm impressed with how he came into a tough situation and made the best out of it. He's a family man. And he loves the people I happen to love the most too."

I'm not sure what to say now. I came here to tell him I've found my mother, but he's gone and said all that stuff about Isaac.

Of everything my dad just said, my mind is focused on one particular word.

Love.

My dad thinks Isaac loves *us*. I know Isaac loves Claire, but me? No way. If my dad only knew about our hours. He may not be so pleased with our arrangement anymore.

I set all his words aside. I came here for a reason, and if I wait any longer I'll chicken out. Because that's exactly what I want to do. I want to bury my head in the sand and pretend I never found her. I liked it better before, when I didn't know where she was. There was certainty in that. The mess was tidy. Now the mess is everywhere.

"Dad, listen." I shake my head. "This isn't about Isaac, though it's good to know you approve of him." I stall for another second, pulling all my hair into my hand and laying it over my left shoulder. "I don't know how to say this, so—"

"Just say it." His voice is gruff. Not because he's mad at me. Because he doesn't do well in the moments right after he realizes he's going to receive news he may not like.

"I found my mom last weekend. She's in Sugar Creek." Best to get it over quickly, like ripping off a Band-Aid.

He's still, the only movement is his head moving back, like he's trying to get away from my words. His expression is nearly unchanged. I wish I were in his head, reading his thoughts and feeling his emotions. This would be a great time for him to suddenly do something totally opposite of my stoic father.

I wait. He clears his throat. Crosses an ankle over the opposite knee so his legs form a box. Then he uncrosses it. Takes off his baseball cap, smooths down his unkempt, graying hair, and slides the hat back on.

"Sugar Creek?" Ironic disbelief fills his words. "I did

some work there last year. Not right there in the town, but nearby. Trouble with a power line."

He shakes his head, pinching the bridge of his nose. I imagine he's thinking of how close he was to her, and he never even knew it.

"What did she say?" he asks.

"I didn't speak to her. I just saw her. She owns the bakery where I went to pick up breakfast."

His head jerks back again. "Blueberry muffins." His eyes are wide. I wonder what he's remembering.

I laugh without feeling happy. "Yep. Other stuff too, but those are her specialty. That's what I was told, anyway."

"I'll be damned. All this time. Sugar Creek."

"I know."

He stands. "I need a beer. You?"

"Please."

When he's in the house, I take three deep breaths. It's over. He knows.

"What do you want to do about all this?" he asks when he comes back out.

I take the beer he's holding out. The neck of the bottle is cold, the beer inside even colder. I take a long drink and set it between my legs.

"I used to imagine finding her one day. Walking somewhere, seeing her out. But she would see me too, and she'd run to me." My words stop. My imagination takes over.

She's in my face, her expression frantic. She's touching my cheeks like she can't believe I'm there. "I'm sorry," she repeats. Tears roll down her cheeks. "I had to go away, but I'm back now. Please let me be a mother to you again. I've never stopped loving you."

I haven't had that daydream in years. Not since Claire was born.

"And that's not what happened?" My dad asks. "She didn't see you?"

I shake my head. "I'm not certain what she saw. She may have glanced my direction, but she didn't recognize me. I ran out of her bakery, so maybe she saw my back." Very different from my fantasy.

"I'd like to pay her a visit," he says in a low growl.

"No." I put my hand up, as though he's going to get up right this second and jump in his truck. "Please, don't. Not for me, anyway. I can't stop you if there are some things you'd like to say to her, but don't do it for me." If his words bring her back... I don't think I can handle her here, in Phoenix, or in my life at all. Resolute peace is still peace, and that's what I've made with her. On my own. Because I've had to. I don't need that rocked any more than it has been.

"Are you OK?" I ask, taking another sip.

"Sure." He answers right away.

I study my dad. He's looking out at the yard. His exterior is tough and strong. Dry like the Arizona soil. But water flows deep down. He's feeling things his face won't show.

We sit quietly, until the sun is almost gone from the sky and the song of the cicadas is more like an orchestra.

Before I leave, I excuse myself to the restroom. Instead, I make a detour to the laundry room to check the lint trap. I'm surprised, and a little sad, to find it empty.

33

ISAAC

I DON'T WANT to move. I'm afraid to breathe too loudly.

She's next to me, on her stomach. Her arm is flung over the pillow, her hair falls down around her. Her lips are parted, begging to be kissed.

We must've fallen asleep last night.

Usually she retreats after our hour is up. Physically and emotionally. I can always tell when it's time. Her gates close, her open eyes shut down.

But not last night. Last night, she was different.

Sixty rolled toward me, not away. She curled into me, ran her fingers over my chest. I tried not to show her how happy that made me.

I kissed her forehead, felt the dampness at her hairline. She'd smiled and buried her face in my neck.

Now it's morning, and I don't know what to do. Will she wake up and feel regret that she didn't leave my bed? She needs that barrier she puts up every day. It keeps her together.

Her eyes flutter a few times, then open. She's alarmed at

first, her shoulders tense. She studies me, her head still on the pillow.

"Hi." Her voice is soft.

"Good morning." I run my hand over her shoulder and down her arm, then back up.

"I fell asleep." She smiles shyly.

"We both did."

"I'm sorry."

I shake my head. "Don't be." My fingers catch in her hair.

She closes her eyes and reaches for me, gripping my shoulders. I move over her as she rolls onto her back. Her hands are in my hair, and I can feel the reverberations of her quiet moans as my mouth roams her chest.

Her hips lift, urging me along. Supporting my weight on my right arm, I hook my left arm under her thigh and hitch up her leg.

Before I go any further, I look into her eyes. I forgot to close the blinds last night, and now the sunlight bounces off everything. It allows me to see her vividly. Hair like dark chocolate, skin creamy, eyes like the ocean. She's breathtaking.

She reaches for me, her fingers trailing the top of my back. Her eyes are bright, wide. The flush on her cheeks is lovely.

"Isaac," she whispers.

I love watching her lips form my name. Especially in this moment.

I love how her chest rises with a sharp intake of breath when I enter her.

I love her slow, rugged exhale when I'm all the way inside her.

Her fingers grip the back of my neck. When her free leg wraps around my backside, I see how this time is different.

In all our other hours, Aubrey gave me her body.

But this, right now, is not one of our *hours*.

This time I can feel Aubrey giving me her heart.

I'M TAKING Aubrey and Claire somewhere today. Somewhere awesome. But first, I have to get through this phone call. Dr. Redmond called again. Another voicemail, another offer. He thinks throwing more money my way will get me to Boston.

He's wrong.

When he doesn't answer, I leave a voicemail. "Dr. Redmond, this is Dr. Isaac Cordova returning your call. I appreciate your secondary offer, and as generous as it is, I remain firm in my choice to decline. My personal life is such that I can't move at this time. Thank you again for considering me. It's an honor." I end the call and set my phone on the desk.

I'm aware I'm not making the best choice for my career, and maybe if things were different with Aubrey, I'd be asking her to move with me to Boston. There's no way I can do that anytime soon. For one, she'd never leave her dad. For two, she has just started taking baby steps with me. We turned our first big corner this morning.

Before I get too carried away by thoughts of waking up next to Aubrey, Claire charges into my office. She bounces up and down in front of my desk, impatient. I'm seeing more of her personality now that she's no longer limited by her cast. Aubrey assures me the sassiness is being resurrected and isn't newly acquired.

"What's up, buttercup?" I smile at my daughter.

"You said you're taking us somewhere special." Her

small hands go to her small hips. I wonder where she picked that up? Aubrey never stands that way.

"And I am. Are you ready?"

Her head bobs up and down. "I'll go get Mommy."

She races out the same way she raced in, her long pony-tail swinging behind her.

When Claire comes in again, she's dragging Aubrey with her.

"Claire tells me we're going somewhere today." Her eyes question me.

"It's a surprise," I say.

Aubrey's lips turn down. She doesn't like surprises.

Forging ahead, I tell her she and Claire will both need swimsuits.

Her eyes narrow.

I give her my best pleading face.

She relents. I can tell by the heave of her chest. "Swim-suits, sunscreen, hats, snacks." She ticks them off on her hands.

"Sure," I agree without hesitation. I'll carry the kitchen sink on my back if it means getting Aubrey to try something new.

We spend the next twenty minutes getting ready, and I pack a bag of snacks and bottles of water.

"Ready?" I ask, when Aubrey comes into the kitchen.

"To go where?" She ask's offhandedly, trying to trip me up.

"Nice try."

She huffs playfully. Tied around her neck are the white straps of her swimsuit. She's in denim cut-offs and a tank top.

We get Claire from her room and climb into my truck.

Aubrey taps her feet to the music that's softly playing, and when she realizes she's doing it, she stops.

"Don't say anything," she warns me with a pointed finger.

"Wasn't going to," I say through a satisfied smile.

It takes a little over an hour to get there. When we pull in, Aubrey raises her eyebrows.

"I don't have a life vest for Claire."

"They do. I double-checked." Ignoring the suspicious look on her face, I hop out of the truck and open the back door for Claire to climb out. Aubrey doesn't know who "they" are, but she's about to.

The lake glitters in the sunlight, and Claire squeals. "It's so shiny."

"Have you been to the lake before?" I ask.

"Nope."

"First time for everything, Claire ."

Aubrey rounds the back of my truck. "A lake day? I'll be honest Cordova, I didn't take you for a lake guy."

"I have all kinds of tricks up my sleeve." Twenty feet away is the marina and our destination. "Come with me." Aubrey and Claire follow me to the white building.

Ten minutes later Aubrey is shaking her head at me. "This is—"

"Going to be fine." I interrupt.

Claire is wearing a life vest, pulled tight and triple-checked by Aubrey, and playing knee deep in the water while our paddle board instructor, Bodie, gives us our first lesson. Aubrey listens closely.

When he's finished, Bodie tells Aubrey to get on, then has me place Claire on the board in front of her.

We paddle out the way we've been taught. Aubrey goes slowly, and I have to keep slowing down for her. After a while, her shoulders drop from her ears. She begins smiling. The wind lifts her ponytail. Claire sits cross-legged in front of Aubrey, pointing at everything she sees.

We paddle to a cove and climb off. Claire stays on until we've walked the boards almost completely out of the water. She hops off and splashes around while Aubrey and I watch from our place on the warm sand.

"Thank you," Aubrey murmurs. With two fists, she gathers sand and buries her feet.

"For bringing you here?"

"Yes. And...for..." She sighs and shakes her head, frustrated.

"You're welcome." I don't need to hear the actual words. Just knowing she's thinking them is enough. Knowing I'm making her feel like that is better than an explanation.

We spend forty more minutes there, splashing with Claire and collecting rocks to leave a message in the sand. *We were here.*

When we arrive back at the marina, Aubrey looks unhappy it's over. "Pick out a place for us where we can eat lunch." I tell her. "I'm going to make sure everything is settled up with Bodie."

Behind the desk in the little white building sits Bodie. In front of the desk is a dog, maybe a lab mix. It lies sleeping but perks up when I set my foot in the place.

Bodie looks up when the dog runs over to me. "Hey, man, how was it? Did your wife have fun?"

My hand, which had been scratching the top of the dogs head, stills. "Uh, yeah, she did." I take my hand back. "She loved it." I don't want to correct him. His assumption does things to my heart and my head. Good things.

I pay Bodie for the lesson and the rental and shake his

hand. He walks out with me to where Aubrey and Claire wait.

"It was nice to meet you both," he says to them. "I love seeing families here. If you play together, you stay together." With a nod at me he disappears back into his shop. Faintly I hear him talking to his dog.

"Did you find a spot for lunch?" I ask Aubrey.

She hands me her phone. On it are a list of choices she found in an internet search. A drop of water runs down the face of the phone, so I flick it off. Aubrey sniffs. I look at her, but she's already turned away.

"Don't," she pleads, her voice quiet.

Like in the truck and at the cove, I don't push for more. And like before, I already know.

I've never been so happy to see a woman cry.

Aubrey's walls won't be vanquished with the force of a wrecking ball or the smack of a sledgehammer.

She needs love.

It's something I've been unknowingly giving her since day one.

God help me, I love her.

34

AUBREY

I'M LETTING ISAAC IN. It was sub-conscious at first. I think. But now it's pretty damn conscious. Getting out of his bed every morning takes superhuman strength.

Five more minutes of warm toes pressed together.

A few more seconds of a smile he hasn't yet given to anybody else that day.

And sometimes, if we're lucky, we pretend we have an hour...

"GOOD MORNING, DOCTOR COWBOY." I grin at Isaac over the island sink. His hair sticks up and his eyes are squinty. He looks sleepy and messy and delicious.

And he's frowning. "You weren't there when I woke up." His voice is petulant. "No Sixty." He grunts, circling the island. I keep washing strawberries like I'm not certain of his intentions.

His hand snakes around my midsection. He buries his face in my hair and inhales.

"That's the smell I need to wake-up. My Aubrey alarm."

He groans happily and places a kiss on the back of my neck. "How much longer are you going to wash those strawberries?"

My hips press into him, and he grips my side with the hand wound around my waist.

My eyes close, enjoying the tease, when Isaac stills.

"Daddy, can we go to the park today?"

My eyes pop open. Claire's standing at the entrance to the hallway, rubbing one eye with a fist.

Isaac's jumps away from me. We're on the far side of the island, and it's too tall for Claire to see anything. But still. We haven't sat down and told her that her mommy and daddy are together now. Then again, we haven't discussed it, so there wouldn't be much to tell her yet.

From the outside, we look like we're together. But on the inside... The official placement of that label feels monumental. As of right now, we're co-parents. If we call ourselves *more*, and it doesn't work out, Claire is officially from a broken home. The opposite of everything I want for her.

Isaac's talking to Claire. He's in front of her, bent down so he's on her level. She's smiling.

She runs to me. I bend down, scoop her up. She's so cute in her nightgown with the mermaid print.

"Daddy said we could go to the park. And then grandma will be here to spend the night with me."

My face is smiling at Claire, but my heart feels a twinge of sadness. I should be grateful she even has one grandma, because six months ago she had zero. But after seeing my mother, it's hard.

I've spent a month pretending she doesn't exist, then imagining what she looked like in The Lost Place eighteen years ago, then hating her, then reminding myself to forget her the way she forgot me.

There's no point in dwelling over what or *who* I've found. Knowing where she is hasn't changed anything. She's still as gone as she ever was.

But there's someone new, and he's *here*. He's present, in every way. And tonight, he's taking me to a benefit gala. Which is why I need to spend the day shopping and getting a manicure and not at the park.

"You both have fun." I smile at the happy picture they make. They're holding hands. Fatherhood looks good on Isaac.

"Mommy's going shopping," Isaac says to Claire.

She sticks out her tongue. Shopping and running errands is far down on the list of things Claire likes to do. Like me, she'd rather be at the park.

It's almost midday by the time I make it to the mall. I try on a dozen things before I decide on a simple floor-length champagne colored dress. And only after I send Britt pictures of me in it do I actually take it to the register.

The last time I got this dressed up was senior prom. Though I couldn't care less about the dress, I can't wait to see Isaac in a tux. Doctor Isaac looks handsome in scrubs, sexy in jeans, but something tells me that in a suit... he might look good enough to eat. Which is why I'm packing a surprise.

I laugh to myself, tapping my fingers on my steering wheel as I head to my nail appointment. There's no way he'll ever expect me to—

What was that?

My car lurches, and my teeth chatter. The front driver's side is lower than the rest of the car. I brake even more and pull off the road. The guy behind me looks pissed, and I don't even have time to say hello with one finger.

I park and climb out.

Flat tire. Ugh.

At least Claire's at the park. It's way too hot to have her sitting on the side of the road with me.

I lean back into my car, turning on the hazards and setting the parking brake.

In the trunk, underneath an emergency backpack and a bag of sand toys, I find my jack, lug wrench, and spare tire.

So much for my manicure.

By the time I'm finished changing the tire, my body is slick with sweat. My hairline is soaked, long rivulets run from between my breasts to my belly button.

My arm muscles yell at me the first time I turn the wheel. I'm tired, hot, and in desperate need of a shower. But at least I have a car with four working wheels.

"AUBREY, WHAT HAPPENED?" Isaac rushes to me.

I've stepped only four feet inside the apartment, but I'm sure my face is bright red. Not to mention the grease on my white shirt. And under my fingernails. The very opposite of the manicure I was supposed to have.

Claire puts down the necklace she's beading and follows Isaac over.

"Mommy, you're dirty."

I bend down, but I don't touch her. "I know, baby. Mommy had some car trouble."

"Car trouble? Did you break down?" Isaac's voice is still alarmed.

I stand and shake my head. "No." I brush away a strand of hair that has fallen into my eyes and wonder if I've left a streak of grease across that side of my face. "Just a flat tire." The rogue hair is back, and this time I use my shoulder to push it aside.

"Why didn't you call?" His eyebrows draw together. He looks angry. And confused.

Claire goes back to her necklace making.

"I need to wash my hands." I hold them up, even though he's probably already noticed the black on them, and walk all the way back to my bedroom. I march into the connected bathroom and turn on the hot water.

Isaac is right behind me.

Pumping soap into my hands, I ask, "What would calling you have accomplished?"

"Help," he says slowly, enunciating every letter.

I scrub a particularly dark spot next to my thumb. "I didn't need help."

Why is this so hard for him to understand?

"Where were you? Camelback? Scottsdale?" His arms cross, and his chin lifts.

I eye him in the mirror. "Roughly. Why?"

"That's a very busy area."

I sigh, shutting off the water. "What's your point?"

He grabs the towel off the rack and tosses it to me. "Do you think that, maybe, in a condensed, crowded area, you could have used some help changing your tire?"

"Honestly? No. I was fine doing it alone. If anything, I was grateful Claire wasn't there to sit in the sun while I did it."

Isaac squints and cocks his head to the side, like he's trying to figure me out.

"You were fine on your own?"

"Yes." I'm exasperated. It's what I've been trying to tell him. Why call for help when you don't need it?

Isaac shakes his head and shifts his weight. "Fine. I get it. You didn't need help. You can do it on your own."

He backs out of the bathroom. "I'm sure you want to get showered. My mom will be here soon."

I watch him go, then undress and turn on the water.

The hot spray hits my skin, pushing the salty sweat off my body. My hands go through the motion of my shower routine, but my mind thinks only of Isaac.

I made him sad. His disappointed eyes stare at me in my memory.

Isaac the fixer wanted to make my bad situation better. But why would I let him when I could do it myself?

35

ISAAC

WHY DIDN'T SHE CALL?

Why didn't she ask for help?

Of all the things about Aubrey, this is what scares me the most. Her total self-reliance.

I don't want to own her. I don't want to control her.

But I do want her to need me.

36

AUBREY

I THINK I'm back in his good graces.

Or maybe, since his mom is here, he's not letting on how mad he is at me.

"You look lovely." Lucia smiles at me as her gaze continues down. She makes a face when she sees my hands.

Despite my best efforts, I haven't been able to clean all the grease from under my nails. I glance at Isaac, who's sitting on the couch next to Claire. He locks eyes with me, then looks away.

Maybe I'm not back in those good graces quite yet.

"I wasn't able to make my manicure appointment today." I dig at my thumb nail, like somehow that will work when soap hasn't.

Lucia laughs. "So instead you rubbed your hands on a tire?"

I laugh too, making it a point not to look at Isaac again. "Something like that."

She takes my hands, studying them. "Do you have a dark red nail polish? I think you could just paint them yourself, and it would be much harder to see the grease."

"Good idea." I hold out my hand to Claire, still not looking at Isaac. I hate that I've upset him. It's even more frustrating that I don't understand how. "Come get dressed for bed, then Mommy and Daddy will leave."

After Claire's dressed, she watches me paint my nails. When she starts her electronic toothbrush, I head for the living room to find the shoes I dropped beside the couch earlier.

I'm still in the hallway when I hear Isaac and his mom. Their voices are soft. Eavesdropping is wrong, but I can't help it.

"It's not that, Mom." Isaac says. "I'm proud she can change a tire. I really don't know if I could. I'm sure I could figure it out, but..." He sighs. "She didn't call me. She didn't even *think* to call me. Not for one second did she think she needed help."

"Maybe she didn't." Lucia says. I detect a bit of pride in her voice. And it makes me proud to know I've made her proud.

"It's not about that, either." Isaac argues. "Her willingness to do it alone bothers me. She's not alone anymore. I'm here. She has me. We're..." His voice trails off.

"You're what?" Lucia asks.

Yes, Isaac, what are we?

"Mommy, why are you standing there?" Claire says to my back. I jump and turn.

I'm about to shush her when I realize I've already been outed. I take Claire's hand and walk out, my face red.

Isaac looks at me with narrowed eyes, but a smile tugs at one corner of his mouth.

Lucia's lips press together like she wants to laugh.

"I was just coming to get my shoes." I throw back my shoulders and retrieve them from the floor.

"Let me take your picture," Lucia says after I've finished winding the last strap around my ankle. She takes her phone from her purse and points it at us.

"Say cheese!" Claire yells.

We smile while Lucia takes what feels like fifty pictures.

We're facing each other, a pose Lucia has carefully placed us in. "So, you no longer believe pictures steal a piece of your soul?" I ask Isaac under my breath.

His face is just inches from mine when he whispers, "Something else has already stolen my soul."

I don't have words. Just one giant, audible gulp.

"Thief," he whispers into my ear.

"I want a picture with Mommy and Daddy too!" Claire shimmies in between us before I can respond.

Faintly I hear Lucia say *cheese*. I'm supposed to be smiling at the camera, but I'm not. I'm staring at Isaac. I watch him smile at Lucia, then laugh with our daughter, and I wonder at what point this all went from hours to *more*.

I THINK it's time for The Talk.

But, considering we shared an Uber with Isaac's friend and his wife, there hasn't been a private moment yet. And another private moment definitely won't be found at this place.

We're forty-five minutes from home in the ballroom of a resort. It's beautiful, I suppose. Gold metal-backed chairs, large flowery centerpieces, a shiny wood dance floor in front of an impressive stage. Too bad I can't appreciate it. I'm distracted by the words I *almost* heard.

I'm here. She has me. We're...

Isaac reaches for me. His hand is warm and soft, and suddenly I want to press my cheek against it.

I gaze at him, wondering if he's on the same wavelength. Maybe it's possible. Last week we both made Claire's lunch for the next day, not realizing the other had already done it. And we'd made the exact same thing. More and more, every day, we're falling into sync.

Except for right now. At this exact moment, Isaac lets go of my hip. He's talking to someone from somewhere, I honestly don't remember, even though he introduced us no less than three minutes ago. I also don't remember the name of someone from somewhere's wife, who's still telling me about how she plans nutritious and healthy meals that are also *so easy* to make. She keeps saying *so easy*. I can't help but tune out. Normally I'm a very good listener, but this is proving too much for me. I nod my head again. I hope I at least *look* interested.

Beside me, Isaac is completely immersed in his conversation. He's motioning with his hands, as though he's using tools, and I assume they're talking about work. I strain to pick up on a few words of their conversation.

"...if you don't take it I will," Dr. Someone says.

The band starts playing louder, and I don't hear Isaac's response. But what I do catch is his look. His eyes dart my way. I smile and rest my hand on his lower back.

"Would you mind if I stole Isaac for a dance?" I ask.

"Go right ahead," Dr. Someone says. He motions to the dance floor.

"Thanks, Craig." Isaac says. "We can pick up that discussion later, if you like."

"I'd like to. I need to know why—"

"Come on, Aubrey." Isaac tugs on my hand and sends an apologetic smile over my head.

Dr. Someone and his wife wave. They both look bewildered.

"What was that about?" I ask, but Isaac either doesn't hear me or doesn't want to answer. We reach the dance floor, and he pulls me in, curling me into his body. It takes a lot of control on my part not to bury my face into his suit jacket. Getting even closer to him might be worth smudging my makeup.

"Sorry about that," Isaac murmurs into my hair. "It didn't look like you were enjoying Craig's wife very much."

I wince. Now I feel bad. I guess I'm not very good at faking.

"What were you and Craig talking about?"

Isaac's shoulders stiffen. The seconds tick by, then he says, "A position that's opening at Boston General."

I look at him. His gaze is somewhere across the room. His shoulders haven't relaxed yet.

"What about it?"

"It's a prestigious role, that's all." He's shrugging like it's no big deal, but the defensive edge to his voice tells me there's more.

"Why do I feel like I'm not getting the full story?" It takes so much effort to keep my voice light, I have no more energy left to keep the sudden nervousness from eating away inside my stomach.

Isaac sighs. Finally, his shoulders drop, but something tells me they are far from relaxed.

"Aubrey, I don't really think this is the place for you to hear about it. I don't want you getting the wrong idea."

I step back, turn, and walk away. Eyes down, I head straight for the doors. Once I'm outside, I walk another twenty feet until I reach a little wooden bench. I sit, tipping my head back, and stare at the teardrop shaped leaves. My heart hammers in my chest.

The air beside me swirls, the bench croaks in protest,

and I don't have to look to see if it's him. Staring up at the pieces of navy blue sky filtering through the leaves, I say "Tell me what you're keeping to yourself."

Now I look at him. He's rubbing his hands over his face. When he's done, he drops them to his knees. "They want me for this job—"

My exhale is angry. "I knew it." I shake my head and look away. This was a mistake. Getting close to Isaac was a mistake. A giant, horrible, life-altering mistake. Not just for me. For my daughter too.

"Aubrey, calm down. You haven't let me finish."

Does he even need to? I can fill in the words for him. "You're going to tell me what a big step up this would be in your career. What an honor it is to be asked to join the team."

"Both of those things are true, but—"

I'm on my feet, furious. With him. With myself. I'm an idiot.

Fool me twice, shame on me.

I whip around. My shaky finger points down at his shocked face. "This is what happens when you love people. *They leave.*"

Isaac stands quickly, knocking me off balance. He grabs my arms above each elbow, catching me. He's in my face, and the shadows make it so that I can barely see his features. His nose presses to mine.

"I turned it down, Aubrey."

Turned it down.

Turned. It. Down.

The words penetrate, and my anger slides away. What replaces it is no better. "For Claire?" My voice is tiny. *For me,* I think. *Say you did it for me.*

"Yes," he breathes. And although I love how much he

loves our daughter, there was a part of me that thought maybe he loved me too. But that was foolish. Isaac and I are a collection of hours. And the very best one was the first hour we spent together.

"I understand," I whisper. And I do. I really do.

I try to smile, but it feels funny on my face, and I'm certain it looks even more painful to him.

"Aubrey, why aren't you happier?"

The tears show up out of nowhere, and it's mortifying. I hate crying. I just have to hope the darkness from the tree keeps them hidden.

"I'm very happy. Claire would be devastated if you moved away." And me too. But I don't say that. Especially not now.

"And you?" Isaac tucks a strand of hair behind my ear. "Would you miss me too? Or would you—" He stops. His hands have come to my face, and my tears have been discovered. "Are you crying?" He pulls me away from the tree so I'm facing the faint light from the building. His big brown eyes pour into mine. "Aubrey, what's wrong?"

"Nothing," I shake my head. "It's stupid."

"Tell me." His fingers flick the tears off my face, and now there are new ones to replace those and I'm so embarrassed I wish I could run away, but that would only make this worse.

"I'm very happy you're sticking around for Claire." I smile through the taste of salt on my lips. "It's important. A girl's dad should be her hero." That's something I know all about.

"I agree. But it's not only Claire I'm staying here for."

My breath catches. "No?"

One side of his mouth turns up. He shakes his head. "I met this woman once, a long time ago. For a while I thought maybe she was just a figment of my imagination. An hour of time I made up. But then one day she appeared out of nowhere. She came, and she brought more than just herself. A piece of me was with her. She'd kept it safe for all those years we were apart." His hand slides to the back of my neck, where his fingers curl through my hair. "She brought me a hand that needs holding. A heart that needs to be loved. And a body that needs to be touched. And I want to do all those things for her. Forever."

He leans further toward me, softly kissing the corner of my lips. My exhale is thick. I turn my head, crushing his lips with my own. I've heard his words. Like a spear, they've sliced through layers of hurts, past the lies I've told myself, and reached their target.

He grabs my waist, pulling me against him. I feel his need, his desire, his *love*. We fit together. There have never been two bodies more meant to become one. Which makes this so much more painful.

Isaac cannot fix me. I am not a body with a broken bone. Tools cannot mend me.

My reaction when I thought he was going to take that job... It tells me just what I've been too blind to see. For years I've been living with a battered and bloodied Band-Aid over my heart, ignoring the pain and hoping the decrepit bandage would keep the pieces together. But it's not my heart that's the problem.

I'm a soul with a wound.

And that wound needs to be healed. It needs to be loved, and cared for, and given the attention it has long been neglected.

I push Isaac away. It takes all the strength I have. I could stay in his arms, and let it happen. It would be so easy.

But I can't. If I know anything about old wounds, it's that

they do not go away. They fester and resurface until their infection is systemic. I have to stop that from happening. If Isaac and I can have a future, I have to confront my past. Claire and Isaac deserve that.

"Isaac," I say, the tears dripping from my chin, "I need to go. I need to see...her."

He reaches for me, but there's already too much space between us. "I'll come with you."

"No," I shake my head, taking another step back. "I need to do this alone."

"You're not alone anymore, Aubrey. Let me be there for you. Let me take care of you."

"I'm fine," I say out of habit. My fingers hit my lips as I realize what I've said.

Isaac's eyes challenge me.

"Give Claire a kiss for me." I choke out the words. "I'll see you both soon."

"You're going now?"

I've been suffering from this wound for eighteen years, but suddenly waiting even one more second to heal it seems inconceivable.

"I can't stand it anymore, Isaac. I have to figure this out. I have to end it."

There's a future for me and Isaac. A family. I want to move forward. Which means first I have to go back.

On quick feet I walk away, and I don't pause until I'm far away, until I'm certain he hasn't followed me.

A brick wall catches me, and I sag against it. I suck in deep breaths of air until I think I'm more or less coherent.

When I'm certain I can speak, I get out my phone and press a button.

"Hi. I need a ride."

37

AUBREY

"THANKS," I say to the driver, sliding out of the backseat. He's old and he looks unhappy. I feel bad that he's out driving people around on a Saturday night. He looks like he should be in a recliner reading a newspaper.

He drives away, leaving me on the street in front of Isaac's place. The light in Claire's bedroom is out, but the living room light is on. What would Lucia say if I went in there right now and told her what I'm planning?

She'd tell me to wait on it, probably. Give it a little thought.

But the time for waiting is over.

I kiss my hand three times and send it out to the lit window. Two for the people inside, one more for the person who's been calling me incessantly. The people I love.

I get in my car, and take my phone from my purse.

"I'm sorry, Isaac," I whisper, and then I turn off my phone. He means well, but he doesn't understand what a lifetime of questions will do to a person. Perfect Isaac from a perfect home. I'm happy he was given a shiny, golden life. I really am. But we don't all get that. Nor do we all get the chance to ask the person who abandoned us *why* they did it.

I'm driving now, almost to the interstate I will stay on for hours. The car is too quiet. I glance at the black face of my phone and put it back in my purse. I turn on the radio, and country music fills my car.

It makes me smile.

I'm doing this for us, Doctor Cowboy.

IT'S ALMOST one in the morning when I pull into the dirt parking lot of a motel. It's in the next town over from Sugar Creek. Briefly I wonder if it's the town my dad worked in, the one with the power line issue.

The desk clerk eyes me suspiciously. I would too, given my attire and the time of night.

"Thanks," I say, taking the key off the cracked counter.

The room is exactly what I expected. A bed I would never want to run a black light over, because sometimes it's best not to know. Everything is in desperate need of an update, or at least a good scrub, but none of that matters.

I take a mylar blanket from the backpack I keep in my trunk. Never have I been so happy to have a hunter for a father. He gave me everything in this backpack. Inside I find freeze-dried foods, matches in a waterproof case, and various other survival supplies. All I really need tonight is the blanket.

I spread it on the bed, lie down, and roll up like a burrito. It takes two hours to fall asleep, despite my exhaustion.

. . .

MY MOUTH TASTES LIKE COTTON. I run my tongue all over, trying to moisten it. I shimmy from my blanket, and walk on stiff legs to the bathroom. Mascara is streaked under my eyes, and my face has long red dents from the blanket.

I can't chase her down like this. I turn on my phone to search for a nearby store. While I'm looking, floods of notifications come in. Text messages, missed calls, voicemails. I ignore them all, but I see the very last text, sent at three a.m.

Good luck.

Thank you, I write. I pause, my fingers hovering above the keys. *I'm sorry I left like that. This is something I need to do. Alone.*

I send the message and grab my purse. Before I walk out, I type and send one more message before I turn off my phone again.

I love you.

It's time he knew that.

I'M ready to go now. At least, I think I am.

Physically, I'm presentable. I'm still in last night's dress and shoes. There was no way around that. But I've cleaned up and brushed my hair and my teeth. I tried to eat breakfast, but the energy bar I bought tasted like chalk in my mouth. Maybe everything tastes like that when you're about to confront your runaway parent. I checked out of the motel under no less scrutiny than I'd checked in with. Different employee, same suspicious, squinty stare.

Sugar Creek is quiet this morning. Nobody out and about. I've passed the bakery twice. The second time I pulled up close enough to see the hours. *Closed on Sundays.*

Is the entire town closed? Are people locked in their homes? Where is everybody?

I drive around, which doesn't take very long, until I see a parking lot with cars.

Church.

Yeah, right.

There's no way she's there.

I drive around the town one more time, even slower, before pulling my car into a spot in the church parking lot. *Well, I suppose church is supposed to be a place for saints and sinners.*

I have no idea how long it will be until the service is over, but it's not like I have anywhere else I could try. This is the most promising lead. So I sit. And I think. Which is something I managed to avoid doing during my drive.

I have so much to say to her. I want to tell her about all the years in grade school when I sat and watched my classmates make Mother's Day gifts. All the colorful, plastic beaded bracelets, the picture frames made from Popsicle sticks, the woven keychains. The training bras I bought with my babysitting money so I didn't have to suffer the embarrassment of telling my dad I needed one.

As hard as that stuff was, they are surface hurts. The worst ones are the ones deep down, the daily subjections that gnaw until they whittle me to nothing. *Sometimes a girl just needs her mom,* the social media posts say. *My mom said...* followed by whatever advice was given. *Now that I'm older, my mom is my best friend,* adult females declare. Or the well-meaning people and their assumption that a mother exists in my life. Of all the daily subjections, those are the worst. Because *of course* I have a mother. Who doesn't? And if a person doesn't have a mother, it's because she died. Never because she voluntarily left.

The more I think, the angrier I feel, until my anger is the color red and the color red is filling the car. I roll down the windows to let it out. When the breeze flows through, it cools me. A little, anyway. The anger is now sharing a stage with the hurt.

I concentrate on breathing. Deep, even breaths, in and out. Claire's little face appears. *My Claire Bear.*

The tiny person who saved me. She took my sad heart and brought it light and love. Now it's easy to see how Isaac and I are meant to be. How much I needed that first hour we spent together.

I'm almost smiling when the wooden church doors swing open. Out walks a man with white hair, and a woman with white hair follows. They stand beside one of the open doors, shaking hands with everyone who walks out.

My breathing picks up. I lean forward. My hands are in my lap, my chin rests against the steering wheel.

Person after person walks out, but I don't see her.

It's like the Dr. Seuss book all over again. *Are You My Mother?*

The congregation flows onto the grass lawn. Some people go to their cars, but instead of leaving they grab things and go back to the lawn. Some have chairs, some hold bags, other's carry things that look like food containers.

There. At the wooden doors.

My mother.

My breath catches in my throat. She's waving her arms and smiling, like she's telling a story, and the two old people at the exit are laughing. She walks down the steps and goes to a car. Confusion fills me for the briefest second, until logic kicks in. Of course she doesn't still own the car she left in.

My brain moves quickly, cataloguing her every motion. *Open trunk, lean one hand on trunk, run other hand along ankle, straighten, pull hair over shoulders, pick up something, close trunk*. The first time I saw her I was too shocked to notice much about her, but now I see everything. How she moves, so gracefully. How she talks to every person she sees. Her smile is easy, relaxed, *and it never leaves her face*. Just like someone else I know.

She carries a large plastic container to an empty table, where she removes the contents and arranges them. *I'd bet my life those are blueberry muffins.*

And I'd be right, based upon the number of people who flock to the table. She's laughing and picking up the box, walking back to her car. I'm hit with the memory of standing on a chair in our kitchen, stirring the batter while she dropped in the berries. She told me to fold them in, so they stay whole, then she placed her hand over mine and showed me how.

I'm out of my car. I don't remember climbing from it, but now I'm beside it. I can see her clearly. She's five cars away, her back to me. She's placing the container back in the trunk.

Someone calls her name and she looks over. She shuts the trunk and takes a step.

This is my chance.

I open my mouth. No sound comes out.

She's walking away, loose gravel being pushed aside with every step. I'm steadily losing my chance. My voice is frozen, and so are my limbs. I watch her. From my spot beside my open car door, I watch her.

She moves through people, talking and laughing. She knows everyone. And they all know her. *Or at least they think they do.* I wonder what story she has told them.

I watch the picnic unfold in front of me until I can't anymore. Because now I understand.

Knowing why she left won't change anything.

Confronting her here, in front of the life she's built for herself, won't change anything for *me*. She can't give back what she has taken away. Telling her what she's done to me won't give me a mother.

Nothing will.

I didn't make her leave, just as I couldn't make her stay. Maybe it was her own ghost that propelled her out the door that day.

The best I can do now is let her be. I've given her enough of my past. There are other people who deserve my future. And I can think of one person in particular who deserves so much more than I've given him.

38

AUBREY

IF LIFE WERE A MOVIE, maybe I would've looked in the rearview mirror just now. So much symbolism in that one gesture. But life isn't a movie, and Sugar Creek doesn't need one last, lingering look.

I turn my phone back on for one minute, to tell Isaac I'm on my way home. When I do that, text messages and voicemail notifications flood my screen. Isaac calls again, just as I'm pulling over to read and listen to the messages.

"Isaac, hi."

"Aubrey, thank god you finally turned your phone on." Relief colors his words. "Your dad was in a hunting accident. He's stable but..."

His words run together for a few seconds, until the fuzziness clears from my head and I can hear again.

"...Are you still in Sugar Creek? Can you come back?"

"Yes." The word is so mixed with salty tears I can barely choke it out.

"Claire and I are here, at the hospital."

"I'm on my way."

"Drive safe," Isaac says. "Don't rush. He's stable. The

mountain didn't kill him, but if anything happened to you, *that* would."

"I'll be there soon. Please give Claire a hug for me." Suddenly all I want is to hold my baby girl, feel her soft, sweet warmth and smell the top of her head.

We hang up and I drive. I'm safe heading down the mountain but I go faster than normal. I'm no doctor, but I think right now my elevated heart rate probably matches the number on my speedometer.

And my mother is the very last thing on my mind.

THE HOSPITAL IS a flurry of activity, and it takes a few minutes for the people at the front desk to tell me what floor my dad's on. My outfit distracted them almost as much as the night clerk at the hotel.

The elevator lets me off on the third floor. I creep past rooms, reading the numbers, until Claire yells, "Mommy!"

I find her down the long, white hall, footsteps thundering. Isaac's a few feet behind her.

Hurrying forward, I gather a leaping Claire into my arms. "Baby," I breathe, the tears springing back up.

"Grandpa is hurt, Mommy." Claire's tone is solemn, her small hands coming to rest on my cheeks. Eyes wide, she continues. "His leg is in a soft cast, and I'm not allowed to touch it. And his face looks funny. It's a different color."

"Bruised," Isaac clarifies, reaching us.

I shift Claire onto my hip and step into him. I want his touch, his smell, I want everything he can give me.

His arms wind around me and Claire, holding us both.

"Hi," he whispers into my ear.

I press my face harder into his chest. "Isaac, I'm so sorry. The way I left—"

"Shh, it's OK. I know." The rumble of his voice in his chest comforts me.

"Aubrey, what can we do for you? Food? Coffee?" A woman speaks up behind Isaac. *Lucia?*

I peel myself off Isaac, and he steps and turns so he's beside me, but his left arm stays around my waist. Lucia and Paul wait for me to say something.

"You guys...are here?"

"Where else would we be?" Lucia smiles, and I know her question isn't one that needs answering. "Here, let me take Claire so you can see your father." She steps forward, hands out.

I hand off my daughter, turning to Isaac. He knows what I'm asking. Grabbing my hand, he leads me four doors down to my father's room. He kisses the top of my head and says softly, "You've got this."

I step in, terrified of what I'm about to see. My dad the ex-Marine, my dad the mountain lion hunter, the man who stepped up when my mother ran.

The bed seems too small for his large frame, or maybe it's his presence that's too large for this small room. Either way, he looks out of place. His eyes are closed, a blanket covers his lower half, but one side is bulky. Claire was right about his face. The left side is swollen, the reddish pink on his cheek beginning to change to dark purple.

I step closer until I'm beside his bed. Bandages crisscross his arms, and more bruises darken his skin.

"Daddy," I whisper, shocked. How many times have I seen him come in from the garage and calmly tell me he's running out to grab a splint because he hit his thumb with a hammer? I've never even seen the man take a sick day.

"Aubs," he says, opening his eyes. His left eye twitches with the effort.

"Dad." My arms rise automatically, but I don't know if I can hug him, so I drop them and place a kiss on the right side of his forehead. "What happened?"

"Oh, you know, took a tumble down a mountain." He grumbles. "Not anything I haven't done before."

I take a deep breath and try not to picture my dad falling. "How did you get help?"

"Another hunter came along after a while. Neither of us could get a signal because we were down in the bottom of a dry creek bed, so he hiked to the top and called for help."

"What did you do while he was doing all that?"

"I stayed put."

I lift my eyes to the ceiling and laugh. "Obviously. I mean, did you take care of yourself? Stop the bleeding on your arms?"

He nods. "My backpack was clipped across my chest, so it stayed on when I fell. Before the guy left to get a call out, he gave me the first aid kit from my pack."

"Where is the person who helped you?"

"I don't know. The last time I saw him was from the inside of the helicopter. He was standing back aways and waved at me."

Helicopter... I didn't even think about how he was rescued. Tears spring to my eyes again as I imagine my dad lying helpless in a creek bed.

"Dad," I say, my voice breaking.

"I'm fine, Aubs. Really. They've got me here, and I'm all doped up. Can't feel a thing. Isaac's been making sure they take real good care of me."

Isaac. The fixer. He was here. And I wasn't. All because I was chasing a ghost.

"Isaac told me where you went. Sounds like I wasn't the

only person hunting in the past twenty-four hours." My dad gives me a look.

I nod slowly, remembering my mother's open face and friendly disposition. It doesn't hurt though. Not like I thought it would.

"Did you talk to her?"

"No. I saw her though. At a church picnic."

My dad scoffs, and I laugh. "Church welcomes sinners and saints."

Dad nods. "They sure do." He tries to adjust himself, but there's really not another position for him to move to. He grimaces and gives up. "So, did you go there with a plan?"

"In my head I had a lot to say. But when I saw her, the words disappeared. Maybe if she'd looked sad, or regretful, it would have been easier to lay into her." In my mind I'm seeing her pulled back shoulders, her easy step, the way her fingers gripped the basket she carried. No sign of a past life anywhere on her. "She looked carefree. Happy. After every-thing she did, everything she took from me, you'd think I could've been strong enough to take a piece of that happi-ness from her by confronting her." My shrug feels heavy. "I couldn't."

My dad leans his head back, so the pillows support his neck, but his eyes remain on me. "It's not in your nature to be vindictive. Children are born loving their parents. It's automatic. Biological. You love her, Aubrey, and that's why you couldn't confront her. Deep down, you don't want to hurt her."

I turn my head, not wanting to absorb his words, but I know he's right. Through all the layers of betrayal, hurt, and anger, there was yearning and warmth. That feeling you feel when you love someone.

"Well, now you know where she is, so you can go talk to

her when you're healthy." I clear my throat, needing desperately to move this conversation off me.

"Oh, I'll be up there, somewhere in the mountains, but I won't be seeking her out. Maybe I'll hunt with someone else from here on out though."

"You're going to keep hunting? Dad, that's ridiculous. Look at yourself." I gesture from his head to his toes.

"Of course I'm going to keep hunting. It was one bad fall. Do you think I should never go out there again?" He makes a disbelieving sound. "Can't let falling down keep you from getting up." He levels me with another pointed look.

"I'm getting the feeling you're not just talking about hunting."

"You need to let him in. If he's not the one for you, then fine. But I think he is. And I think you know it too." His words are slow, measured.

"When did you start thinking so much about this?" And when did he get so wise?

"I had a lot of time on my hands in the past day."

"Oh, Dad. I can't stand thinking about what you've gone through." I push down the great big heave my chest wants to make. At this point, I'm certain that would embarrass both of us. Isn't it enough to know the feeling is there? Do we really have to show the emotion to feel it?

"Everything's all right now, Aubs." His fingers brush the hand I've laid on his bed.

"Excuse me?" A women's voice speaks up behind me. My dad peers beyond me, smiling, and I follow his gaze.

"Hi, I'm Cheryl." A middle-age woman in scrubs approaches me, her hand out. "I've been with your dad since he came in last night." I shake her hand and introduce myself. Cheryl has shoulder-length dirty blonde hair and a round, inviting face.

She steps around me, smiling warmly at my dad. "My shift will be ending soon. Is there anything you need right now?"

"No, we're good," I say.

At the same time my dad says, "Actually, I'm ready for a nap."

"Dad, I'm sorry," Quickly I step back from his bed. "I didn't know."

"Knock it off, Aubs. You're never an imposition." He raises his arms, and Nurse Cheryl frowns. How much pain does this one action cause him? According to him, he doesn't feel much, but I'm not inclined to believe he feels nothing.

Gently I fold myself into his waiting arms, careful not to squeeze. I only linger a few seconds. Pulling myself upright, I say "Let me know what you need. I can run home and grab stuff for you."

"Maybe some clothes." He scratches his jaw. Cheryl is checking monitors and bags hanging on the other side of his bed. "I don't think I can wear what I came here in." He glances at Cheryl, and she smirks.

"Not unless you can sew." They laugh together at her joke.

"I'll bring you clothes. Shorts. For your cast." I grab my purse from where I left it on the ground. "Anything else?"

He shakes his head no. "Cheryl's taking good care of me."

"OK. I'll see you soon." I go to leave, but he calls my name and I turn back. His eyes are on me, and they look full, with emotion or words or maybe some combination. They both live inside him, but they don't often make any sort of grand appearance.

"You're a person worth loving, Aubrey. I've always known that."

I'm so overcome I can hardly manage a nod. His words deserve my full acknowledgment, but I've never been good at receiving compliments.

"I love you too, Dad," I say on my way out the door. The air I'm leaving on feels immensely different than the frightened, sad air I walked in on.

39

AUBREY

I GRABBED MORE than clothes for my dad. I took everything he would like to have but wouldn't think to ask for. And I added cologne to the bag. Nurse Cheryl is cute.

I took something from my old room, too, and traded it for the evening gown I've been wearing for too long. I don't need *just in case* clothes anymore.

I'm nearly to the hospital when I stop for coffee. After last night, I need the strongest blend they have.

That's exactly what I order, size large. I add the cream myself at their little station in the corner. Lips to the brim of the cup, I'm blowing across the top of the coffee when someone steps in front of me.

I look up. Shock rolls through me.

"Owen, hi." I lift my bent neck from my coffee.

His hair is longer now, blond waves that tuck behind his ears. He's dressed in navy blue slacks and a crisp blue-and-white gingham shirt with a sheep embroidered over the left breast.

"Aubrey!" His arm goes around my shoulders as we navigate an awkward side hug. Coffee sloshes onto my hand. I use the napkin in my other hand to clean up, trying to ignore the burning sensation.

"How are you?" I ask, pushing away the immediate bad feelings I have toward him. He broke my heart, but I wouldn't have Claire if he hadn't. Or Isaac. Owen set that whole night into motion.

"I'm great." He nods and rocks back on his feet, shoving his hands in his pockets. "Working for the family business. Real estate," he adds, like I may not remember. It's an unnecessary reminder. "How are you?"

"Wonderful," I say, momentarily forgetting about the current upheaval in my life. "I'm an underwriter at Bridgewater. I have a daughter. She's four." Just mentioning Claire makes my cheeks spread into a grin. The barista calls out a complicated coffee order, and Owen spins to grab it from the counter.

He motions to a nearby table. "Do you have time to sit?"

"Um, sure." I sit down with my drink while Owen grabs a sleeve from the counter and slips his coffee into it.

When he sits, his eyes are soft with apology. "I'm really glad I ran into you. I've always told myself if I ever saw you again I would say this to you." He sighs deeply while one hand spins the napkin on the table. "I shouldn't have broken up with you over the phone. That was shitty. I'm sorry."

With one finger I tap the wooden tabletop, evaluating his contrite expression. The apology is nice, but there's something else I want. I'm never going to know why my mother left, but at this exact moment it's possible for me to learn Owen's reason.

I nod. "Thanks, but... What I really need is to know why you broke up with me."

He twists his lips. Sips from his coffee. Squints his eyes.

I lean forward. "Just tell me. It won't hurt my feelings. I need to know why. It's important to me. Please."

He sighs again. He's probably wishing he'd turned around the second he saw me today.

"You were...so intense." He pinches the bridge of his nose and scrunches his eyes. When he opens them, they look wary. "Are you sure this is a good idea?"

My chin is propped on my hand, and I nod into it. "It's better than any apology."

Owen seems to understand I mean it, because he opens his mouth. "We were young, and you soaked up everything about me. About us. You were like a sponge. And the way you loved, it was so hard. You loved with force. It was too heavy for me." One hand runs through his hair. "Is this what you want to hear? I feel bad."

My head shakes. "Don't. This is good. This is what I've been needing since the day your balls retracted into your body and you broke up with me by phone. On April Fools Day." I sip from my drink, eyes on him, and smirk.

He groans, but he's half-smiling. "I deserved that."

"You did."

"So you have a daughter? Four?" He sits back in the chair, relaxed. Suddenly his eyebrows draw together. I can almost see his brain trying to fit the puzzle pieces together.

I sip my drink and let him sweat for a couple seconds. "Not yours," I say as I lower my cup.

He lets out a shaky, relieved laugh. "For a second there..."

I shake my head. "Nope. No secret baby reveals happening today." Once in a lifetime was enough for me.

We talk for a few more minutes before Owen says he has a showing he needs to get to. "I'm glad I ran into you," he says as he stands. "You look good. Happy. Different."

"Good luck at your showing today." I smile up at him.

"Thanks. Let me know if you're ever in the market for a house." His voice turns eager, the tone of a sales guy.

I lock my eyes in place so they won't roll. "Will do. Bye."

He pats my shoulder as he walks past. For the first time since I saw Owen, my tense muscles relax.

I love too hard. That was Owen's reason. And it says more about him than it does about me. It tells me he needs plain vanilla. White plates.

But Isaac...

He wants my color. He wants to take our hours and turn them into a life together. He's not afraid of my intensity.

It's not until I'm in my car and driving again that I realize something.

Broken people love harder.

So why does Isaac love the way he does?

40

ISAAC

FOUR DAYS after he was found, John was discharged from the hospital with instructions to rest. Aubrey is finally back at work after taking the week off to be at the hospital and then help him settle in at home. I don't say anything to Aubrey about it, but I think Nurse Cheryl will be making some house calls. John morphed into a witty, personable man every time Cheryl came into his room, and she seemed just as smitten. I'm a big believer in fated outcomes, and both Aubrey and John finding love in a hospital isn't a coincidence.

We've all been working together to take care of Claire so Aubrey can be with John. At first she balked, unsure of what to do with a team of people ready to help her, but then she accepted the help without too much of a fight. This is a win for me, because just two weeks ago she would've insisted she was fine doing it all on her own.

On Monday night when she came home from visiting John, she told me about her mom.

Aubrey's face doesn't show much emotion, but if I keep

my focus on her eyes, I can see it all, swimming just beneath the surface.

I saw her confusion and her pain.

I saw her choice and what it cost her to make it.

I know she still wonders, even if she doesn't admit it, about the reasons why.

And I know she feels alone.

That's why I'm taking her there today. Because she's not alone, and she needs to know that.

Aubrey needs to know my ugly truth. She deserves to know why I was really at the bar the night we met.

And now, with my mom's blessing, Aubrey's going to understand how we're more alike than she could've ever imagined.

Claire and I are waiting for her to come home. Last night Aubrey cooked a week of meals and this morning she took them over to John's house.

I've been keeping Claire busy all morning. I need her to fall asleep in the car this afternoon. I've just set her up with a smock and laid out her watercolor paint set when Aubrey opens the front door.

"Mommy!" Claire runs for her like it has been days and not hours since she last saw her.

Aubrey opens her arms. She doesn't check to see if Claire has paint on her. She takes her and holds her tight. She buries her face in her hair.

"I love you so much, Claire."

"Mommy, why are you crying?"

Aubrey pulls back but keeps her arms on Claire's shoulders. She smiles through her tears, brushes Claire's hair from her face. "You're very special. That's all. And sometimes knowing that overwhelms me."

She stands and walks to me. Physically, Aubrey's the

same, but emotionally she's different. Maybe it's her energy. She's looser, calmer. Open. Less like steel and more like silk.

She puts her hand on my chest. "That goes for you, too. You're special. And it overwhelms me."

I know how hard this is for her. How every word of love fights its way out of her. Declarations come as naturally to her as allowing herself to feel at all. That's what makes every word she utters meaningful.

It makes what I'm taking her to see today even more important.

Lifting her hand from my chest, I kiss her bent fingers. "I need to show you something."

She gives me a confused smile. "OK."

I turn to Claire. "Can we save the painting for another day?"

She nods, taking off her smock and dropping it where she stands. She runs over to the bookshelf I set up for her and starts looking through her books.

"Do I have time to change first?" Aubrey looks down at herself. She's wearing cotton shorts and a T-shirt, both of which could pass as pajamas, but I happen to know she didn't sleep in that last night. She wore nothing, and she slept in my arms.

We smile together, remembering the way our bodies melted into one another. Aubrey is everything I need. Everything I want.

When she leaves the room to change, I whip up a quick sandwich for Claire. I've recently learned that a full belly plus lots of morning activities equals a nap.

My efforts are rewarded when we're in the car less than ten minutes and Claire passes out with an open book on her lap.

Aubrey reaches back, taking the book and placing it beside her car seat.

"Was that your plan? For her to fall asleep?"

I laugh. "I ran her ragged this morning. Park, foot races, jumping races. I need her asleep for this. She doesn't need to know what I'm going to tell you. Not yet, anyway."

Aubrey sobers when I say that. She straightens in her seat. "Should I be worried?"

"Not at all. It has nothing to do with you. Or me, really." I frown. "Well, it does have to do with me, but..." I'm really butchering this. "Everything is fine, OK? I promise."

My words do nothing to relieve the worried look on her face.

She's quiet.

"Sixty?"

She looks at me. Her hair falls in her face, and she brushes it back with her fingers.

"We're good." My assurance's probably won't help, but at least I can try.

She nods, but stays quiet until we arrive.

The parking lot is empty, like I expected it would be. It's Sunday, and this is an office building. I park in the middle of the lot, between two rows.

"Isaac, why are we here?" She looks around, first out my window, then hers, and finally in front.

The steering wheel supports my forearm as I gaze out the windshield. The building in front of us is impressive. Twisted steel beams, big glass windows, deep green ivy growing up one side. I once read it was ahead of its time. As was its creator.

I get out of the car, leaving it running for Claire, and walk around to the front. Aubrey follows and stands beside me. I point up at the building. "My dad built this. He was the architect."

Aubrey makes a sound, a disbelieving snort. "Your dad is a scientist."

I shake my head. *Here goes.*

"Not Paul. My real dad."

I watch her face as I tell her. Her head moves slowly from side to side.

"Paul isn't your real dad?"

"No. My real dad is a man named Lee Martin."

"But... your parents. They've been married longer than you've been alive." Her eyes grow wide after she says it.

"My mom had an affair. Lee Martin was her college sweetheart. He moved away after they graduated and she met my dad. When Lee came back, he called her. And then"—I take Aubrey's hand—"they had an affair. Which produced me. My mom told Lee everything, and he said he didn't want a child." Even old wounds can still bleed, and this one hurts. Aubrey needs to hear this, so I keep going. "My mom wanted me, and Paul wanted my mom. He forgave her, and Lee gave up all parental rights. Paul adopted me, and he's never been anything but my dad."

Aubrey lets out a heavy breath. "I don't know what to say."

"That was why I was at the bar the night we met. That was the day my mom told me about Lee Martin." I tear my gaze from Aubrey and look at the building in front of me. It's a work of art, a masterpiece of clean lines, cold steel, and glass, all juxtaposed with the earthy warmth of the ivy. It makes me wonder about the person who designed it.

"I always thought it was a girl who hurt you and sent you there that night." Her smile is ironic. "Can you believe I was even a teensy bit jealous?" She shakes her head, blinking up at the structure.

"You were right, technically."

"I...I don't know what to say. Your mom..." Aubrey squeezes her eyes shut. When she opens them, they're shiny. "I feel so bad for your dad. Paul, I mean. And you, too." Her fingers drift over my forearm.

"You can still call him my dad. That's what he is. And don't worry about me. I've gotten over it."

"How?" She makes a face. "I don't mean that you shouldn't have. I just feel silly now, knowing all this. It took me until now to forgive my mom for what she did, and I've known about it my whole life. How did you go from shock to forgiveness so quickly?"

"It took some time. That night with you helped. When I heard your story, I realized I wasn't alone. And it wasn't anything I did wrong. I watched you leave after our hour—"

"You watched me go?"

I feel a twinge of guilt. I hadn't wanted her to feel embarrassed about the way we'd used each other, so I pretended to be asleep.

"Our time was up, and when you got out of my bed, I knew you were going to leave. I watched you get dressed. And then you picked up my family picture from a box and looked at it." I can see it so clearly, her finger tracing the people in the photograph, the light from that night's full moon illuminating her body. "I realized how lucky I was to have my dad. Someone who wanted me so much he adopted the lovechild of his wife's affair."

Aubrey takes a deep breath. Her eyes follow two quail running across the parking lot. When they disappear into a bush, she murmurs, "I don't know what to say."

I understand that. How long was it before I could form a sentence after I first found out?

"It's a lot to take in," I tell her.

"Where do we go from here, Isaac?" She blinks up at me, shielding her eyes from the sun.

"That depends on you, Sixty."

"Me?" Her eyes show me the fear she feels, but there's happiness there too.

I nod once. "I'm all in. Are you?"

Her eyes roam my face, then her hands follow the trails her eyes just made. I close my eyes and lean into her touch.

When she says the word, I hear it, but I can't believe it, so I ask her to say it again.

"Yes," she yells, laughing.

I laugh with her, and pull her face to mine. When my lips slide over hers, I know our hours are finished. The clock is wide open, and I'm going to love her every hour of every day until there are no more hours left.

41

EPILOGUE

PERFECTION ISN'T ATTAINABLE, I know that now. It doesn't even exist. But when I look out at the scene in front of me, I know this is the best it could ever be.

Claire flies up into the air, her knees tucked into her body, and comes back down, sending a wall of water cascading over Isaac. She laughs and swims away. Isaac glides to where I sit on the second pool step, leaning in to kiss me on the lips.

"What do you think about giving Claire a little brother or sister?" he murmurs against my cheek.

"Only if we can spend more than one hour trying," I whisper.

Our back door opens, and my dad steps out. Isaac straightens but holds his hand up. I smack his offered high-five and wink.

"Dad, where's Cheryl?" I ask as he comes up behind me.

"In the kitchen. She brought over an appetizer. And a dessert."

I smile. He tries to hide it, but I can tell he really likes her. I like her too, and I especially like that he goes hunting a lot less than he used to. I consider it a win from all angles.

"Hi, John." Isaac comes out of the pool, dries off, and shakes hands with my dad.

"Hello, son-in-law." He claps Isaac on the back, then wipes the pool water off on his shorts. "You two ready for that honeymoon yet?"

Isaac looks at me. "Maybe soon, but for right now I think we're just happy to be together in our new place."

"You let me know. I'm ready to have Claire back at my house for a few nights. Get in some good Claire Bear time."

At this Claire runs over, attaching herself to his leg. When she pulls away, he's left with a big wet spot on his shorts.

"Where's Cheryl?" Claire asks.

"Let's go find her," he says, and they set off through the yard.

Isaac lowers himself onto the step beside me. "Tonight," he says quietly.

"What happens tonight?" I feign innocence.

"The baby making begins."

"The baby making began a long time ago," I wiggle my eyebrows.

Sometimes I think about what led me to that night in the cowboy bar. I can see the road that took me there, and easily remember the cracks in my heart that seemed too wide to ever be filled.

I'll never forget the day I realized I was fighting a war against someone who didn't know she'd waged one on me.

Beneath the surface of the water my hand finds Isaac's, and I squeeze.

"Thank you."

"For?"

Fixing me, I want to say, but I know I fixed myself the day I chose forgiveness over anger.

"For being you," I say to him.

"Mommy, Daddy, come inside," Claire yells. "You should see what Cheryl made for dessert."

"Be right there," Isaac yells back, quickly climbing from the pool.

I can't contain my laughter as I follow and wrap a towel around my waist.

"What? I'm excited to see what Cheryl made." Isaac hastily runs a towel over himself. "Hurry up, Mrs. Cordova." Playfully he cuts in front of me as we walk through the pool fence.

Reaching back for my hand, he pulls me alongside him, and we follow the sound of our daughter's laughter into our home.

The End

THE TIME SERIES CONTINUES...

Magic Minutes
(The Time Series Book Two)

Yesterday, I got engaged. I said yes to a man who loves me, and I love him. Happiness should shine brightly from my head to my toes.

But that's not happening.

Despite this ring on my finger, I can't stop looking back at my life, back to the boy who cast a spell on me a long time ago.

It's true, there is no love like your first.

I was eighteen when Noah Sutton stole my heart. He was destined for greatness, and I could barely scrape together enough money to help my mother pay our rent.

We spent that summer pushing limits, breaking rules, and living in moments I thought would last forever.

None of that stopped us from breaking each other's hearts.

I could tell you we were too different.

That we were doomed from day one.

You would probably agree with me when I say first loves are rarely last loves.

Or, I could start at the beginning, and tell you our story.

There's just one little problem: the more I think about Noah, the more certain I become that I'm marrying the wrong man.

Oh, boy. I think this is going to get messy.

Turn the page for the entire first chapter of Magic Minutes…

MAGIC MINUTES
CHAPTER ONE

Noah

I didn't come to the lake for this.

Running without a purpose. That's why I came. And I would've kept on running too, except for the violent splashes, the thrashing arms.

"Hey!" I stand on the shore and yell, panic edging my voice. I pull off my shoes and toss them aside, walking in a few feet. Water splashes the tops of my calves. I pause, waiting to see if the person will stop when she hears me. I'm desperately hoping she's just goofing off.

The movement doesn't stop.

I know it's a girl because of all the hair. It floats on the surface of the water, and when she comes up again, it's slicked halfway down her head. It's red, like a flame.

The water is on fire.

"Hey," I yell again. No response. Fine. I jog in a few more feet and dive under the surface. It's not all that deep here, and there are no waves. I could stand, but it's faster to swim.

I keep my eyes open in the fresh water. I'm not sure how

long it takes me to reach her. Twenty, maybe thirty seconds? I'm a fast swimmer. My lung capacity is larger than most.

She arches above the water again, just a foot away from me. I reach out, wrap my arm around her waist, and tug her to my side. With one arm I keep her locked against my side and above the surface, with the other I tow us through the water. It's slow going, not to mention cold, and it doesn't help that the girl is still struggling. She's twisting and pushing against my forearm, which is wrapped around her. She's probably scared. Maybe she still thinks she's fighting for her life. My one-armed strokes are enough to get us to a place where I can stand. The muddy bottom wedges between my toes. Trudging toward the shore, I glance down at the girl I'm towing along.

Her body has gone slack, and she's looking at me. Her lips are taut and her eyebrows are pulled together. She's pissed?

"What?" I say sharply, but I'm panting, so it doesn't come out as strongly as I'd hoped. I can play ninety minutes of soccer with hardly a break, but this rescuing someone from a lake thing is harder than it looks.

She doesn't respond. When the water is only to my knees, I let her go. It laps to the middle of her thighs, but I figure she's okay in that depth.

Her arms cross her chest, and she stares at me. Her mouth is still a straight line and her eyes are bright. Full of something. I don't know what.

The longer she stares, the more my stomach starts to feel weird. She's not just staring... she's evaluating. And for the first time in my life, I'm afraid I'm not measuring up.

"I wasn't drowning," she says, as though it's no big deal. She starts for the shore.

"Looked like it to me." I follow. My voice isn't as calm as

hers. The wind picks up, and my wet T-shirt clings to my skin. She's wearing a dress, bluer than the water that surrounds us, and it clings to her. "What were you doing out there if you weren't drowning?" If anybody's keeping score, let it be known I don't believe the girl. "Wait." A horrible thought slams into me. "Were you...drowning on purpose?" I can't bring myself to ask her if she was trying to commit suicide.

"No," she says quickly, looking back at me. "I'm not suicidal." Softly, she says, "I was dancing."

She resumes trudging through the water, and again I follow. In no time my long strides easily overtake hers.

"Dancing?" I ask.

"Ever heard of it?"

"Nope. Never."

She laughs, and I'm struck by the feeling that I know her from somewhere. She's around my age, I think. It's possible she goes to my high school.

Once on shore, she heads for a cluster of rocks and sits down on the flattest one. Her head dips back, face lifted to the sun, and she stretches out.

"No soccer practice today?" she asks, eyes still closed.

So, she does go to my high school. Or maybe a neighboring one, but that's a stretch. I'm not that well-known.

"Practice finished up a while ago." My mind races to figure out who she is. I walk closer, looking harder at her under the safety of her closed gaze, as though proximity will increase recognition.

She's beautiful in an unconventional way. If the red hair weren't enough of a differentiator, she wears a tiny diamond in her right nostril. How many girls in my class wear a nose ring? I catch sight of her left ear and count. Seven earrings. Why only seven? Why not eight? And why aren't there any earrings in her right ear? Does one nose ring equal seven earrings, so that now the left and right are balanced?

Despite the excessive earrings, she looks better than any half-drowned possibly suicidal person has a right to. The blue fabric drapes against her creamy skin, and the shocking red hair fans out around her. Her chest rises and falls with her breath, and my eyes are drawn to her collarbone. I've never noticed that part of a girl before. On her, it's captivating.

"Don't you have a girlfriend?" She's got one eye cocked open, and her hand comes up to shield it from the sun.

"Sort of," I say. My unease has more to do with the fact that she knows me, yet I have no idea who she is, and way less to do with the fact that my break-up with Kelsey is still secret, and I've just lied to this girl.

Before she can ask me to explain my *sort of* relationship status, I ask "How do you dance in water?" If that's what she was really doing.

"The same way you dance on land." She gives me a perplexed look, as though I'm the one who needs help.

"Sure," I say, nodding. I turn, heading to the shoes I threw off before running into the water.

"You don't believe me?" The wind takes her voice and throws it, but I catch what she's asked. With goosebumps covering my arms, I spin around.

"Not really."

Rising gracefully from the boulder, she comes toward me. Her gait is lithe, the wet dress clings to the insides of her thighs. The sun has dried some of her hair, and it falls around her face in waves.

"Put your hands above your head," she instructs.

"You can't be serious."

"I am."

I sigh and look at the lake. It's so calm now.

Raising my hands, I look back at her. The girl whose name I still don't know.

She nods her approval and lifts her own arms. "Now," she says, "close your eyes and think of your favorite song." As I watch she closes her eyes, and in seconds her hips are swaying. A smile plays on her lips, and she turns in place, until she's facing me again. She looks free. And happy.

Her eyes narrow after she opens them and looks at me. "You didn't do it."

"I...uh...I meant to." I can't confess I was too busy watching her. "I don't know how to dance by myself."

She stares at me again, and again the feeling of being evaluated comes over me. She holds out a hand. "Dance with me?"

I take her open palm and curl my fingers around hers. She steps into me, bringing with her a rush of nerves. Her other hand comes to rest on the back of my neck, and it's her, not me, who makes us move.

It's slow, so slow, and there's nothing to move to. No beat, no timing, no constraints. Nothing to tell us when to start. Nothing to tell us when to stop. She lays her head against my chest, and when I look down at the shock of red, I feel nothing short of wonder. It's a color I've never been this close to.

We sway together until she says against my chest, "I know you don't know who I am."

I opt for silence. Nothing I say will make it better.

With her head still in place on my chest, she says "I'm not mad. I wouldn't expect you to know me."

Suddenly I wish I did. She's everything I want to be, and everything I don't have the guts to admit I am. She is all the things.

At some point, she decides our dance is finished. When she steps away from me, I fight the urge to pull her back in. Then, when she picks up her sandals and walks away, I want to ask her to come back.

She pauses just before stepping onto the trail and looks back at me. Tree branches hang down around her, some low enough to brush her shoulders, and she looks like she stepped from a fairy tale. "My name is Ember." Then she turns around, and in a few seconds I can't see her anymore.

I want to chase her, take her hand in mine, and tell her I'll never hear music the same way again.

Download Now

ALSO BY JENNIFER MILLIKIN

Coming May 10th, 2021
Preorder The Maverick (Hayden Family Book Two)

The Patriot (Hayden Family Book One)

One Good Thing

Beyond The Pale

Good On Paper

Full of Fire

The Day He Went Away

Magic Minutes (The Time Series Book Two)

The Lifetime of A Second (The Time Series Book Three)

To be in the know about new releases, receive exclusive
sneak peeks, and get
Full of Fury: A Full of Fire novella for free,
visit jennifermillikinwrites.com and get on the mailing list.

ACKNOWLEDGMENTS

Luke. From day one you knew my ugly truth, and you've spent the past twelve years slowly, sometimes painstakingly, helping me move past it. And when I stumble, you're either catching me or helping me up.

To my dad. Chevy days were the best days. Thanks for passing on your love of Seger. I'll never stop checking your lint trap. And thank you, thank you, thank you for that other really big thing you did thirty years ago.

My soul sister Kristan. I love you and your meticulous error-spotting ways.

To my son. You don't know it, but the five page books you've been writing kept me from quitting. When I see your creations, it reminds me that I'm the one who inspired you, and that I need to keep inspiring you.

To my Village Moms. You ladies are amazing. You are mommies, friends, and lady bosses. I admire each and every one of you.

Readers. Where would I be without you? Your encouraging words make the blood, sweat, and tears worthwhile.

Is it weird to acknowledge my ugly truth? Well, I'm going to. It's OK to be ugly, it's OK to be scarred, it's OK to be imperfect. Acknowledging the ugly truth takes away it's power.

CPSIA information can be obtained
at www.ICGtesting.com
Printed in the USA
LVHW010019200421
684914LV00001B/1